BULLETPROOF

LUKE McCAFFREY

Black Rose Writing | Texas

ISBN: 978-1-68513-638-3
LIBRARY OF CONGRESS CONTROL NUMBER: 2025934574
PUBLISHED BY BLACK ROSE WRITING
www.blackrosewriting.com

Printed in the United States of America
Suggested Retail Price (SRP) $20.95

Bulletproof is printed in EB Garamond

Dedicated to

Cairo,
who I miss more than anything

&

Kevin Farrell,
who showed us all what true courage looks like

BULLETPROOF

And this is more the story on how I survived my lowest,
When you're side by side with O. it's like it's ride or die and you know it,
Please excuse the killers, just the kind of guys I roll with.
—OT the Real, "Invisible Trampolines"

PROLOGUE

Guinea, West Africa - 2023

Steam rose from a glass of mint tea resting atop the wrought iron balcony rail above the small courtyard. Tapestries and rugs of intricately stitched patterns hung vertically along pockmarked cement walls below. Beside a doorless opening a vendor sat perched on a stool, smoking hashish to pass the time. The sky above was the blue of the sea where sparse clouds stretched long and thin, as if on the verge of disappearing.

O'Hara sipped his tea and inhaled deeply, if only to remember the slight ache in his rib that surfaced with certain changes in weather. He stared down one of the footpaths to where he could see the coast of Ile Kassa between the buildings. It was his first time seeing the ocean since Bel-Air.

He pulled the photograph from his pocket and studied it, as he had so many times before. The barrel-chested gangster. Slicked back hair. Ponytail. A thick gold chain hanging from his neck. He drank the last of his tea and closed his eyes, allowing himself to return to the haunted memories, like watching clips of disconnected film reel. The dialogue was vague but for six simple sentences. Lines of song that had since reverberated within his mind. Ever present. A soundtrack to the blurred montage that remained with him. That ballad was all he had left, and remembering its words was akin to the nostalgic, self-immolation of his soul...

Twilight. A pink sky stretched across the pale turquoise sea whose water was as clear as quartz. The setting sun appeared exaggerated in size, hanging just above the horizon and highlighting the crests of waves. Crowds of locals gathered in pockets along Bel-Air Beach, some dancing to the rhythmic beat from a distant drum circle. Amjad was yards away, kicking a soccer ball with a group of children as others sat around campfires cheering them on.

After the most recent period in the mountains near Simondou, O'Hara found this stretch of the coast to be a paradise like no other. He wrapped his arm around Dina's waist and pulled her close. The way she looked at him, her eyes were like gemstones, capturing the shades of the sky as if lit from within.

They hadn't seen one another in months, with the mountains being too volatile a setting for her to ever visit. The treacherous landscape. The coups that seemed always on the horizon. She didn't want to risk anything happening to him in the final months before he was due to meet her in Australia, and begged him to consider coming sooner than they had planned.

"*When you think about me...*" he sang softly, pausing to lean in and kiss her on the cheek. "*Mama please don't worry... 'Cause I'll be back with no injury... Before you can call upon me... There's not an army that can stop my path....*"

"*Cause love's all around me...*" she continued singing the Matisyahu ballad in a far more beautiful voice than his, then returned a kiss. Her lips were soft. Pulling her head away she smiled, filling his chest with the warmth of an African sun...

They showered with the lights off, holding one another under the water stream as a warm breeze blew in off the moonlit ocean. Their conversation slipped seamlessly between English and French, her speaking in the refined, educated tongue she had grown up with in the private schools of Beirut and Paris, and he in a broken mix of the Guinean street, laced with slang and colloquialisms. He soaped her back and listened to the way she described Queensland, where they hoped to one day start a family. The hinterlands, an untamed paradise of anonymity. She spoke of the dense bushland. The vibrant green of palm fronds and gray trunks of eucalyptus gums, where sightings of kangaroos and koalas were commonplace, as were the unwelcome red bellies and eastern browns that the workers would often encounter while first clearing the land. Knowing all that she described belonged to them, regardless of whether he had ever laid eyes on it, gave purpose to what he had endured in Africa…

He was dressed in linen slacks and a loose-fitting shirt that concealed the Glock he kept tucked at his waist. She wore his favorite cotton dress from their days in Lebanon. It was close to midnight by the time they left Li Yong's bar after a feast of steamed pork buns and char sui, washed down with several bottles of South African red wine. The leaves of the surrounding trees hung still in the warm air. O'Hara felt oddly lucid despite the effects of alcohol, as if the barometric pressure had changed to heighten his perception. He looked back over his shoulder where through the bar windows he could see Li Yong switching the lights off one at a time. Some of the street lamps had been busted out, causing a shroud of darkness to settle over much of the block. The only sounds were of the crashing surf just out of sight beyond the nearest buildings.

That was when he first noticed the slow purring of an engine. He heard a slight whistle followed by a crackle. Before he could process what had occurred, he saw four black-clad men step from the shadows with pistols aimed in his direction. He turned to shield Dina but she was no longer there.

He recognized the puffing sounds of suppressed gunfire and was knocked forward with stabbing pain through his left shoulder. As he stumbled, he saw Dina lying in the street, clutching her chest with one hand. A thunderous clap echoed among the low buildings and one of the attackers dropped. O'Hara looked up to find Li Yong standing in the bar entrance with a shotgun in his hands. Amjad dove atop Dina to cover her.

O'Hara dropped to a knee and drew the Glock from his waist, firing three shots in the direction of the nearest attacker. The man spasmed and fell facedown. Motorcycle engines revved. O'Hara was hit twice more in his ribs and thigh, and was spun around on axis by the blows. Unable to catch his breath, he shot once more and fell. The weight of a body held him down and he felt Li take the Glock from his hand and begin shooting. Empty shell casings landed on his skin, leaving small stings of burn as he heard the violent crunching sound of a car wreck. Glass breaking. The roaring surf.

O'Hara tried to roll to one side but Li pinned him down. He realized he was in trouble when he no longer had the strength to overpower the small Asian man. He was exhausted. He wanted to sleep. The West African air was uncharacteristically chilled. His teeth chattered. Amjad was moaning in the distance. Another gunshot crackled. Li was looking down at him, screaming in Mandarin. He slapped O'Hara across the cheek. Shouted some more. His words were miles away now, and blended into a long string of muffled sounds.

Shivering, he coughed once, felt sharp pain and had trouble catching his breath. He was so tired, needing sleep more than anything. But he understood that submitting to it would mean never waking again. He strained his neck to find Dina. Amjad was still covering her. There was blood everywhere and neither of them were moving. O'Hara coughed once more and felt another stabbing pain in his ribcage. Then came a sinking feeling, as if dropping to the depths of the ocean. The camera lens of broken film-reel montage closed in on him. Then darkness...

ONE

Amsterdam, The Netherlands – 2023

Snow was falling heavy over the cobblestone walkway that lined one of the lesser canals. The red glow from the display windows of working-girls reflected along the black water surface. Upstream houseboats floated in the shadows. O'Hara stood leaning against the guardrail of a small pedestrian bridge, pretending to take in the serene setting. From his vantage point he had a clear view of the front of the bar a block away.

It was called Sailor's, with a neon-lit sign set down a block too narrow for vehicles to travel. A crowd was gathered outside the main entrance, holding beers and smoking cigarettes. O'Hara could hear the thumps of bass every time the front door opened.

He breathed into his hands to warm them and felt butterflies in his stomach as he recognized the man he knew as Dmitri Smidovich exit the bar and light up a smoke, looking just as he did in the photograph.

O'Hara turned and walked along the canal path so as to approach Sailor's from the opposite side. He stopped under the shadow of a store awning to remove a *balisong* from his pocket, keeping it folded as he continued on toward the bar. Any nervousness was now gone. He felt nothing. Numb. As he approached the last turn before Sailor's came into view, he imagined Dina's face.

That was all it took, envisioning her so vividly. He laid eyes on the man, who was now busy talking to an Arab with a hood drawn up over his head.

The Arab handed him something and walked away. As O'Hara drew near, Smidovich pulled out a cellphone and brought it to his ear.

Without breaking stride, O'Hara flicked the knife open so that the blade was exposed. Once close enough he stepped toward the man and hit him twice in the chest, near the heart. Smidovich let out a grunt and dropped his phone. O'Hara then swung the blade across his neck opening up a deep gash from under his ear to his Adam's apple.

The last thing O'Hara saw as he walked away was the man collapse to the sidewalk. As he kept walking, he could hear commotion, yelling. He fought the urge to run so as not to attract attention. As he reached the street that ran parallel to the waterway, he heard footsteps coming up behind him at a quickening pace. He turned to find the hooded Arab that had been standing with Smidovich. There was a pistol in his hand. O'Hara held the knife up to defend himself, then heard a click and a puff of air. A dime-sized hole and blood spatter appeared on the man's forehead and he fell face-down on the sidewalk.

O'Hara turned to find a familiar face he hadn't seen in years. The unmistakable brown eyes and dark skin, now masked by an even longer, woolier beard. He was wearing a leather bomber jacket that made him look huskier than he had remembered him to be.

"*Yalla*," Omar Al Awamleh said as he tucked his handgun at the small of his back. He turned and walked away. O'Hara followed him. Once they had crossed the nearest canal and turned a corner, the man picked his pace up to a jog. O'Hara noticed a limp in his stride, and thought of the shootout with Hezbollah where he had taken several rounds to the knee. When they reached Damrak, the main thoroughfare of the city, Omar used an electronic key fob to unlock the doors of a parked black sedan.

"Get in," he said, and climbed into the driver's seat.

O'Hara circled around and hopped in the passenger side.

Omar pressed the ignition button and the engine roared. He pulled the car onto the road and drove south out of the city.

"What are you doing here?"

The Israeli glanced sideways at him, then turned his attention to the road ahead. "I would be asking you the same thing if I didn't just witness the answer."

They rode in silence until they had left the city behind. Outside the window, snow blanketed the moonlit rolling hills of the Dutch countryside. In the distance giant windmills spun slowly in the night sky.

"How the hell did you track me down?" O'Hara finally asked.

"It's what I do."

"Are you here to kill me?" He thought of Yoni Kaplan.

"You'd already be dead if so." He glanced at O'Hara's blood-stained knife, then reached to an inner pocket of his jacket and removed a bandana, which he tossed on his lap. "Clean that up and put it away." He then extended his arm. "I'm sorry about Dina," he said.

O'Hara clasped his hand.

"I would have found you sooner, but you've obviously been taught to cover your tracks."

"Foreplay was never your thing, Omar."

Omar clucked his tongue. "Omar died in Beirut." He patted O'Hara's thigh. "You've earned the right to know my birth name. Call me Rafi."

O'Hara nodded.

"What name are you going by, these days?"

"O'Hara."

He clucked his tongue once more. "You won't make it across any border with that name."

O'Hara didn't respond.

"Do you have documents?"

He shook his head.

"*Beseder*," Rafi said. He drummed his fingers against the steering wheel. "I will help you with this. You will have to cross the next border in the trunk, though."

"Which border?"

"Belgium. We can stop there until I get you identification." He pulled a cigarette pack down from where it was pinched between the overhead visor and the roof. He fished one from the box and stuck it in his mouth, then pulled a plastic lighter from one of the cup holders and lit it. He drew hard and rolled down his window, letting in a blast of cold winter air as he blew a stream of smoke out into the night. "We have a long drive ahead and much to discuss."

O'Hara unzipped his coat. "I wondered what happened to you."

"I've been keeping an eye on Dina's parents, thinking they might lead me to you."

O'Hara stared out the side window. "I haven't been to see them."

Rafi looked at him. "They're in Paris."

O'Hara nodded. "I wouldn't know the first thing to say to them."

"Have you never met them?"

O'Hara shook his head.

"They're your last living connection to her. It would help with the healing."

O'Hara looked back out the window. "Do you know why Smidovich put the hit out on me?" he asked, changing the subject.

"Why would I?"

O'Hara nodded. "You know something, or you wouldn't have found me in Amsterdam."

Rafi pulled from the cigarette.

"You move with a limp, now," O'Hara said.

"I won't be running marathons anytime soon, but I'm still quick when I need to be." He punched buttons on the dashboard and turned the heat up in the car. "How did you learn of Smidovich? The Malaysian?"

"You know about Li," he said.

Rafi didn't answer.

O'Hara frowned, to which his friend gave a slight nod.

"This Li helped get you to Holland?" he asked.

"Yeah," O'Hara said.

"You know he's Sam Gor."

"I only know him as Li Yong."

"Sam Gor. Chinese triad."

"I know he has connects, is all I know." O'Hara adjusted the seat to recline some. "And they are his own business."

"Let's find somewhere to fill our stomachs. It won't be long before you have to get in the trunk."

The coffee warmed O'Hara. What he did in Amsterdam was already beginning to feel imagined, like a dream. He slipped his hand in his pocket and felt the folded knife.

"In what capacity did you come find me?"

"What does this mean?"

"Professional?"

"Professional?"

"Mossad. Shin Bet. Whoever you're with."

Rafi interrupted him by clucking his tongue. "It is important that we are honest with one another. I am here as your friend."

"Do they know you came looking for me."

Rafi gave a non-committal shrug.

"What would they think about what you did back there?"

"They wouldn't lose any sleep. Just as I don't lose sleep over the fact that you killed Yoni in Beirut."

O'Hara was caught off-guard by the accusation and had the sudden urge to jump from the moving vehicle. He took a sip of coffee to appear unfazed.

"He was found with an entry wound behind his ear."

"I know nothing about that." Over the years he often wondered who might have discovered Yoni's body.

"Israel wasn't behind what occurred in Beirut."

"Yoni knew it was gonna happen," O'Hara said.

Rafi nodded. "He was acting independently from the state."

"You were meant to be at the port."

"He sent me there. It is only by luck I wasn't there when it exploded." He sipped his coffee. "Which is why I don't care about what happened to him."

"What about others in your organization?"

"I never told anyone that you were there."

"Do they know what he was up to?"

"The ones that need to, do. And they know he was working with American extremists."

O'Hara thought of Preston Knox and Idaho.

"But everything is still very compartmentalized. There are ongoing concerns that some within my government remain loyal to Yoni's cause."

"Maybe your own people took him out."

He clucked his tongue three times. "He was revered. If he was alive, he might be running the institute by now."

"When was he exposed?"

"I learned of it when I returned to Israel for the first time in years. After I left you." He pulled the cigarette pack down from the visor and lit another one. When he rolled the window down, he turned the heat to full blast. "As I said, I am here as your friend. You are in danger, but not from us. Yoni was given a martyr's death. A story was disseminated throughout the government that placed him at the seat of the explosion, where he was running an op. He allegedly died alongside the one you knew as Layla."

"You stopped trusting her toward the end."

Rafi nodded. "She was one of Yoni's disciples."

"He didn't try to recruit you to his cause?"

"He used me. But he knew if he told me everything, I wouldn't have gone along with it."

"I hope you have been rewarded for your integrity." O'Hara gestured toward Rafi's knee. "And all you've endured."

"I am here with a proposition, and can make you promises that I know I will keep. I'm in a better position than before."

"You've been promoted?"

Rafi nodded.

"What's the proposition?"

"A working relationship."

"Me and you?"

Rafi nodded once more. "When was the last time you saw the Saudis?"

"The night I was shot. Amjad was there."

"What about the others. Prince Ahmed bin Tarek."

"Not since before it all went down."

"He didn't send anyone for you?"

"Someone came for Amjad's body, was asking around about me. But Li lied to them. He didn't trust them. You know how the Chinese are."

"Where were you at the time?"

"In the bush, recovering."

"And you haven't reached out to the prince since getting healthy?"

"I don't have the contacts, anymore. You can't just ring up a palace and ask for a prince."

"Why not contact them through a Saudi consulate?"

"I was given a clean slate." O'Hara sighed. "I guess I wanted to let sleeping dogs lie."

"What does this mean?"

"Why are you asking about the Saudis?" O'Hara asked.

"I want you to make contact with them. Try to work your way back into that circle."

"Is that part of your proposition?"

"Yes."

"What's in it for me?"

"Money. A new identity. The best of the best watching your back." He touched his chest with the hand that held a cigarette. "And I personally will find out everyone else connected to the attack in Guinea. Smidovich was just the tip of the iceberg."

O'Hara looked out the window. He knew there were more people involved. Men tied to Uncle Nikolai, or Viktor. It didn't make sense that a Russian gangster in the Netherlands would be the end of it. He also knew his trail had gone cold unless he received some outside help. The kind Rafi's contacts and access could provide.

"If you got back in with ABT—"

"What's that?"

"It's what we call Prince Ahmed bin Tarek. If you rekindled your relationship with him, you'd be back to being only once-removed from the Crown Prince."

"I've only met the Crown Prince. I don't know the guy."

"Even so… We've been given a taste of who he really is with the Kashoggi incident. And he's been up to some real dodgy stuff ever since Russia invaded Ukraine and set the world on edge. Geopolitical chess moves." He touched his chest again. "As I said, you would have to deal with nobody other than me. Think about it."

O'Hara looked out the window.

When he realized he wasn't getting an answer, Rafi cleared his throat. "Why Guinea?" he asked.

"What do you mean?"

"Why did you trade in the pampered life of Riyadh for a hard scrabble African one?"

"A year in Saudi was enough. They were pains in the ass about us living together, unmarried."

"Why not just marry?"

"She wanted to do it the right way."

Rafi nodded.

"Amjad was gifted a position overseeing two African mines. Up in the mountains, tasked with making sure gold and iron-ore actually reached the port of Conakry without being intercepted by militias or bandits."

"Rough job for a pampered Arab."

"He had trouble with it."

"He struck me as the type that would rather be receiving manicures."

"Prince Ahmed offered me the chance to go help him out." He finished the last of his coffee.

"Makes sense." Rafi exited the motorway at the next off-ramp and idled the car in the shadows beneath the trees of what appeared to be a barren orchard. "Time for you to get comfortable." He gestured toward the back of the car. "First piss. You'll be in there a while."

"What if they decide to search the car?"

"We will be crossing at a checkpoint that is usually only manned by a handful of officers."

"That didn't answer my question."

"Let's just hope for the best, yeah?" Rafi said as he opened his door and stepped out of the vehicle.

Rafi left O'Hara in the trunk until he found a small hotel along the outskirts of Antwerp where he paid cash for a private room with two beds and a kitchenette.

O'Hara smelled as one would expect, after having spent several hours sweating in the boot of a car, and he wanted a shower. As he pulled his shirt off over his head, Rafi observed the scars on his shoulder and torso.

"How many times were you hit?"

"A few."

"How does it feel, now?"

"In this weather? Pretty shit. I'm in the best shape of my life, otherwise."

"You look to be." He straightened his leg and O'Hara heard a popping sound. "Where in the bush was this place you recovered?"

O'Hara shrugged. "I woke up there a few days later." He hung his shirt over the back of a chair in the corner of the room. "Deep in, though. Outside of some of the hired guns that guarded the perimeter, I didn't encounter a single African the entire time. The Chinese in Africa only ride with their own."

"How many people lived there?"

"Half-dozen. We had little mud-brick dwellings." He kicked his shoes off and started removing his socks. "Li was in and out. He still had business to tend to in Conakry and Bel-Air. The doctor and a cook were the only constants. Some others cycled through, caretakers and what not." He pulled his burner phone and the balisong from his jeans and set them on the table. "Then Li brought in this one-armed Malaysian to train me up."

"Train you up?"

"Silat."

"What happened to his other arm?"

"Who knows. All I know is this little guy... you'd think you could knock him over with a slap, but once he had a blade in that hand, he became about the last guy I'd ever want to be up against."

"Is that where you got the butterfly knife?" Rafi asked.

O'Hara nodded.

"How did you communicate with them?"

"Li and the doctor spoke English." O'Hara pulled his jeans off and hung them over the same chair that his shirt was on. "The rest of them only spoke Mandarin or Malay."

"Did you pick any up?"

"Mandarin, a bit. It's all I heard for long stretches."

"Still remember any?"

"I could probably get a point across. It's been a minute, though."

Rafi laughed and shook his head. "You missed your calling, my friend. You should have gotten into my line of work."

"You guys are all fucked."

Rafi's grin widened.

"Enough reminiscing," O'Hara said. "What's the plan from here on out?"

"You'll lay low here while I head back and secure you a new passport. We'll have to take what we can get on such short notice. Build a backstory."

"I've done it before."

"I know. Once we have all that sorted, we'll work out a plan to put you back in touch with ABT."

O'Hara nodded. He had spent years locked in smaller rooms than the one they were now in. "Shower time," he said, and stepped into the bathroom.

Rafi was gone for the next three days. O'Hara laid low in his hotel room. He ordered meals to be left outside his door, drank coffee, exercised and read. At night he'd watch the news in French, to see if anything was mentioned about Smidovich. There was nothing. He kept the do-not-disturb sign hanging from outside the door the entire time, and saw nobody.

On the fourth morning he awoke to the smell of brewed coffee. When he opened his eyes, Rafi was leaning against the window, watching a pair of pigeons pecking at crumbs on the ledge outside. He was dressed in jeans and boots and his leather bomber jacket.

"It's cold out there, today," he said without looking at O'Hara.

"Pour me a cup, will ya."

Rafi pulled two mugs down from the overhead cabinet and filled them with black coffee. He handed one to O'Hara, who sat up, then took a seat at the opposite end of the couch.

"How was your trip?" O'Hara asked as he tasted the coffee.

Rafi slipped a hand inside his jacket and removed an envelope, then tossed it on O'Hara's lap.

O'Hara tore it open and pulled out a navy-blue passport booklet. Across the top of the cover read *Canada* in gold lettering, and below it a national crest. Beneath that were the words passport, in both English and French. O'Hara opened it to find the photo that Rafi had taken of him the first night in the hotel, alongside the name Daniel Marrero and a series of identification numbers. His age was accurate with a listed birthplace of Toronto.

"Toronto?"

"The passport is authentic. Canada works with you knowing a bit of French."

"Are there any supporting documents?"

Rafi handed him a credit card. "You'll be able to cross borders. We have a fake exit stamp from Toronto, and an entry one for Brussels that will pass any quick inspections. It has been processed to show up in the digital travel records, in case they dig deeper.

"You sure?"

"*Habibi*, do you think I'm here under my real identity?" He nodded toward the passport.

"Do I have an address? Any other details I need to memorize?"

"You have some room to write your own story. Just study a map online and familiarize yourself with some of the streets in that area. You know the deal." He smiled. "You were as good a liar as anyone I have worked with."

O'Hara studied the passport.

"If you stay out of trouble and dress unassuming, you are unlikely to be grilled by any border agents. Know enough of your backstory to make it believable. The document will hold up."

O'Hara tapped the passport against his open palm. "Thank you."

"You're welcome, Danny," Rafi said.

"Danny Marrero," O'Hara repeated, as if trying on the name for size.

He spent the next few days keeping a low profile under his new Canadian alias. He went for runs through the neighborhood and found an outdoor park where he used the playground equipment to do pull-ups. He ate out twice a day, a late breakfast around noon, and an early dinner, never visiting the same café or restaurant twice. He'd drink coffee and read books from the lending library in the hotel lobby, or use his new cellphone's web browser to search for news reports about the death of Dmitri Smidovich. Only one article mentioned the man by name. There didn't appear to be many leads regarding the investigation.

One morning he awoke at dusk. Outside the window, the empty street below was pale shades of black and grays, like a photograph lifted from an aged newspaper. He brewed a pot of coffee, poured himself a cup and pulled a stool up to the windowsill. A woman in a bathrobe, with a wool hat and a scarf wrapped around her neck smoked a cigarette on an upper floor balcony across the way. He sat and observed her, imagining who she might be. He remembered enjoying doing this as a young kid. Observing. A life of trauma and neglect will do that to a person. Turn them into a watcher. Detail-oriented. Strong memory. What happened to that child over the decades, he wondered? He looked back at the upper floor balcony but the woman was gone.

He showered, dressed and walked the streets for the next few hours as the city came to life. He bought a newspaper from a kiosk and sat at a café, where he ordered a buttered croissant and a cappuccino. He folded the newspaper back on itself and lay it on the table beside his plate in case he needed to use it to avoid conversations with strangers at the nearest tables. He people-watched, imagining a teenage Dina living in a European city like this, spending her high school years hanging out in similar streets while having no clue where her life would end up taking her or how it would be cut so short.

That was when he noticed Rafi approaching from across the square. The limping gait. The broad shoulders. The beard. He had traded in the bomber jacket for a black pea coat, on which he had the collar turned up to keep his neck warm against the winter breeze. He pulled the empty chair out from under the table and sat, catching the waiter's attention and ordering two more cappuccinos.

"Getting used to the new name?" he asked.

"So far so good," O'Hara said.

"Good." He rested a pale blue pack of Gauloises cigarettes on the table.

"Changing flavors?" O'Hara asked.

"They're shit."

"They're all shit. You learn anything new?"

Rafi shrugged.

O'Hara waited for more.

"As we assumed. There's more Russians beyond our friend in Holland."

"I want them all."

Rafi held his hand over the table, as if to suggest O'Hara calm down. The waiter arrived and set the fresh drinks on the table. O'Hara lifted his and took a sip.

"I have a contact number for ABT," he said, once the waiter had left. "You need to reconnect with him before you go risk getting yourself killed by a *Ruski*. Hitting some of these other guys won't be a matter of just walking up on them with a knife."

After a long pause O'Hara said, "Our arrangement also included me getting paid."

Rafi reached in his jacket pocket and removed a white envelope. "That should hold you over."

O'Hara slipped the envelope in his pocket without opening it. "Euros?" he asked.

Rafi nodded.

"I'll have to find a money exchange."

"Why?"

"I want to go to Australia."

Rafi removed a cigarette from the pack and stuck it between his teeth. He searched his pocket for a light, before cursing and flagging down a waiter to request one.

"I want to see where she was living."

Rafi gave a nod, but said nothing.

"I need closure."

The waiter returned with a lighter, sparked the flame and held it to the end of Rafi's cigarette until it caught. Rafi took a long drag, and said "*Merci,*" with smoke escaping his lips. He looked at O'Hara.

"I suppose you can wait and contact ABT from Australia." He rested his hand with the cigarette on the tabletop. "It's credible."

"What about these other Russians you mentioned?"

"Let's follow the trail a bit more instead of eating every crumb as we come to it."

O'Hara tapped his pocket that contained the envelope. "Can you help me with the flight, or should I use this?"

"I'll book the flight."

O'Hara sipped his coffee. "How soon can you do that?"

"How soon do you need me to?"

"There's nothing keeping me here."

Rafi looked off in the distance and drew hard on his cigarette. He looked back at O'Hara and blew a hard stream of smoke out of the side of his mouth, then nodded.

TWO

Queensland, Australia

It was a ninety-minute drive north from the airport in Brisbane, along a highway lined by dense, tropical bushland. Through the open window of the taxi O'Hara could smell the salty ocean air. His Canadian passport had withstood the test of Australian customs and the unease he felt on the long flight over, the nausea that came with wondering if those airplane meals would be his last as a free man, were behind him. At least for now.

With the southern hemisphere's seasons reversed, the summer air was sweltering and humid. The taxi exited the highway and they rode along a series of heavily forested backroads. A sad smile found its way onto O'Hara's face as he began to understand why Dina chose this setting as the place to put down roots.

They passed through a rural town consisting of a pub and a service station, before climbing a partially paved road into the hills, through woodland so thick the canopy formed a tunnel overhead. Yellow and black koala-crossing signs were posted along the route, and O'Hara noticed his first kangaroo standing among the pale trunks of gum trees that lined the road. Fifteen minutes into the bush, they turned off onto a gravel road that descended along a creek into a clearing where chopped timber was piled off to one side of a small log cabin. Damp smells of algae and moss filled the air of the property and he could hear the distant roar of a waterfall.

O'Hara added a generous tip to the driver's metered fare, and waited for the man to leave. Once alone, he closed his eyes and breathed in the forest, paying attention to birdsong from a flock of multi-colored lorikeets on the branches above. He had never felt closer to Dina since losing her, and could sense her presence in all aspects of the forest. Dropping to his knees, he wept. Somewhere along the way, he had changed from a man who rarely knew how to cry, to one who couldn't seem to prevent it. He allowed the tears to flow. He wanted her to understand how broken he was without her.

After some time, he climbed to his feet and walked toward the cabin. It felt like returning to a home he knew from a dream. He was relieved to discover the key beneath the lone garden statue of Ganesh. He thanked the deity aloud, unlocked the front door and let himself in. He paused for a moment to take it all in and appreciate every last detail of the state in which Dina had left the cabin before journeying to meet him in Africa for the final time. An empty glass mug on the table nearest the sofa with the teabag still in it. Faint traces of burnt incense, as if absorbed into the timber walls.

"Hey Momma," he said aloud. The air felt thick and heavy like being under water. "I miss you so much," he whispered. He walked over to the table and picked up the empty mug, smelled it, and held it up to the light that shone through the window. Faint lip marks could be seen along the edge of the glass. He sighed and set it back down.

Tapestries covered many of the walls, faeries and unicorns stitched among the designs. He smiled at how much she had grown into herself since Beirut. As if the forest enabled the true Dina to evolve. As he stood to walk into the bedroom, something caught his eye. Standing on a recessed shelf to one side of the bedroom doorway was a bronze statue of an Egyptian deity with the muscular body of a man, and the head of an Ibis. The statue held a quill in one hand and a scroll in the other with a moon resting above its head.

Entering the bedroom, he sat down on the mattress. There were a series of three framed photographs, each of him and Dina in different settings. The first was taken at one of Prince Ahmed's yacht parties off the coast of Beirut. They were chest deep in the pool, holding bottles of beer, smiling. The second was in Riyadh, at a dinner party in Amjad's home.

He observed the third photograph, one that had been taken in Sierra Leone during one of their holidays while he had been working abroad. The sadness was so heavy in his chest that for a moment it was difficult to breathe. He wanted to remember and relive his memories of her, but couldn't escape the emptiness that she left behind. He lay back on the bed with his feet still draped over the side, and closed his eyes. He inhaled and held his breath for a long moment, until he could feel his pulse pounding in his ears. When he could hold it no longer, he let the air out slow. Before he had fully exhaled, he was asleep…

Few remaining stars dotted the upper portions of the indigo sky as vibrant shades of pink and orange had begun to climb the lowest edges of the horizon. The summit was a plateau of level blocks, giving the impression that an original capstone had been removed. From the center, poles had been erected to form a skeleton point. Scattered names of previous visitors were etched into the stone like graffiti.

Across the valley, the sunrise reflected against the eastern face of a neighboring pyramid. Beyond it, the Sphinx rested like a guardian of the land. O'Hara leaned back on his arms. His palms felt the stone vibrating.

Sound is the source of everything. Vibration. Creation.

The red sun now hung low over the horizon. It was much larger than any sun O'Hara had ever witnessed. The sands were illuminated, vibrant, and technicolor as though captured in an altered photograph. His eyes were drawn toward the back of the Sphinx, as if by magnetic pull.

Do you know who they are? It was not his own thoughts, but a distinct, unfamiliar voice within his head. *They of the monuments?*

The intrusive thoughts startled him, yet he was unafraid. Somehow, he knew this was a place he had been before. He looked over his shoulder, where a man now sat behind him, crouched on a block at the western edge. He was olive skinned with a shaved head, and wore sandals and a tunic of sorts. His face was broad, noticeably in the brow and cheekbones, and he wore a golden hoop through one of his nostrils. His limbs were lean and long, and around his wrists he wore white gemstone bracelets.

Have no fear. You have made it this far, the voice spoke. *Come*. His lips curled into a slight grin.

O'Hara stood and crossed the stone blocks.

The man's skin now took on an orange hue under the sun's rays and his eyes were the same pale violet color as the western sky beyond him. The gemstone bracelets illuminated.

"Who are you?" O'Hara asked. His voice echoed through the valley below.

Close your eyes and trust, the voice spoke. *You are safe.*

He hesitated for a moment, then closed his eyes. When he did, he saw a much larger being, with muscular limbs and shoulders, wearing a metallic helmet that made his head look like that of a long-beaked bird. He thought of the statue he had recently seen somewhere he could not recall, and opened his eyes to find the man smiling.

Is that more familiar? the voice asked. *I am often interpreted in such a way.* The man motioned for him to sit. *Yet, I have many forms across many densities. Close your eyes once more.*

O'Hara sat and closed his eyes. Before him stood a bearded Norse warrior, with long braided hair and a patch over one eye, holding a spear. Sitting on either shoulder of this man were two large, black ravens. He opened his eyes.

We are one and the same. The man moved his hands in a circular motion and when he stopped, they were each holding a translucent green tablet. *It has all been recorded*, the voice said. He moved his hands once more in the same manner and the tablets vanished.

A wave of warmth passed over O'Hara.

You are not here by accident, the voice said. He held his open palm turned up toward the sky, and a rose-colored orb appeared and hovered. *And this is no dream.* He then pushed the orb in O'Hara's direction. It floated toward him. As it grew near, he heard Dina's familiar voice whisper, "I love you."

Goosebumps crawled along his flesh.

"Can I be with her?" He asked.

The man nodded. *When you are ready.* He placed his palms flat against the stone block he sat on. *These monuments were constructed as power plants. They are the perfect geometry and location to generate zero-point energy, and are far older than your historians think. And the one that honored Sekhmet is more than twice as old as they are.* The man looked below, toward the sphinx. *There was once two of them. They were lions.*

The human face was carved from the original cat's head many centuries after it was constructed. It is a keeper of the records. The secrets. He patted the stone block beneath him. *And these... the energy generated by these monuments bring a specific frequency to the planet that will raise its density. Some of you will be prepared for that.* The man gestured toward O'Hara with a nod of his head, and a translucent image of Dina appeared before them. *She is of the old. Those who inhabited the planet during the years the lion was constructed in what your people call the age of Leo.*

O'Hara glanced at Dina, then back at the man.

You both originate... he paused and smiled, then pointed a long finger up toward the sky. *This monument was once used as a portal. Both for astral travel, and sometimes physical transportation as well. She has used it.* The man pointed at him. *You have.*

The man again began moving his hands in a circular motion. When he steadied them, they cradled a hovering holographic image of two pyramids interlocked, one inverted within the other, a multidimensional Star of David. The geometric design was the violet color of the man's eyes. *Do you know of the merkaba? The sacred tetrahedron?*

O'Hara shook his head.

Visualizing yourself in a merkaba is a tool for interdimensional travel. It triggers the transmutation of personal energy of the self, into another dimension with all intention. Do not forget I told you this. It is a tool you may use. All pyramids you see are actually merkabas. The inverted one is vibrational and unseen to the naked eye, which perceives at a lower density.

O'Hara was unsure of what this meant, although he felt a resonance with the man's message, as if understanding it on a subconscious level. He was transfixed by the design that hovered over the man's hands, now beginning to slowly rotate on its axis.

Sacred geometry creates a spiral of high frequency energy, an amplifier of consciousness, that will activate an intention, and increase connection with source. Truth. The man pulled his hands apart, causing the merkaba to expand in size, until it was larger than both of them. *Step inside. You will be immersed in a much higher density, and see what you are missing in your current matrix.*

O'Hara stood. He studied the man's violet eyes, then stepped into the merkaba hologram.

The land was suddenly flat and the night sky above was littered with the largest, brightest stars that O'Hara had ever seen. He scanned the horizon, which felt familiar, yet was nowhere he recognized. He stood among grassland, where occasional trees sprouted, acacia and eucalyptus. A star traversed the sky, leaving a trail of white in its wake.

He inhaled deeply, and with the exhalation, he heard a deep, gravely hum of vibration.

He closed his eyes and savored the restorative, healing sensation it brought with it.

You may ask me anything you would like. Simply think it.

"Am I really here?"

You are. As am I. For there is no such thing as time, or death. We are all everywhere, at once. We are all one. You awaken in what you call reality and partake in the holographic interpretation.

"Who are you?"

For purposes of your understanding, I have many names, in many lands, across many forgotten times. For you to most easily understand, you may call me Thoth. The man tilted his head to one side and closed his eyes, as if listening for something. His eyes opened and he nodded toward the sun. *Awaken, before you are trapped in this illusion you call 'time'.*

"I want to know more."

You will...

His eyes had yet to adjust to the light that was shining in through the bedroom window and all he could make out for a long moment was a silhouette standing in the doorway. At first, he wondered whether he was still dreaming. He slid his hand to his waist for the sidearm that hadn't been there since Africa. As his eyes began to focus, he realized he was looking at the outline of a woman.

"Who are you?" O'Hara asked, sitting upright.

"You came," the woman said in a sad whisper. She spoke with an Australian accent.

"Who are you?" he repeated.

She stepped into a slice of sunlight that shone in through the window.

"Teagan," she said. She wore loose fitting shorts and a tank top, and her dark blonde hair was dreadlocked and tied up above her head in a loose bun. She offered a slight smile that caused dimples to form in the taut skin of her face.

Tattoos of geometric patterns and Polynesian designs ran the length of her arms and shoulders and she wore a golden hoop through one of her nostrils. What caught O'Hara's attention most, however, was the pale gray color of her eyes under the light, and how similar they were to Dina's in the way she observed him. It lent her a familiar feeling, like running into a distant relative for the first time in ages.

"I have been looking forward to meeting you for a long time," she said. "Would you like something to drink?"

"I should be asking you that." He looked around.

She smiled, as if embarrassed. "Of course."

"Have you been living here?"

She nodded.

A confused look came over O'Hara's face. "You knew Dina," he said.

She sat on the bed beside him. "I was the one she came down here seeking."

"She was after an aboriginal elder. A man."

She smiled. "In another lifetime, yes."

"What the fuck," O'Hara said under his breath.

She placed a hand on his shoulder. "Dina and I were sisters," she said.

"Sisters," he repeated.

"Of the same soul group." She took hold of his hand. "I know how it probably sounds."

"Do you," he said.

"Please know that you are safe with me."

"Safe?"

"We are connected," she said. "Just as you were with her."

"Look..." he began. "I'm not interested in anything like that."

A look of embarrassment came over her. "I am not suggesting anything physical." She laughed and shook her head. "She is still here among us, and is the reason you found me."

"I'm not here to find you."

"She drew you here." She touched his knee. "Would you like a glass of wine?"

O'Hara already felt drunk from listening to her.

When he didn't answer, she stood and walked toward the kitchen. He heard cabinets opening and closing, listened to the cap of a wine bottle being twisted open and the sounds of glasses being filled. It was all so surreal. This cabin in which he was meant to grow old with Dina. This strange woman more comfortable on the property than he ever would be. She entered the room holding two glasses of red wine and handed him one.

"Dina never once mentioned you," he said.

"I understand."

He waited for her to elaborate. "You understand what?"

A long silence descended between them.

"She was gifted," she said.

"Gifted," he repeated.

"Very much so. But it was untaught. Unharnessed. Her gift evolved down here."

"Do you have a similar gift?"

She nodded, then gestured toward his glass. "Are you going to try it?"

O'Hara looked at the glass.

"It was her favorite wine."

He felt insecure, as though he should have known her favorite wine. He took a sip, feeling the tension in his forehead relax. He closed his eyes and sensed Dina close by.

"From the Clare Valley." When he didn't respond, she continued. "You and I needed to meet this way. I believe she knew that all along, even if only intuitively."

For a moment her comment upset him, as though suggesting Dina only played a supporting role in something bigger. Sensing this, she touched his arm.

"I intend no disrespect." She patted his skin. "There's more in store for you. Things you could never see coming."

"I'm done," he replied, having no interest in her words. "Broken."

"You are stronger than you think. It's only by going into the dark that you can emerge to truly appreciate the light."

"Dina was the only light I've known."

A slight smile appeared on Teagan's face. "But not the last."

He shook his head, suddenly uncomfortable with how vulnerable he had allowed himself to become.

"Give yourself permission to know me," she said in barely more than a whisper.

Had he ever encountered her prior to Beirut there would have been no denying Teagan's attractiveness, but he felt nothing for her in that way. He couldn't. What he did feel, however, was that he needed her friendship like he needed air in his lungs. Here was a living bridge into Dina's world. Someone with the keys to a door that might lead to a better understanding of what she was down here seeking.

* * *

It was an old feed barn that had been converted into a trendy cafe. Corrugated metal exterior walls were covered with spraypainted murals and the whole front of the venue was open walls, facing railroad tracks. Behind the café, through the doors of a refurbished silo O'Hara noticed the large stainless-steel drum machinery of a coffee roasting operation.

When they entered, the waitresses all knew Teagan by name and she introduced O'Hara as Danny. There was an artsy, bohemian vibe to the crowd.

"This was Dina's favorite place to grab breakfast," Teagan said.

More painted murals stretched the length of the interior walls of the café. The tables and chairs were a mismatch of styles, from wooden stools, to love seats and recliners.

"I painted that," Teagan said when she noticed him looking at one of the murals.

"No kiddin'," he said, impressed.

"What kind of coffee do you like?"

"Black's fine."

They walked to a wooden counter where a pair of baristas were working a set of espresso machines. Beyond them was a small kitchenette where eggs and bacon fried on a steel flattop grill. Teagan ordered two 'long blacks' and 'breaky sandwiches' and they walked to the far corner where the cushioned loveseat and chair were arranged around a small circular table.

"I dig the vibe in this place," O'Hara said.

"It's a hidden gem. Amazing nature around here, too. I'll take you on a bushwalk after we eat."

O'Hara watched her as she waved at one of the employees across the room. There was something enigmatic about her. Beautiful in all the traditional ways a man would desire in a woman, the yogi physique and the pretty smile, but with a confidence that suggested she hadn't a care in the world if anyone noticed her for it. He wondered if she even realized it herself. She reminded him of Dina in that regard. He studied the tattoos that covered her shoulders and ran down each of her arms, the geometric designs. A merkaba, that same multidimensional star of two interlocking pyramids, covered her right shoulder. Remembering it from his dream gave him the chills.

"Is that a merkaba?" he asked, pointing to her tattoo.

"Not many people know what it's called," she said and smiled. "It's a very sacred and powerful design."

A waitress wearing a rainbow bandana brought over their coffees and food.

"Thanks for this," O'Hara said and bit into the sandwich.

"Thanks for finally showing up."

He washed the food down with coffee. "You knew I'd come, did you?"

She nodded as she chewed. "I'd have known who you were anywhere in the world. But where it happened... you lying in her bed... it was overwhelming."

"I can't lie, it feels as if I've known you for longer than an hour."

She laughed. "Kindred souls really do exist," she said.

"I want you to take me to all her favorite spots down here."

"Too easy. There's one place she used to especially love to go. Almost every sunset she'd be out there."

"Where's that?"

"By the ocean."

She reached out and placed her hand atop his. Her eyes were so similar to Dina's that he had to look away.

"It's kind of crazy she ended up in a town that had her name in it," he said awkwardly, hoping to offset the heaviness of the moment. "Yan-dina."

"That's probably why I loved the name long before I ever crossed paths with her or knew her earth name."

"You're not from around here?"

She shook her head. "Far from it." She smiled, bringing out her dimples. "But to answer what I think you're asking; I was born down in Tasmania. I bounced around during my younger years. Tassie up to Cairns. Slowly made my way back down the coast, stopping and finding random work, you know. When I got to Sunny Coast, I decided to post up, though. The land spoke to me."

He understood how Teagan was the kind of person Dina would befriend. They felt so much alike. But he couldn't wrap his head around how she could have gone so long without ever once mentioning her. It saddened him to think she had kept such a secret and he hoped there weren't others to be discovered.

"That's the beautiful thing about this region, whether you want enchanted forest or pristine ocean beaches, you're never far from either." She sipped her coffee.

"Dina used to say that. I always thought she was exaggerating."

Teagan clucked her tongue.

This made O'Hara grin. "You learn that from her?"

"What?"

"The tongue thing."

She smiled. Her eyes took on a distant, sad look. "I have a few things I need to take care of this afternoon. If you're up for killing some time at the beach, I can show you that favorite spot of hers a bit later?"

After a long silence, he nodded.

* * *

He took a seat at a table on the outside terrace, facing the calm turquoise waters where the Mooloolah River met the sea. The stretch of peninsula that extended toward Point Cartwright was narrow enough that even from where he sat, with the high dunes blocking any view of the ocean, he could hear the roaring of the surf.

Washing down fried Barramundi and beer battered chips with a locally brewed lager, he read an article on his phone about Dmitri Smidovich's death and was comforted by the fact that the internet search results weren't many. Among those he found, only one mentioned the Russian gangster by name. The common assumption among the articles was that he was likely taken out by a rival organized crime outfit. Only one of the stories even mentioned the second man who Rafi had shot.

He put his phone back in his pocket and watched the locals who gathered on the promenade below. Once he finished his meal, he ordered another beer and took it to a paved path that ran parallel to the dunes. The pandanas trees, with their phallus-like roots growing from the base of their trunks, formed a natural tunnel where their overhead branches intertwined above. He traveled the path past runners and dog walkers, feeling a serenity that can only be discovered among the sounds and salty breeze that rolled in off the sea.

At a shop a few blocks away, he purchased swim trunks and found a quiet stretch of coastline where he sat with the sun on his shoulders and watched the ocean, feeling its energy. For the first time since losing Dina, he experienced a moment of genuine gratitude for all he still had in life.

He hung his clothes on a bush atop the dune and walked toward the water, performing a silent meditation with the heat of the sand against his bare feet. He entered the cool water, walking out until he was waist deep and dove into a wave. Submitting to the weightlessness of being underwater, the sweep and pull of the rip put him at the mercy of its power and allowed him to release all of the tension that he had been carrying since Africa. He was fully present, undistracted and in the moment. Part of him wanted to remain there, and let the tide take him for good. He didn't resurface until his lungs burned, aching for air, and the salty tears from his eyes had mixed with that of the sea.

He swam against the rip, and then allowed himself to be drawn back by it. Standing neck deep in the water, he performed a series of exercises he had learned at the river near Li's compound in the African bush. He loved the burning sensation he felt in his muscles while practicing the movements and felt alive and invigorated. When he exited the water and sat on the hot sand, his body, mind and soul were in alignment, relaxed to the point of exhaustion.

He dressed and walked to the cliffs at the northernmost stretch of the peninsula, where he watched paragliders make wide sweeps across the sky. Down below, clusters of surfers straddled their boards in the water, awaiting the perfect wave. This was a lifestyle he could get used to, he thought. A part of the world where he could see himself finally hitting the brakes and laying low.

As the sun began its slide down toward the horizon, his phone buzzed. It was a message from Teagan, who directed him the rest of the way up the cliffside walk toward a blue lighthouse he could now see in the distance. It stood tall along a high cliff overlook among the backdrop of the cloudless pink sky. He walked in its direction.

When he arrived, she was standing at the railing that overlooked the wide expanse of sea. To one side, across the inlet was the suburb of Mooloolaba. In the other direction was nothing but ocean. Sailboats glided across the waters in the foreground, and far beyond them he spotted the lights of a barge.

"You can see whales during the migration months," she said as he walked up beside her. "You hear the slapping of their tails against the water. Such magical creatures." She put a hand on his back and handed him a bundle of herbs tied together by string.

As he accepted it, he felt a mix of gratitude and discomfort. He put his arm around her shoulder and gave a slight squeeze.

"Thank you for doing this with me."

"Thank you," she replied, then added, "We are all one in the end." She used a lighter to burn the end of the bushel that he held. There were tears welled up in her eyes, causing ripples of pink reflection.

O'Hara felt pressure building in his own eyes and blinked to clear his vision. "I love you," he said to the breeze.

Together they watched the smoke ride the wind. He felt Dina's presence and was comforted by this realization. She would always be with him, but now she was free.

THREE

He had the cabin to himself for the next few days. Teagan was commissioned to paint a mural for a tattoo studio in the Gold Coast, and decided to stay down there in a hotel until she had finished the job. She left her black Ford Territory with O'Hara and caught a train from the old-town Landsborough railway station.

He spent his first day alone, getting used to driving on the other side of the road, exploring the Sunshine Coast. He found a beach town called Mudjimba where he went for a long swim in the surf, ate fried fish and drank a beer at a café across the street. Down the coast in Mooloolaba he discovered a used bookstore where he was surprised to find an Eddie Bunker memoir among the stacks. He bought it and brought it to Buddina where he read it under the shade of a tree, facing the ocean.

As the gloam hours neared, twilight banked down over the coast like a blanket. O'Hara walked the paved path up toward the lighthouse just in time to catch the setting sun. The ocean glowed a pale blue, with wave crests of pink sea foam. The sky to the west was a deep shade of violet with thin clouds mirroring the red sun, now somewhere out of sight.

He leaned against the railing, looking out toward the horizon, thinking of Dina in the spot at which they burned the offering in her memory. He expressed his love and imagined what it might have been like to spend just one day with her in this beautiful landscape. Down below at the base of the cliffs, crowds were gathered. Blankets were spread along the sand and kids were playing cricket while adults enjoyed sundowners. Music could be heard echoing across the water from The Spit in Mooloolaba.

He didn't notice he had company until he heard a wheezing sigh and turned to find an elderly man with thick-framed eyeglasses, sitting down on the nearest wooden bench. He was dressed in a white linen shirt, khaki pants and a pair of boat shoes. A fringe of gray hair wrapped the sides of his head, connecting to a well-groomed beard, just a shade darker.

They met eyes and the man smiled. O'Hara acknowledged him with a nod, then turned his attention back to the sea. He let Dina know he'd return in a day or two and started down the paved path.

"Beautiful up here," the older man said in what didn't seem to be an Australian accent. He was holding the flame of a Zippo lighter to the end of a cigar, and spoke with it clamped between his teeth. Once the flame caught, he snapped the lighter shut and slipped it in his pocket.

"Sure is," O'Hara responded.

"New Yorker?" the man asked, causing O'Hara to stop and look at him. When he said nothing, the man continued. "Only two places on earth say 'sure' that way. The Big Apple and Jersey."

A nauseous feeling settled in O'Hara's gut as he realized the man spoke with an American accent.

"Bob," he said, extending his hand.

O'Hara clasped it, taking note of his firm grip.

"Danny."

"What's got you so far from home?"

"Take a wild guess?" He gestured out toward the ocean.

Bob pulled the cigar from his mouth with one hand. "It's a good part of the world." He pointed a finger at him. "So, which is it, New York or Jersey?"

"Neither. What about you?"

"Colorado." He raised the cigar back to his lips, and drew from it. "I spent thirty years calling the East Coast home, though."

O'Hara didn't reply.

"You going to tell me?" Bob asked with a smile.

O'Hara looked around to see if anyone else was present. "Sorry to disappoint, I'm actually from Canada."

Bob said something unfamiliar in French.

"You have a good night." O'Hara turned to walk down the path.

Bob closed one eye as he drew from his cigar. "Rafi..."

O'Hara stopped and looked at the old man.

Bob stood from the bench. "Have time for a walk?"

They strolled barefoot along the sands of Buddina, holding their shoes in their hand. The night wind off the ocean was strong and the waves broke hard. The high tide brought the water within feet of the dunes, and because of this, they had the beach to themselves for as far as they could see ahead under the moonlight.

Bob walked slow, and stopped to rest often. He had the long-limbed appearance of a man who could have been taller had he just fixed his posture. O'Hara noticed discoloration in the skin of his hands and neck, and couldn't determine if it was bruising or liver spots.

"We have known one another for years. Since he was young and making a name for himself." He glanced sideways at O'Hara. "Before Beirut."

O'Hara didn't indicate that he knew what Bob was talking about.

"We had a liaison relationship back then. I dealt with his mentor." When O'Hara didn't speak, he added, "Yoni."

Just as the silence had begun to grow uncomfortable, Bob continued. "He turned out to be a bad egg, huh?"

"I don't know what you mean," O'Hara said.

"Yoni." He stopped walking, breathing heavily. "You're a smart guy. I'm sure you're piecing together an idea of what I might be."

O'Hara gave an apologetic shrug of his shoulders.

"You know this little breadcrumb trail you're trying to follow," Bob said. "Ever wonder where Rafi gets his intel?"

O'Hara stared at him. "You're Israeli."

Bob shook his head. "I just told you what I am. I even told you what state I'm from."

"You guys lie for a living."

"As do you, Poit." He started walking. "I really am from Colorado. And did spend over three decades calling the East Coast home." He let out a wheezy cough. "You caught me in the twilight of life. Otherwise, you'd never have gotten that much truth out of me."

"Why would Rafi need a foreigner for help? His people are the best in the game."

"The people you're looking for are likely to be from a part of the world that happens to be my wheelhouse."

When he didn't elaborate, O'Hara looked over at him.

Bob coughed, then cleared his throat and spat.

"Were you in Lebanon?"

He shook his head. "Our way of life is very compartmentalized. Everything is divided up by need-to-know." He stepped toward O'Hara. "I was next door in Syria. Heavy Russian presence there."

O'Hara was suspicious of being provided with even this little bit of information. He knew guys like Bob didn't suffer loose lips without a motive.

"Which is why Rafi approached me about your situation. When it comes to Russia, I've been the guy for quite some time." He continued walking. "The explosion. You were there for it, yeah?" He glanced over at O'Hara, who didn't respond. "I lost friends there, too."

O'Hara could hear the sadness in his voice.

"They're now engraved stars on a wall." Bob frowned. "You were sent over there to track down Jared Ingleton."

"Were you a part of that?"

Bob shook his head. "I know guys who were."

"Sounds like you'd be pretty high up the work ladder."

"You wouldn't be wrong in assuming that."

"Then others must know you're here."

The man shook his head. "I'm dying."

O'Hara stopped walking and studied him. The poor posture and lack of endurance made more sense now. They continued walking.

"I'm sorry to hear it," O'Hara said.

"Appreciate that." He brought the cigar to his mouth and stopped. "We all go eventually. I've had a good run." The cigar bounced as he spoke. He removed the zippo from his pocket and struck a flame, which blew out immediately. He turned his back to block the wind and relit it, then snapped the lighter shut and returned it to his pocket.

"Tell me then. Was it Nikolai Semenov's people who tried to kill me?"

"Not to feed your ego, but your situation looks like it goes higher than the Russian mob." He put a hand on O'Hara's shoulder, as if to hold himself up. "We have a lot to discuss. You up for letting me buy you a drink?"

"Sure."

Bob gestured toward a set of wooden stairs that cut through the sand dune toward the nearest road beyond.

La Balsa Park was a stretch of grass and gazebos where locals enjoyed picnics along the calm waterfront of the marina, just a short walk inland from the coast.

O'Hara and Bob took a seat on a wooden bench near the rocky embankment that led down to the water. They each held plastic tumblers of wine half-filled with a South Australian red, the bottle of which rested on the pavement near their feet.

The marina was empty of people, as it always was once the sun had set. A long stripe of white reflected the waxing moon along the still water's surface, where the red dots of buoy lights bobbed up and down. Across the marina, fishing vessels and private boats were moored in rows.

"When Rafi dialed me in on your situation, I also assumed it would've had to do with Nikolai Semenov," Bob said. "He had connections all the way to the Kremlin."

O'Hara sipped his wine and listened.

"I know about the Albanians. I don't know which one of you killed the fat fuck, but I know you were present when it happened, so Semenov's people were the obvious ones to suspect." He slapped at a mosquito on his forearm.

"If not for Uncle Nikolai, what other reason would Russians have to want me dead? Viktor?"

"Kusnetsov?" He shook his head. "That psycho was a liability. They would have ended up killing him, themselves, eventually." He shook his head again. "The militia that was training your buddy up in the Bekka. The guy at the head of that organization, The Baker, they call him. He is one of the president's oldest friends."

"The guy behind the Volk Group."

"*Da*," Bob replied in Russian with a slight nod of his head. "His name is Oleg Annenkov."

"I've heard of him."

He tapped O'Hara's knee with the back of his hand. "The Baker's younger brother was the guy who actually ran the training camp in Lebanon. You would have probably seen him in Kusnetsov's bar in Beirut with all the militia members when they went down to get drunk and laid."

O'Hara remembered the muscular Russian with the arm sleeve tattoos that would come into Bar Sofia.

"Little bro was at the port when it exploded."

O'Hara looked over at Bob, who picked up the bottle of wine and refilled his tumbler.

"Now as good as we may be... we being my people. Your people, too, but my colleagues." He topped off his own wine and set the bottle down beside his feet. "As good as we are. I'd say the Russians are more efficient at the game. The best practice is to assume they know everything."

"Everything about what?"

"About the explosion. Whether or not it was an accident. Who was behind it if it wasn't."

"For all I know it was your people behind it."

Bob shrugged. "It wasn't, but point taken." He sipped his wine. "Let me put it this way, you know at least one individual that was connected to it. Rafi's old mentor."

"You guys are fucked." He looked at Bob. "How do you even know you can trust Rafi?"

"I don't."

"How do I know I can trust you?"

"You don't."

"This kind of cloak-and-dagger talk may have once impressed me, but I've been around the block a few times since then."

"You sure have." Bob smoothed his pant leg with his free hand. "Listen, let's just accept that we have vested interests that complement one another's end goals. And fast forward to the fact that what I'm telling you is that the men behind what happened to you in Bel-Air were not the Red Mafia, but the Russian government." He pointed toward the sky, and whistled softly. "All the way to the top. The little judoka that's out there on a warpath..."

O'Hara frowned. "Get fucked," he said with a slight laugh, and stood. "Whatever manipulative plan I'm being sucked into this time, count me out." He finished off his drink.

"Don't get cocky. I'm sure you're not renting any space in Little Judoka's head." Bob looked out toward the water. "But if his good pal holds you accountable for his younger brother's death, LJ will green light you without skipping a beat."

"LJ?" O'Hara asked, before figuring out what it stood for. He felt chills run through his body, thinking about being on that man's hitlist.

"Tell Rafi I need to see him," O'Hara said. "I can't just sit around, down here in the dark."

"Yeah, it's gotta be tough spending your days in the Sunshine Coast," Bob said. He placed a hand on O'Hara's shoulder. "I'm sorry... I know why you're really here."

"Maybe this is where you casually slip off into the shadows as smoothly as you appeared."

"Those days are gone, kid. I'm too old and broken for that shit." He leaned down and grabbed the bottle of wine and poured the last of it into O'Hara's empty tumbler, and stood. "I will now slowly and noisily hobble toward the shadows. We'll be in touch."

"How?" O'Hara asked, without looking at him.

"I'll find you."

Bob walked away from the waterfront, softly whistling the tune to the Irish ballad, *Fields of Athenry*. O'Hara turned and almost called out to him, but instead watched him until he had turned a corner out of sight.

The song brought back memories of an old life. One that now felt like it could have belonged to a stranger. He drank the wine left in his tumbler and looked out at the moored boats in the harbor. As he thought of the song, he thought of Red and the old neighborhood in the borough he once knew. It felt like a place he once read about in a book.

FOUR

When Teagan returned, she took him up the coast, an hour and a half to a town called Rainbow Beach where they took the Ford off-road along the sands for several miles to a secluded spot set between the surf and a high rock cliff.

They spread a blanket and ate a lunch of boiled prawns and sliced cheese, and split a bottle of Shiraz. After their picnic, in the cool breeze coming in off the ocean O'Hara finished the Eddie Bunker memoir he had bought a few days earlier, feeling like he had just spent time with an old friend. Teagan did yoga stretches down near the water's edge where the sand was wet and firm. When she was finished, they swam together, watching a pod of dolphins breach the water in the distance.

The guilt he had been feeling about spending time with her didn't seem to follow him on this particular afternoon. He felt safe in her presence, in a way he had not felt around anyone since losing Dina. She seemed to sense his desire to not speak of her, almost as though she were able to read his mind. He guessed that she probably could to some degree. They stuck to light topics, discussing her childhood down in Tasmania, and laughed about how different it was to his in the Bronx. The landscape she described sounded like another planet in its beauty. She made him promise to let her take him there, someday. Once the second bottle of wine had been opened and the buzz began to hit, he was all about the plans.

They allowed themselves to fall asleep under the shade cast by the high cliffs that blocked out the waning sun to the west. He was unsure of how much time had passed when he awoke, but when he did Teagan was sitting over a small propane campfire, brewing a pot of coffee. He lay there on the blanket, listening to the surf and watching an osprey glide overhead against the backdrop of a cloudless sky. When the percolator began to gurgle, she poured the coffee into two tin mugs and carried them over.

She handed one to him and sat. He wanted to speak but didn't have the words, and wondered if she felt the same. The moment was interrupted when his phone began to vibrate. He picked it up off the blanket and saw a blocked number on the screen.

"Hello?" he answered.

"Danny," Rafi's voice said, with the slightest of an accent.

"I was wondering when I'd hear from you. I met your boy the other day."

"What?"

"Your man."

Silence followed. "Not over the phone. Are you still where you planned on being?"

"Close enough."

"I need you to get to Alexandra Headlands."

"When?"

"Tomorrow. Be there at six. Alone."

"Be where?"

"Beware of what?" Rafi asked.

"Be where at six?"

"The Oaks."

He went to answer but Rafi had already hung up.

"Everything alright?" Teagan asked.

"Where's Alexandra Headlands?"

"Sunny Coast. Not far from where we live."

Something about her saying 'where we live' was comforting.

"What about it?"

He sipped his coffee, wondering what information Rafi had for him.

When he didn't answer she added, "I can take you there."

"I'm meeting someone."

"Oh," she said.

"A guy," he clarified.

"That's not my business, either way."

"Right."

"I can give you a lift."

"Thanks."

"Shall we go grab a drink in town before we head home? They've probably got some happy hour deals going at a few of the pubs."

O'Hara finished his coffee and stood. "Yeah, that sounds good."

They began packing up the Ford. As he carried the metal percolator and propane burner, he watched her shake the sand from the picnic blanket.

"Hey..." he said, and waited for her to look at him. "Thank you."

"What for?"

"You know, everything." He thought for a moment, searching for the right words. "All of this would have been a lot harder without you around."

Teagan smiled in a way that O'Hara could see in her eyes that she was touched by his words. She walked over and set the folded blanket in the trunk and held her arms wide. He set down what he was holding on top of the blanket and hugged her.

"We're going through this together," she said. She closed her eyes and rested her head against his shoulder.

The corner pub along the main street in the town of Rainbow Beach sat high above the sidewalk and without walls so that the music echoed down past the block of tourist shops, eateries and ice cream parlors.

Eighties rock played from a jukebox beside a row of female backpackers, all perched on stools belly up to the bar with their large knapsacks resting on the floor at their feet. A group of burly men, with long bushy beards and an assortment of auto-racing themed shirts gathered around a tall table in the middle, gawking at the women and making comments to one another. The only other person in the pub, aside from the bar staff was a middle-aged man with a horseshoe mustache, leaning against the corner railing that overlooked the main street. He wore a tank-top with a gold rope chain around his neck, and aviator sunglasses resting atop his forehead. His arms were covered in an assortment of tattoos from wrist to shoulder, and he was holding a pint glass of beer.

"This is a one-and-done spot," O'Hara said as they walked up to the bar.

"What'll it be?" the man behind the bar asked them, sliding two napkins forward.

"Your favorite beer," O'Hara said.

"Two," Teagan added.

The man nodded and reached out of sight, producing two bottles of Byron Bay lager which he set on napkins. O'Hara handed the man a twenty-dollar bill. "Keep the change."

"Cheers," the bartender said.

"Will ya look at the ass beneath those dreadlocks!" a loud voice called out from behind.

Laughs followed.

O'Hara looked over his shoulder at the group of beards around the table where the voice originated. One man nodded upward with his chin, as if to tempt O'Hara to speak.

"Should we just go?" Teagan suggested.

"Nah." O'Hara picked up the bottles and handed one to Teagan. "Let's go over there, though. I can't drink with my back to these jerkoffs."

They crossed the room, with the beards making no attempt to conceal their interest in Teagan. One of them said something that caused the others to laugh.

"It's not typically a town with this kind of vibe to it," Teagan said.

"You never know what you'll get in a tourist trap."

He glanced over at the tattooed man in the tank top, who was watching the group of beards with an unimpressed expression. The man nodded when he noticed O'Hara looking at him.

Skid Row was playing from the speakers, and Teagan began moving her head with the music. O'Hara noticed one of them stand from his stool as the others clapped him on the back, egging him on. He was looking at Teagan.

"Here we go," O'Hara said, as the man approached them. He was a large, thick in the neck and shoulders, and his ginger beard grew down over his chest. His forearms and hands were covered with ink.

"Would the two of you like to join us?"

"We're just having one and hitting the road."

"You're a yank?" the man said with surprise. He looked at Teagan. "And you, dear?"

She shook her head.

The man called back over his shoulder to his friends. "He's a fucking yank. What a wank!" He looked back at O'Hara. "Where are you from, mate?"

O'Hara sipped his beer and said nothing.

"I think I've scared the cunt." The man let out a giggle. "Speechless."

"We're just trying to have a quiet drink," Teagan said.

"Just one? No way. Why don't you come dance with me," the man said. "Assuming the mute doesn't mind." He shot O'Hara a goofy grin. "You don't mind, do ya, mate?"

"Listen," O'Hara said.

"To what?" the man repeated.

"This front," O'Hara said, and gestured with his hands to the man's tattoos, his beard. "What's the point of it?"

"What's the point of it?"

"What are you a parrot?" O'Hara asked.

"Mate—" the man said, sternly and pointed a thick finger at O'Hara.

"I'm not your mate," O'Hara interrupted him. "Fuck off back off to your table, before you get more than you came over for."

"You looking to get smacked, are ya?"

O'Hara grinned.

"Show the yank what happens to mouthy cunts," one of the man's friends said.

"Let's go," Teagan said, and put her beer down on a table.

"Let's not, dear," the man said. "You're a hard cunt, yeah?" he asked O'Hara.

When O'Hara didn't reply he pushed him. The railing broke O'Hara's fall. He planted his back foot and hit the man with a straight right to the jaw that starched him stiff. The man's legs buckled and he hit the floor in stages, as if going down in slow motion. The abrupt sounds of chairs being knocked aside drew all eyes in the room, and the unconscious man's friends rushed forward. One was holding an empty beer bottle by the neck.

"What the fuck!" another yelled.

O'Hara reached into his back pocket and pulled the balisong, swinging it in one fluid motion so that it snapped together with the blade pointing directly at the man with the bottle.

"What's up?" he asked him.

The downed man let out a long moan on the floor between them. O'Hara leaned down and hit him upside the head with an open hand, knocking him back out.

Cackling could be heard coming from the corner. O'Hara glanced over to find the man in the tank top with the gold chain and aviator sunglasses grinning widely.

"What a bunch of pussies," the man said while clapping his hands together. He walked toward them all. "Well done, mate," he said to O'Hara before turning to the beard with the bottle. "Put the bottle down, ya big goof. Your man just talked himself into an early bed time, is all." He let out another exaggerated laugh. "For fuck's sake, mate. You forgot to tuck him in for the night."

"Who the fuck are you?" one of the beards said.

The man in the tank top suddenly stopped laughing and stared at him. "It's a shame you don't know. Because you wouldn't be opening that little cock-hole of a mouth if you did." He pointed a finger at each of the three remaining men in the group. "Now, if I can count correctly, there's three of you bogan cunts left standing. And after what I just saw this bloke do to your friend, I'd say a two-against-three is fair odds." He gestured at the man with his chin. "Shall we finish what sleeping beauty here, started?"

Teagan stepped between them and leaned her head close to the man with the bottle and whispered something into his ear. The man's eyes widened and he pulled his head back to look at her. She nodded her head and the man suddenly looked as though he was on the verge of tears. She placed her palm on his chest, and said "She's alright."

The man took a step back. Then set the bottle down on the nearest table. He looked at O'Hara briefly, then turned and leaned his hand against the back of a stool, as if to keep himself from stumbling.

"Help Jase up," he said to his friends. He looked at Teagan, then at his friends. "Let's go."

"What, the party's over?" the man in the tank top asked. "I was hoping to bash one or two of you wombats, myself." He laughed.

O'Hara swung the knife closed and slipped it into his pocket. He nodded at the man in the tank top. "Thanks."

"You're alright," the man said. "Can I buy you and the missus another round?"

O'Hara looked at the two men trying to help Jase back to his feet. A patch of blood was matted in his beard like a soaked sponge.

"We're just friends," he said about Teagan, as if to convince himself of the fact more than to tell the man.

"What a pity," the man said with a grin. A few of his teeth were gold capped. "I'm Mick." He extended his hand.

"Danny," O'Hara shook it.

"*Oh Danny Boy*," Mick sang in an exaggerated voice.

"This is Teagan," O'Hara said.

"Pleasure," Mick said to Teagan. "There's a brewery about fifteen minutes out of town. Which way are you headed?"

O'Hara looked at Teagan for the answer.

"Sunny Coast," she said.

"That's the way," the man said. "How about we fuck off, outta here before any coppers show up?"

O'Hara looked at Teagan, wondering what she could have possibly whispered into the other man's ear to shake him up like that. "Yeah, alright," he said to Mick.

"I told him his sister is safe, and happy," Teagan said as they pulled off the treelined road of high pine forest into the gravel parking lot where a lone building sat. "That she is with him every moment of every day."

"He lost his sister? Poor bastard."

She nodded. "She didn't want her brother to get hurt, and stepped forward to give me the message."

"How often can you do that? Communicate?"

"As often as I want to make myself available. Dina talks to me."

"Can you read people's minds?"

She laughed, then shook her head. "I can feel the energy and intentions of a person. It helps me read them on a whole. But I can't hear someone's actual thoughts."

"Thank God for that," he said, making her laugh.

Mick was standing at the front entrance to the building, which looked like an old airplane hangar with a sign mounted over the doorway that read *Leperchaun Landing*.

"There they are," Mick said as they reached him. "Let's go wet our throats."

They entered the brewery, which was mostly empty aside from a family with children that were eating a meal at one of the wooden picnic tables inside the large room.

"What'll it be? I'm buying."

"Whatever you're having," O'Hara said.

"Same. Thanks," Teagan added.

Mick walked toward the bar while the two of them took a seat along the bench of an empty wooden table.

"Seems like a character," O'Hara said. "What vibes are you picking up about him?" he asked, playfully.

She hit him with the back of her hand. "Are you making fun?"

"A bit."

"Nothing suspicious," she said about Mick.

"That's good." He looked over at where he was paying the bartender. "I've had my fill of suspicious characters."

Mick brought three beers over and set them on the table, before raising his. "Cheers," he said.

O'Hara and Teagan lifted theirs and they all touched glasses before taking a drink.

"So, where're you from? That's a thick accent you've got." Mick then nodded toward Teagan. "You're obviously an Aussie."

"Tassie, originally," she said.

"I'm from Canada," O'Hara said.

"Get fucked!" Mick said with a giggle. "I would have pegged you for a Yank. Was going to ask you how you felt about this whole country wearing American sports team hats and shirts while not knowing a bloody thing about the games."

O'Hara laughed.

"I bet you like ice hockey."

"Yeah."

"I don't understand the rules, but I love that they let them fight."

"Yeah, it's a real man's sport. Where are you from?"

"Originally from down in Western Sydney. But I've been in Queensland for ages." He frowned and looked toward the ceiling. A thick, wormy scar could be seen on the underside of his jawline. "Shit, it'll be twenty-five years next month."

"Where do you live?" Teagan asked.

"Brisbane." He leaned forward. "You?"

"Yandina."

"That's a hinterland town, yeah?"

She nodded.

"Right."

"So, what do you do in Brissy?" Teagan asked.

"What do I do?" Mick shrugged. "Whatever I want."

O'Hara grinned.

"I mean–," she began.

"I know what you mean, I'm just taking the piss." He sipped his beer. "I do a bit of this, a bit of that. Odd jobs. I'm good with me hands." He nodded toward O'Hara. "Sometimes I come upon jobs I bet you'd be good at, Canucky."

O'Hara didn't respond.

"Isn't that what they call Canadians?" Mick winked.

O'Hara had known more than a few Micks in prison, and from the block back in New York.

"Hockey man with the heavy hands," Mick said, and laughed. "You touched him. Bang! Dreamtime, as the Abos say." He laughed harder. "Then with the butterfly knife." He mimicked the movements, swinging his hand back and forth.

"I appreciate what you did back there," O'Hara said.

"I'm a true-blue Aussie, mate. I'm always game for a good punch up." He drained the last of his beer. "Plus, we can smell our own." He winked.

A loud rumbling of rolling thunder could be heard outside. Mick looked past them toward the windows in the brewery wall.

"Fuck me, it's gotten dark, hey?"

"Looks like a storm's brewing."

"I'm on a bike, too." He reached across the table and patted the back of Teagan's hand. "I hate to love and leave you both, but I better head or I'll be buggered riding in the rain." He extended his hand to O'Hara, who clasped it. "Take down my number. If you find yourself down Brissy way, give us a shout and we'll pick up where we left off."

"Will do," O'Hara said and entered Mick's number into his phone, as he told it. He raised his glass. "Thanks for these."

Mick nodded.

"Cheers Mick," Teagan said.

"Chow, says the wog." He walked across the bar and left. A few minutes later they heard the grumbling of a motorcycle engine.

O'Hara turned to Teagan. "A real one."

She nodded. "We should get going, too. Some of the roads back can flood if it gets bad enough."

O'Hara was feeling good from the beer. He grinned and shook his head. "What?"

"What do you mean, what? You're probably reading my mind as we sit here."

"I told you it doesn't work that way."

"What is it, about an hour to Yandina?"

"A bit more than that."

O'Hara nodded. "That should be enough time for you to explain how it does work."

* * *

The suite was a one-bedroom flat with a kitchen and bathroom, and floor to ceiling windows. Sliding doors opened onto a fourth-floor balcony facing the ocean across the Alexandra Parade coastal thoroughfare. On a glass dining table was a laptop and a mobile phone with an attachment clipped onto the back of it. It was plugged into a wall outlet.

"Bob," O'Hara said as Rafi let him in, closing the door behind him.

Rafi narrowed his eyes as if studying him, waiting for more.

"Did you send him?"

He clucked his tongue.

"Did you know he was going to come see me?"

Rafi poured two glass mugs of tea from a pot and carried them to the table. "Where did he catch up with you?" He set the mugs down on either side of the laptop.

"Buddina."

Rafi gave a slight nod. "Does he know you're here meeting with me tonight?"

"Not unless you told him."

Rafi clucked his tongue again.

"Am I good to deal with him?"

Rafi nodded. "Of course." He picked up his tea. "How's he looking, these days? It's been a while since I've actually seen him in person."

"Beard. Glasses. I don't know how he looked when he was healthy." O'Hara sipped his tea. "Do you know what he has?"

"Has?"

"What he's sick with."

"Yeah. Poor guy." He paused as if in thought, then gestured to the laptop. "The reason I asked to meet you was to tell you in person that I have a contact number for ABT. Turns out he's been spending most of his time in Egypt, lately." He walked to the sliding doors and surveyed the street below.

"Why Egypt?"

"The Neom project. He's got something to do with it extending into the Sinai."

O'Hara looked around the room. "Will you be staying here?"

"I'll be in and out."

"So, will it be you or Bob I'll be dealing with, mostly."

Rafi seemed distracted by something. He picked up the mobile phone and checked the screen.

"You guys haven't met up at all down here?" O'Hara asked.

"I only landed a couple hours ago. Came straight here." He was reading something on his phone as he spoke. "I'm sorry, *Habibi*, I'm going to have to cut this one short. There is something I must tend to." He reached into his pocket and handed him an index card. "ABT's number. Memorize it and dispose of the card once you have."

"When do you want me to call him?"

"Hold off for now. We will meet again in a few days." He put an arm around O'Hara's shoulder and ushered him toward the door. "We'll sort it out then."

At the door Rafi slapped hands with O'Hara and they hugged.

"It's great to see you," he said.

"You too, brother," O'Hara replied.

"I'll be in touch."

O'Hara nodded and walked out.

FIVE

Not far from the cabin, off the Nambour-Yandina connection road sat a caravan park. It was set down an embankment alongside a lazy creek, among the first trees of the forest. From the road it looked like a shantytown of mismatched panels and corrugated tin roofs. Where the mobile homes ended, a row of tents could be seen along a dirt path down to the water's edge.

O'Hara knew the deal with trailer park life, and the unspoken rules that governed it. One didn't have to travel too far north out of New York City before you hit some of the upstate towns, with small communities that lived life according to their own ways.

He followed Teagan through a road patched with overgrown weeds, past a tipped tricycle and a half-deflated soccer ball, to a mobile home with faded maroon wood panels and a freshly painted white door. She knocked and the door swung open to reveal a thin, bearded man, covered in tattoos, with long hair tied back in a loose bun. The smell of cannabis was strong coming from within.

"How ya goin'?" he said.

"Figured I'd stop by before the new batch is gone."

The man looked at O'Hara and nodded. O'Hara returned a nod.

"Chocolate?"

She replied with an affirmative hum. "Two."

"Yeah, right." He closed the door for a moment, and when he opened it, he handed her two circular chocolates wrapped in tinfoil.

"Cheers," Teagan said with a smile, and handed the man folded Australian bills.

"Too easy," the man replied. "Catch ya." He closed the door.

They climbed the hill back toward the connection road.

"How long have you been dealing with that guy?"

"His mother makes the best psilocybin candies," she replied.

"Dude looked like he had a taste for meth."

"Yeah, that's an issue around here."

"Do you mess with it?"

"Ice? God no. Just mushrooms for spiritual practice." She looked over at him. "It's great for raising one's vibration. Dina and I would take them once a month."

O'Hara stopped and looked at her, wondering what else he didn't know about Dina.

"Everything becomes enhanced. Sounds, colors, your perception and connection to source. It'll be good for you. It's helped me a lot since losing her."

They reached Teagan's Ford and climbed in.

They sat facing one another on a flannel blanket that was spread over the grass. The scents of local flora and vines of jasmine that grew along a fence at the nearest timber garden bed lingered within the thick moisture of the humid air and added to the peaceful ambiance of the setting.

The air glowed a hazy green with speckled patterns of light that penetrated the thick forest canopy. She was dressed in a loose t-shirt and baggy harem pants and the locks of her hair were twisted up above her head. A bronze singing bowl and wand rested on her lap and a tea pot with two cups was set to one side.

"Let's clear the air and set our intentions before we begin," she said. "It's important to know what we are after." She struck the bowl with the wand and drew it in a circular motion along the rim, creating a humming sound that O'Hara could feel in his cells as much as he could hear it. The frequency of the vibration put him at instant ease, and he felt his body begin to relax.

"We operate on frequencies, and when we delve into the psychedelic and meditative states, we actually raise our vibration to where we can see and hear and communicate with those of other densities. You'd be amazed by what's actually right in front of you at all times, but which you just don't see while operating from a third density perspective. You create your own reality, and your own reality is all there is."

O'Hara nodded, having no clue what she was talking about but not wanting to embarrass her.

"We incarnate on earth to learn, and evolve. To help humans as a collective." She reached a hand out and gently touched the side of his face. "Set your intentions for this experience. Clear your mind and meditate on what you'd like to receive from it. I am grateful to experience this with you."

He took a deep breath as she continued making the bowl hum.

"It will take twenty minutes or so, to begin feeling the effects."

She pulled the two pieces of chocolate from her pocket and unwrapped the tinfoil from around one, then handed it to him. It resembled a thick coin with bits of exposed mushroom mixed within. He accepted it and waited as she unwrapped the second one. She smiled and popped it into her mouth and began to chew. He did the same. She picked up both cups of tea and handed him one. He sipped it.

"Here we go," she said. "Lie down now and relax. Ride wherever the wave takes you."

He closed his eyes so that he could better focus on the sounds of the birds, the rushing waterfall in the distance. He knew a switch had been hit within him since Africa. The ability to shut off his emotions the way he did in Amsterdam. He wanted to feel remorse, guilt, anything when he remembered Dmitri Smidovich, but there was nothing.

"Treat yourself the way you would treat your best friend," Teagan said from where she lay with her eyes closed.

O'Hara contemplated her words. There had been no harsher judge than himself. He wondered how he would treat someone else he cared about had they endured all that he had gone through. Would he have more empathy?

After some time, she took hold of his hand and he heard a familiar humming sound that he swore was coming from the earth beneath him. The primordial *OM*, he wondered. He turned his head and could hear the whistle of the wind passing through each of the individual blades of grass. With this he knew the mushrooms were beginning to take effect. The sky that poked through the holes in the green foliage above was an iridescent blue. He felt a burst of warmth in his gut, which spread outward through his body and filled his chest, his limbs, eventually his head.

"A good batch," Teagan said.

When O'Hara looked over, she was smiling with her eyes closed. O'Hara heard a deep rumbling emanating from the earth. He could feel the ground vibrating against his back and thought he might be able to absorb it into his body. He soon realized that what he was hearing were the ethereal vibrations of the aboriginal digeridoo. His mind was on the move now, and he didn't have time to make sense of where the sounds originated or whether what he was thinking made any sense at all, but the hypnotic humming of the earth was carrying him deeper into a state of consciousness he had never experienced in his awakened life.

"Teagan," he said, to make sure she was still present, but his own voice sounded far off and echoed.

Have no fear. You are never alone, a man's voice responded.

O'Hara looked around for the origin of the voice but found nobody other than Teagan, who was crouched a few yards away and now caressing the tall grass as it danced and licked toward the air like living coral.

Do you remember me? the voice asked.

"Yes," he answered aloud. His words echoed. He noticed a koala sitting up high in a gum tree, watching him. "I'm feeling it," he added, speaking of the mushrooms.

You're connected, the voice replied. *Close your eyes.*

O'Hara closed his eyes. In the blackness he began to see small purple orbs floating in different directions. Then he noticed something start to take form. It began as an iridescent marking, similar to the trail of a shooting star. It slowly formed into a larger shape. He kept his eyes closed, doing his best to focus on what it was he was witnessing, until he realized it had taken the shape of an eye. The iris was a shade of deep mahogany on the outer edges and violet at its core, and by now O'Hara was able to make out all the fine details within it. It was like no human eye he had ever seen, yet shared many similarities.

As he acknowledged this thought, he felt an explosion of pure bliss within his core, and had the subconscious understanding that the feeling was not his own, but had been gifted to him.

You are a spiritual being having a human experience. Time is an illusion. There is only now. Be in the now.

O'Hara felt connected to something that was more powerful than he could comprehend. He somehow understood that, while in this state, he could create anything by simply thinking it. He focused on the image of Dina, remembering her face in all of its detail. The gray storm cloud eyes. The scar beneath her jawline. The enchanting smile. He felt the caress of fingertips being dragged along the skin of his forearm, and opened his eyes. She was there, kneeling beside him with her hand on his.

He wanted to speak. Years' worth of words he never had a chance to say before losing her. Messages he had spoken since, but never knew whether she had actually heard. His voice was gone. A flood of tears came from his eyes as he struggled to speak, fearing she would vanish at any moment.

He was not dreaming. He could feel her. He looked around for Teagan, to ask for help, but she was gone. He looked back at Dina.

"Shhhh," she said, and pulled his face to her chest, hugging him softly.

He was safe there. Like a child. Nothing else in the world mattered. He wrapped his arms around her and held her as if he would never let go. She leaned her head down and whispered into his ear. "You never have to worry. I am with you and always will be. We have found each other in every incarnation. We will never be apart."

Still unable to find his voice, he leaned his forehead against hers and closed his eyes. He felt her lips against his, soft and familiar. Their tongues met and warmth overtook his entire body, like slipping into a bath. They lay back on the blanket, wrapped in one another's embrace. He closed his eyes and breathed in her scent, felt her skin against his face. He wanted to cross over to where she came from, to leave this life behind and go with her.

You are never without her, the male voice said. *Time is an illusion.*

O'Hara took comfort in believing this. Comfort he had desired since his earliest years. He felt looked-after by another, protected. He submitted to it and sank into the earth where they lay holding one another. There was no need to struggle for words. They were in sync. Their bodies and breaths were communicating as if their minds shared a single subconscious. All they had to do was think for the other to understand. At one point he was unsure if he was even awake. His eyes were closed and she was curled up within his arms with her back against his chest. He felt her body shift and opened his eyes.

He was staring into the eyes of Teagan, who must have recognized his disappointment when her smile faded. He shrugged her off.

"What did I do?" he asked.

She didn't respond.

He looked around.

She reached a hand out toward him but he batted it away.

O'Hara stood. "You knew what you were doing?"

"I'm on my own trip."

He rubbed his eyes.

"It's okay," she said.

He looked at her coldly. "How could you say that?"

She lay on her back and stared at the tree cover above. It angered him that she didn't seem bothered by what had happened. He felt as though they had betrayed Dina, and it enraged him. He kicked one of the empty tea mugs across the property.

Teagan frowned, but remained silent.

"No," he said and walked toward the house.

She didn't follow him, which upset him more. He entered their bedroom closet and grabbed his Canadian passport and cellphone and pocketed them. On his way out of the house with just the clothes on his back, he refused to look over at where she sat on the grass.

"Where are you going?" she asked.

He ignored her and walked up the drive to the nearest dirt road. As he trekked toward the town of Yandina, still tripping hard from the mushrooms, his mind was flooded with so many conflicting emotions he found it hard to focus on a single thought. The weight of having been disloyal to Dina of all people was almost too much to bear and he hated himself for it. In all of his years, loyalty was the one code he had never wavered from. It was the glue that had always kept him from falling apart.

SIX

They sat at a table outside a fish and chips shop that looked out across Moreton Bay. Sailboats slid along the calm waters out toward the islands while slow electronic music echoed from one of the lounge bars at the base of a nearby hotel.

An attractive waitress with intricate Polynesian tattoos running up both legs brought two long-stemmed glasses and set them on the table along with a bottle of Barossa Valley red, from which she removed the cap.

"What's this news you've got for me?" O'Hara asked. His mood had yet to bounce back from what had occurred with Teagan.

There was a heaviness to Rafi's expression. He lifted the bottle and poured two glasses full.

"Come out with it." O'Hara tasted the wine. "This dude Mick'll be here soon. I don't feel like having to explain who you are."

"We might need to get you out of Australia." Rafi gestured with his chin toward an elderly couple at the nearest table who was paying their bill. "Once they're gone, I'll explain."

"You learn something new from Bob?"

Rafi looked at him. "Something like that," he said and watched the older couple, who stood.

They looked out across the bay. A group of women in bikini tops and shorts were dancing at the base of a boardwalk. The melody coming from the lounge bar fit the setting perfectly. If the track being played had an album cover, O'Hara thought it could be a photo of this stretch near Redcliffe.

A man came walking along the promenade path just beyond the outdoor tables. He had designer sunglasses on, a ball cap pulled down low and an unbuttoned linen shirt with his arms crossed. He caught O'Hara's attention because of how much he resembled the Yankees legend Jorge Posada who, for a few long moments, he believed it actually might have been. That's when he noticed the black tube poking out from under the man's armpit.

He heard two puffs of air as the man passed them and looked over in time to see Rafi's chest take the second of two hits. A burst of red exploded from his back. O'Hara lunged toward the man, managing to grab hold of the pistol with one hand. The gunman headbutted O'Hara and fired a shot at the floor. O'Hara didn't have a firm grip as the slide jerked back, causing him to let go.

O'Hara brought his elbow hard across the side of the man's head, dropping him to a knee. The gun fell. Before O'Hara could reach for it, the man was back on his feet and had pulled a curved kerambit knife from his belt. He swung his arm in a quick, snapping motion. O'Hara jumped back as the blade missed his neck by inches. The man kept swinging from obscure angles that O'Hara recognized as the trained movements of a professional. All he could do was stay on the defensive, using cross arm blocks and parries, trying not to be cut. There wasn't a single opportunity to strike back.

In all of the commotion the man's sunglasses slipped from his face and O'Hara glanced up at the dead gaze of his eyes. Calm and focused, void of emotion. They were mismatched in color, one eye brown while the other was such a pale shade of blue it was barely darker than the white around it.

Men and women were shouting and screaming in the background. Without missing a beat, the attacker snuck in a lunge kick that caught O'Hara clean in the solar plexus, dropping him and knocking the wind from his lungs.

He heard the growling of a motorcycle engine and for a moment his mind was back in the streets of Bel-Air. Loud crackles of gunshots followed, just like in Guinea. The attacker looked in the direction they had come from, then turned and tipped the table O'Hara and Rafi had been sitting at moments earlier. He took cover behind it, then ran and disappeared around the nearest corner.

O'Hara felt someone grab him by the collar and try to lift him. The fabric ripped and O'Hara climbed to his feet, turning to find Mick Hanna with a pistol in one hand.

"Oi! Let's go!" he yelled at O'Hara. His words were muffled from the after effects of the gunfire.

O'Hara looked down at Rafi, still sitting in the chair, dull eyes staring off in the distance with two entry holes in his chest. He turned and ran after Mick who swung a leg up and over his Harley. "Get on," he said.

O'Hara straddled the bike behind him and they sped off down the street. He could hear sirens in the distance. He held on tight and thought about Rafi. How something so traumatic as losing a friend had become so familiar a feeling.

Mick dropped O'Hara off at the hotel he had been staying at on Roma Street in Brisbane and returned twenty minutes later having swapped the Harley for an old Lexus sedan.

As they made their way north along the Bruce Highway, O'Hara reclined in the passenger seat and used his thumb and forefinger to massage the tension from his temples. He had yet to wrap his head around the fact that Rafi was gone and what that might mean going forward. He wondered who the attacker could have been, but knew any assumptions were in vain. Once he resigned himself to this fact, he found he could only think of one face. One person he wanted to see. The realization caught him off-guard.

The sky had grown dark and heavy clouds banked down over the southern suburbs as they drove past the exit leading toward Bribie Island. 'Dumb Things' by Paul Kelly played from the stereo system. Alongside the highway trees bent under the force of the winds, as if moving to the rhythm. A bolt of lightning cut a jagged path through the sky, followed by a distinct crackle, then a slow rumble of rolling thunder.

"How long do you think we'll have to lay low?"

"Mate, the whole thing was over in a flash but the odds that nobody caught us on camera phones is slim these days." Mick lowered the volume on the music. "We'll have to change our appearance. Have a shave, maybe change our hair color. Shit like that."

"I'm sorry."

"Yeah, nah, you were fucked," Mick said. "The guy with the knife was swinging like he had an extra pair of arms on him." He shook his head. "Then old mate there with two holes in his chest. I didn't really have time to worry about the details. Someone was out there shooting." He stopped talking and shrugged. "Time to go on walkabout."

O'Hara studied the randomness and poor quality of many of the tattoos that ran along Mick's thick forearm to the hand that guided the steering wheel. No doubt prison ink. "Thank you," he said.

Mick looked over at him and nodded. "You're alright."

"So much for nobody owning guns in this country."

Mick laughed. "The good guys don't." He looked over at O'Hara, then back at the road. "I can't afford not to. There are plenty of blokes that aren't the biggest fans of Mick Hanna."

He pointed a ringed finger at O'Hara without looking away from the road. "Tell me a story, Canucky. You're there sitting with some Wog-looking fella on the edge of Redcliffe, knowing I'm coming to meet you for a coffee. I'm thinking you'll be alone. When I arrive, your Wog's dead and a knife fight is taking place in front of the corpse."

O'Hara didn't respond. He hadn't had a moment of clear thinking to come up with a lie.

"Why don't we start with the Wog..." Mick said.

By the time they made it to the edges of Yandina O'Hara had made one of the riskiest decisions of his life and had told Mick everything, going back as far as Africa. He was exhausted. Tired of running, of having to keep track of all his lies. Of wondering who had tried to kill him in Guinea, and whether or not they were the same people still trying to do so. It was a spontaneous, gut-based decision to come clean to the Aussie hardman, but if there was one calculated thought that went into it, it was that Mick didn't hesitate to put his life and freedom on the line for him. He at least deserved to know what it had all been done for.

When Mick matched him with his own life story, it put O'Hara's nerves more at ease. What would have been immediate red flags in the eyes of most were the marks of a kindred soul for him. The forty-six-year-old Australian turned out to have made a career out of what he called 'expropriating the money and belongings' of drug dealers and criminals. He spent nearly half his life serving hard time in several prisons for bank robbery, kidnapping and a load of other violent offenses he committed once inside. Mick was feared among the country's criminal underworld, who viewed him as a loose cannon, and as a result he had his share of enemies. This was all confirmed when O'Hara typed his name into the search engine of his phone and it returned a long list of old Sydney Morning Herald articles about his exploits and court cases.

"There's no doubt coppers won't take long to recognize me in any video footage that gets submitted," Mick said.

"We can lay low at the cabin," O'Hara replied. He had yet to decide how he would explain the situation to Teagan.

He directed Mick up the hill road, into the forest where they drove until the pavement gave way to gravel. At the turn off that lead to the cabin, O'Hara noticed an old, white Toyota pick-up truck parked in the driveway. He held his hand out, and Mick stopped at the top of the slope.

"Is the ute Teagan's?"

"Not unless she just bought it. Go slow."

Mick rode the brake down the path to keep as quiet as possible. Gravel crunched and wood-fall snapped under the Lexus tires as they rolled. He parked the car behind the truck to block it in, and they climbed out of the car. Mick had his pistol drawn.

"No need for that," a man's familiar voice called out in an American accent from inside the screen door. Bob stepped out onto the front stoop. O'Hara held his hand up to Mick, who tucked the pistol at his waist.

"Who the fuck's he?" Mick asked.

"My last hope for some answers."

"I sent your lady friend to a secure location." Bob pushed the door open and stepped out. "We have to assume this spot is compromised. Same goes for the flat at Alexandra Headlands." He had been looking at O'Hara the entire time. He turned his attention to Mick and extended his hand. "Bob."

"Mick," he said and clasped the man's hand.

"How'd you hear about it?" O'Hara asked.

Bob frowned, but said nothing.

"Who the fuck was it?"

"Whoever it was, if they found you in Redcliffe, they'll sure as hell find you here." Bob gestured over his shoulder toward the cabin. "If you didn't show soon, I wasn't going to wait."

"Where's Teagan?" O'Hara asked.

"Bli Bli." He pulled the screen door open. "If there's anything you need, grab it now."

O'Hara entered the cabin first and looked around. None of it felt like his to begin with.

Bob saw him looking at a framed photo of Dina. "I'll get rid of all those."

O'Hara looked at the small shelf where the statue of Thoth no longer was.

"I don't need anything."

"Let's go, then. You can follow me to the safe house."

They were a few steps outside of the cabin when Bob stopped and turned to them. "Nothing personal, but I don't know you."

"Tell the old cunt he doesn't want to know me," Mick said to O'Hara.

"I'm only alive because of this man," O'Hara said. "He knows everything, now, anyway."

Bob stared at O'Hara for a long moment. "Alright," he said.

The house was a one-story brick dwelling on a cul-de-sac with only one neighbor and backed by dense eucalyptus gums that covered the hills like green clouds of billowing smoke. The neighborhood only had one road in and one road out, and among the homes there were a fish and chips shop and a liquor store.

They all agreed that Mick should park the Lexus inside the garage, out of sight since it was registered in his sister's name and easily traced. Bob then left his truck on the paved driveway and brought them into the house.

Inside O'Hara found Teagan sitting on an oversized suede couch in a large living room connected to an open kitchen with an island counter. She stood as he walked toward her.

"Are you okay?" he asked.

She nodded and touched the side of his face, as if assessing him for injuries.

"I'm gonna make a store run," Bob said. "When I get back, you and I need to talk."

O'Hara nodded. "Get some shaving razors."

"And hair dye," Mick added.

"Any particular color?"

"What am I a poof, mate? Pick one."

Bob nodded and pulled his truck keys from his pocket. "Get comfortable. This'll be home for a while." He then turned and left.

O'Hara could sense that Teagan wanted to say something.

"I'll give you two a moment," Mick said. "Where's the shower in this place?"

Teagan pointed down a hallway.

"Cheers," he said and left the room.

O'Hara gestured to the open doorway of a bedroom. They entered and he closed the door.

"Look, I don't know what to say other than I'm sorry for my behavior."

She shook her head and took hold of his hand.

"You didn't deserve any of it."

"Forget it," she said. "Are you okay? I kept getting these terrifying downloads that a life was lost. Then Bob came and found me at the cabin."

"What did he say?"

"A man was killed and you were in danger. The cabin wasn't safe."

"Did he say if you were in danger?"

"He said we should assume so until we know more."

O'Hara sighed. He felt exhausted. "Is there any coffee?"

She nodded. "I'll make some." She turned and left the room, closing the door behind her.

He sat on the edge of the bed and rested his face in his hands. There was no denying the fact that he was feeling relieved to be back with her. She brought a sense of comfort to his life where that hadn't existed for years.

She returned holding two mugs of coffee and handed him one, then sat beside him on the bed. They drank in silence for some time. He then proceeded to tell her everything, starting with his release from prison in New York and finishing with the incident in Redcliffe. When he explained that Mick had likely been the only reason he survived the encounter, she reminded him that this was a plan they had all agreed to, long before incarnating. He was getting a bit tired of that kind of talk, but accepted it.

They heard Bob return and walked back out into the living room, where he and Mick had the news playing on the television. A female reporter was standing along the promenade in Redcliffe with Morton Bay in the background, discussing a murder that had occurred earlier in the afternoon. Rafi's identity was not mentioned, nor were any details of the killer, however she confirmed that the Queensland Police Service were reviewing video footage of the incident and following leads based on eyewitness accounts.

Mick looked over at O'Hara and fluttered his eyebrows, then took a swig of beer and let out a belch.

"On that note, I got your razors and hair dye." Bob held up a plastic shopping bag.

"Cheers," Mick said without looking back at him. "We should probably get a few long sleeve tees, too." He held up his arms. "Cover these tats if we need to leave the house."

"You'll want to keep the trips out to a minimum," Bob said.

"Too easy," Mick replied. "This place is cozy as. Reminds me of the killing fields."

"The what?" Teagan asked.

"Goulburn." Mick said. He stood and walked to the kitchen and got another beer.

"Let me get one of those razors," O'Hara said.

Bob removed the package from the bag, tore it open and handed him one, along with a tube of shaving cream. "When you're finished, you and I need to take a ride somewhere."

"Sure," he said and walked back into the bedroom he had been in with Teagan. He went in the attached bathroom and stripped off his clothes. He took the can and sprayed a generous amount of cream on one palm and lathered his entire head, then took the razor, ran it under a stream of hot water and began shaving off his hair.

Once alone, the heaviness of all that had occurred since Redcliffe finally caught up with him and it became hard to breathe, as if there were a weighted vest over his chest and shoulders. He managed to shave his whole head before the emotions caught up with him in full, at which point he doubled over and the muscles of his face tightened as he tried to sob silently so that the others wouldn't hear him. He ran the shower water and stepped under the hot stream, letting it rinse the steady flow of tears from his face.

He thought he had been hardened to loss and death, emotionally calloused from having experienced so much of it throughout his life. This was how he justified his lack of a reaction to Rafi's murder. He now understood he had just been running from it. Hiding. The image of Rafi's lifeless body was once again fresh in his mind's eye. He sat on the floor of the shower for almost an hour and wept until he heard Teagan knocking on the door. He climbed out, toweled off and dressed in a clean pair of clothes.

* * *

Somewhere out at sea not far from the coast, he stood beside Bob aboard an old fishing vessel, leaning against the gunwale and staring back toward the Alexandra Headlands coastline. Under a three-quarters moon he studied Bob who held a pair of high-powered lenses to his face. To the naked eye, O'Hara couldn't see anything but a few dots of light in the distance. The red of an ember glowed as Bob drew smoke from the cigar clamped between his teeth. He turned and handed O'Hara the binoculars.

"It's rented out for a month, still," Bob said. "This will be a safe way to keep an eye on it. See who comes and goes."

O'Hara held the lenses to his eyes and was now able to see the windows along the front of The Oaks resort, where Rafi had rented the flat. He found what he thought was the right balcony. The lights were off inside the flat. He turned to Bob. The old man pulled on his cigar with one eye closed and nodded his head.

"I'd say Redcliffe clarified quite a bit," Bob said.

"That was a professional," O'Hara said.

"Can you describe him?"

"My height maybe. Looked like Jorge Posada."

"Who?"

"Come on." O'Hara shot him a look of disbelief. "He knew what he was doing with that blade."

"What happened to the gun?"

"I caught him with a clean shot and he dropped it. That's when he pulled the kerambit." O'Hara looked out toward the ocean as he recalled the fight. "That elbow would have put most men out cold. It barely fazed him."

"Then Mick started shooting?"

O'Hara nodded. "And the guy hit the bricks."

"Was he hit?"

"I don't think so. He took cover for a sec and was gone."

"Do you remember him having any markings? Tattoos? Scars?"

"He had two different colored eyes. One was pale blue and the other brown." O'Hara looked back at Bob. "Psycho eyes."

Bob frowned, as if remembering something.

"What?" O'Hara asked.

"Nothing."

O'Hara cleared his throat and spit over the side of the boat and glanced up at the wheelhouse, which sat a level above the rear deck. "I still can't believe Rafi's gone."

"Yeah," Bob said.

He snapped his fingers. "Just like that."

"It can happen like that in our way of life." Bob rested a hand on O'Hara's shoulder. "It's time I bring you up to speed on some things."

O'Hara looked at him.

"You want a beer?" The old man gestured to the wheelhouse.

The room smelled of old cigar smoke and dampness. There was a bench along the wall on which a cooler of beers rested. After handing a can of Bent Spoke to O'Hara, Bob carried his over to the wheel. There was a digital GPS map screen and radio equipment with a mic on a long cord, hanging from a hook in the wall.

The boat rose and fell with the swells, and through the window it was impossible to distinguish the sea from the sky in the darkness. Bob hit a switch on an overhead lamp and the room became dimly lit.

O'Hara sat down on the bench, and waited for him to speak.

"You know what Rafi was," Bob said. "You know what I was." In the silence that followed, O'Hara could hear the lapping of waves against the outside of the boat.

"Was?"

"Was," Bob repeated. "It's all that ever mattered to me. The craft. The mission. All I have cared about since day one on the job. Three marriages later. Grown children, some of whom I rarely see. Grand-children spread out all over the world..." He held his arms out and looked down at his chest. "A body that's failing me. I still wouldn't change a thing about how it all played out." He sipped his beer and seemed lost in thought for a moment. "I did well. Accomplished some really important things over the decades. Been to places you likely wouldn't even recognize the names of. Recruited and ran agents. Some of whom you might recognize the names of. Eventually started promoting. Rose high in the organization." He steadied the wheel and turned and looked O'Hara in the eyes. "You're getting the backstory because it's cathartic for me to offload. I've carried it around bottled up for long enough. And quite honestly, because I don't have very much time left on this earth... So frankly, it doesn't matter if I tell you." He pointed at O'Hara with the lip of his beer bottle. "There's nothing you can do with this information that can harm me, at this point. My legacy, maybe... but not me."

O'Hara knew when to stay quiet and let a man talk. He sipped his beer.

"I spent the better part of my career focused on the Soviets, then the Russians. Made my bones in Moscow station and a bunch of the 'stans during the Cold War, before ending up back stateside climbing the bureaucratic ladder while being one of the go-to guys for anything related to that part of the globe."

Bob stopped talking and stared out the window, which now reflected the image of what the lamp illuminated within the cabin.

"At some point I took a wrong turn. We all do." He looked at O'Hara. "But this was one of those turns you can't back-track from." He took a long drink from his beer, his eyes appearing distant as if in his mind he was somewhere back in time. Reliving the wrong turn.

"How high up were you in rank?" O'Hara asked.

"High." Bob said this, as if it might not be so good of a thing. "My wrong turn was never noticed. We're talking decades, nobody had a clue. Until one day it was."

O'Hara narrowed his eyes.

"Even a broken clock is right twice a day."

"Did you betray your country?" O'Hara asked, figuring it to be the only thing an intelligence officer could actually do wrong in their own eyes.

"The cooked story will tell it that way," Bob replied. "But nothing is ever as it seems in our line of work, kid."

"Where does Rafi come into this?"

"Rafi," Bob said, as if remembering that was where the conversation began. "One of the finest intelligence officers I've ever met." He paused to drink his beer.

O'Hara set his bottle down on a desktop and turned to Bob. "I trusted him."

"Rightly so." Bob stroked his beard. "I have a guy that can pick up some of the pieces. Continue where you and Rafi left off."

"Who?"

"His name is Nate Killeen. The guy's been under my wing since day one."

"How does that work, if Rafi was Israeli?"

"Rafi was handling you for me."

"America?"

"For me."

"What, are you running your own private spy ring?" he asked, half-kidding.

"Something like that."

O'Hara hadn't realized how much he had been riding on adrenaline until he felt the sudden energy dump. It was as if he had been drugged. "Why?"

"My wrong turn from years ago has built me some very unique relationships that gave me access to people and things that most don't have." He pulled out a fresh cigar and stuck it in his mouth, then slid a window open. "The world is a dangerous place, my friend. We are living in scary times where the good and bad guys aren't so easily distinguished from one another."

O'Hara ran his palm over his head as he tried to make sense of what was being said.

"Rafi had information he needed to pass me, in Redcliffe," he said. "He said he needed to get me out of Australia."

O'Hara thought he noticed a look of confusion on Bob's face, until he nodded and said, "That's right."

"He was killed before he could tell me why."

Bob cleared his throat and adjusted a dial on the boat's communication equipment.

"We believe you might have been betrayed by the Saudis."

O'Hara felt a cold chill run through his body. "Betrayed?"

"That they traded knowledge of your whereabouts in Africa to Russians."

"Which Russians, exactly? The Baker?"

Bob slightly tilted his head. "Still working on those finer details."

"Fuck," he said under his breath. "How credible is this?"

"Rafi wouldn't have been willing to pass it on, otherwise. He was a professional."

"Professional liar. Like you." He was stunned by the thought of it. "Is that information what got him killed?"

"I'm as blindsided by it as you are, kid," Bob said. "A guy like Rafi doesn't get caught with his guard down."

"Who was it, then?"

Bob shrugged. "It's all speculation at this point."

O'Hara finished his beer and dropped his empty bottle into a trash can. He picked up the binoculars from a shelf beside the wheel and looked through them in the direction of The Oaks as if the answer might be out there. "Speculate, then."

"There's been some Russians visiting your friend the prince, out in Cairo," Bob said.

"If the prince is tied to what happened in Guinea, he's a dead man."

"Slow down. All I'm saying at this point is everyone's a suspect, and whoever it is, they know you're in Australia."

O'Hara thought of the possibility of Prince Ahmed having betrayed him. Of him being responsible for Dina's murder. This would have also made him responsible for getting Amjad killed, though, which made it hard to believe. He turned to Bob. "Why are you doing all this? What's the end goal?"

Bob looked out the window and drew smoke, as if contemplating the right answer. "Redemption," he said.

SEVEN

"I like it. It suits you," she said, running a hand over the smooth skin of his head. He hadn't shaved his face yet, and stubble grew along his chin and lip.

"I wish I had the head shape for it," Mick said. "I'm over here looking like a fat Billy Idol."

O'Hara laughed for what felt like the first time in ages. He looked over at his friend, who was now clean shaven with his hair dyed blonde.

"It did the trick," O'Hara said. "Just keep the tats covered."

Mick stood. "Where does Bob keep his stogies?"

"Under the drawer near the coffee pot," Bob said as he entered the room. He picked up the remote control that had been resting on the living room table and turned the television on. The news was playing, and a spokesperson for the Australian Federal Police was standing at a podium beside a member of the Queensland Police Service.

"The victim was an Israeli national. His identity is being withheld at this time, as the investigation continues and we work with the Israeli government to notify his next of kin. There are believed to be at least three other people involved in the incident, and we are reviewing all evidence as a nationwide manhunt has been put into place to track down these individuals. More information will be made available to the public as time goes on. Thank you for your patience." The man left the podium without taking any questions from reporters.

O'Hara looked at Bob, who nodded.

"Won't be long," Mick said with one of Bob's cigars clamped between his teeth.

"When the neighbors start calling in about the four new adults that moved in?"

Bob shook his head. "If you keep quiet and off the front lawn, I don't see it being an issue."

"Right," Mick said. He grabbed a lighter off the kitchen counter and walked out the sliding door to the backyard patio.

"Is he going to be alright?" Bob asked, looking at Mick through the window.

"I wouldn't worry," O'Hara said. "He's solid."

Bob leaned his hands on his knees and stood with a groan. "Let me know if that changes. We can't have any loose ends down here."

"Where are you headed?"

"To catch a flight."

"To where?"

"I'm going to see if I can find out anything about your funny-eyed fellow."

"Are you going to sort out Rafi getting home?"

Bob sighed. "Unfortunately, not."

"Who will?"

"Israeli government, as they just mentioned on the news."

O'Hara looked at him with disappointment. Bob offered an apologetic shrug.

"When will you be back?"

"No more than a couple of days. I wouldn't stray too far from home, if I were you. The kitchen's stocked." Bob looked at Teagan. "If anyone needs to make a run, it should be you."

She nodded.

"Lock the door behind me," Bob said. He walked across the room and picked up a leather briefcase from an armchair and left.

"What vibes do you pick up about him?" O'Hara asked Teagan.

"About every vibe you can imagine." She looked at O'Hara, forced a smile and shrugged her shoulders. "I'm so sorry about your friend. Everyone's so worried about being caught they forget about the loss."

O'Hara averted his eyes. He found it most uncomfortable when people showed him empathy.

"Just know that all of these difficult situations… trials and tribulations…" She waited for him to look up at her. "They are forging you into what you need to be, for something much bigger. It is not by accident that you are the one still standing."

He placed his hand on hers as a gesture of gratitude, and looked out the sliding glass door that led to the backyard where Mick was smoking, staring up at the trees. "Poor bastard thought he was meeting me for a coffee." He looked back at Teagan. "You might not want to get too close to me."

"I can look after myself," she said.

O'Hara touched her cheek and stood, turned and walked out to the backyard.

"You good?" he asked Mick, as he stepped outside and slid the door shut behind him.

Mick puffed on his cigar, still watching the dense canopy of tree tops that hid the house from that direction. "All good, mate." He pointed upwards. "Kookaburra. I love them."

O'Hara looked up but couldn't see it. Then he heard the bird's maniacal laugh. He looked at Mick, who was grinning and began to mimic the call. "Such an Aussie bird."

"I'm sorry you're trapped in this mess."

"I'm not trapped," Mick said. "I can walk out that front door anytime I choose to." He tapped his cigar with a finger and dropped ash onto the paved stones. "But that would be stupid of me."

"I keep pulling people into these shit storms everywhere I go."

"Mate, I learned a long time ago to just submit."

"What do you mean?"

"Submit. Go with the flow of the universe." Mick looked at him, his dark eyebrows stood out against the dyed hair of his head. "I considered leaving the gun at home when I was off to meet you for a simple coffee.

Figured, I had a good feeling about you in my gut. None of these wankers that still had it out for me were going to go through the trouble to send a guy from," he made quotations with his fingers, "Toronto to do the job. And Redcliffe is weak as piss."

"Thank God you brought it."

"Fuckin' oath. And when I arrived, I was barely off the bike when I saw you having what looked like a punch-up with the cunt. But you guys were swinging all funny like..." He pressed a ringed finger to his temple. "This is how the mind works in real time, right? Everything slows. So, I am wondering why the other bloke's swinging his arms so weird and you're just blocking and moving. I thought, stop blocking and punch the cunt!" He stopped talking to pull from his cigar, then blew a stream of smoke. "That's when I realized it looked just like a knife attack in prison. He had a blade. So, I said, fuck it, that's my new mate he's after. Started squeezing."

O'Hara thumped his chest softly.

"You act... and then submit to the outcome," Mick continued. He held his arms wide, looking around at the backyard and the house behind him. "I've lived in a concrete cell with some of the scum of this country. You're a top bloke. Teagan is a beautiful Sheila. This will be like a resort." He looked at O'Hara. "The path I've traveled hasn't left me with many true friends, if any. You'd be hard pressed to have enough fingers and toes to count the drug dealers and gangsters of Sydney I haven't stood over. Robbed. Bashed. Shot." He giggled. "A few of the Lebbos down there want me the worst. They've probably got one of those fatwas out on me, the cunts." He batted his hand at the air.

"I knew you were a tough bastard, but you've caught me off guard with the Zen philosophy."

"Zen and the art of being a crim," Mick said with a grin. He pointed at O'Hara. "I knew you and I were cut from the same cloth when I saw you bash the bearded cunt up in Rainbow Beach. We ride together, now. No regrets."

O'Hara walked over to him and hugged him, clapping him on the back.

"Only thing you do need to be sorry for is this fucking hair I'm walking around with," the big man said. "That is your fault."

"Yeah," O'Hara said with a laugh. "You may wanna think about getting the eyebrows to match."

"Fuck off!" Mick said with a grin and pushed him away.

* * *

He found her in the bedroom, sitting cross-legged on the floor with her eyes closed and her hands resting, palms up on her knees. Her dreadlocks were twisted back into that wild bun she was wearing when they had first met. There was a worn copy of the Bhagavad Gita on the rug.

"Join me," she said without opening her eyes.

He closed the door and crossed the room, removed his shoes and sat with his back against one of the walls so that he was facing her.

"They're coming forward. Wanting their chance to communicate." One side of her mouth curled. "Wow, you've lost more than I was aware of." She inhaled deeply, held her breath for a long beat, and exhaled slowly. "Okay."

O'Hara observed her, the bone structure of her face under the passive lighting that shone in through the floor to ceiling windows. Her lips. The serenity of her relaxed expression, like a Buddha.

"Dina's letting the others have a moment, first," Teagan said with a soft smile. She nodded her head and her smile widened. "The grandmother figure is here. She's funny. Sassy." She pursed her lips. "She's saying something about Russia. Did you go to Russia?" Keeping her eyes shut, she frowned quizzically and cocked her head at an angle. "It's like she's showing me you sneaking into Russia."

O'Hara grinned. There was no doubt that she was communicating with Nan. He wondered if Red was with her.

"Does this make sense?"

"I snuck into the grounds of the Russian mission in the Bronx when I was a kid. It's like the residential part of the embassy, where all the diplomats and their families lived."

"She's laughing about it. Saying, 'Boy I knew you were going to be sneaking into other countries long before you even knew!'." Teagan laughed. "She said she's colorblind. Does this make sense?"

"Wow," O'Hara said in barely more than a whisper. "That was her line. Nan was black."

"Oh," Teagan said, as if surprised. "Because she came forward to me as if she were your grandmother. This is how she thought of you."

"She was."

His response caused Teagan to smile. "She appreciates you saying that. Know that she has been with you since she crossed over and she protects you now in ways she could not while she was alive."

O'Hara smiled, appreciating the thought that she might be present in the room.

"I've got another one, now. A man."

"Red?"

Teagan didn't respond. "Strong man. Beard. Oh," she said as her face took on a surprised expression. "I think this is the man who recently crossed over. Was he bearded?"

"Rafi?"

She nodded. "He wants you to know he is okay. He was welcomed by his family. Kids and I think his wife." She cocked her head at an angle. "Did he lose his family?"

"Not that I was aware of. But anything's possible with him. He didn't reveal too much about himself, and what he did reveal may not have been the truth."

She let out a slight laugh. "He says now you know."

O'Hara smiled. "Can you ask him who did it? Who shot him?"

Her expression faded. She took a deep breath. "He isn't giving me anything. He says stay the course." She nodded. "Almost like, complete the mission. If this makes sense."

"Yeah."

She remained still for a long moment, as if listening for something. "Let go of any guilt over his passing. It was his time and he chose it. He wanted to be with his family." She nodded as if in agreement with whatever message she was receiving. "He says, you got this from here."

Suddenly her face softened again and she sighed long and slow. "Okay, it's Dina's time. The others are moving aside for her."

O'Hara felt butterflies in his stomach, like he was meeting her for the first time all over again. Teagan said nothing for a long stretch. A tear slid down one of her cheeks.

"She wants to speak through me," Teagan said. "She wants me to channel her." Her face tightened as if about to cry, but she let out a slow breath and nodded. "I have never done this before. She wants to know if this is okay with you."

"Of course," O'Hara said, trying to hide how nervous he was to receive any message from Dina.

She did not speak for some time. O'Hara could hear Mick rustling around in the kitchen. Her eyes opened and she looked at him. The intensity of her stare was disarming, and made O'Hara feel exposed and vulnerable.

She smiled, and reached a hand out and caressed the side of his face. He let her.

"I chose my exit point, stop holding yourself responsible. I am with you forever. Always have been. Always will be."

O'Hara remained silent. He closed his eyes and focused on the feeling of Teagan's hand against his face, imagining it to be Dina's.

"Like Lord Sananda and Lady Nada found one another in their incarnations, so did we." Teagan inhaled deeply and exhaled.

"Who?" he mouthed without sound.

"Yeshua and the Lady Magdalene," Teagan said. Her voice sounded different to him. "And as they returned to Merope and reunited when their work was done... so will we."

"Where?"

"You already know the answer to this question. And every other question. But if I help you discover it, your contractual path will be altered. You must discover it on your own. It is a part of what you agreed to."

"I don't understand."

She smiled. "Everything has happened the way it was supposed to. You have manifested, and succeeded so far. Your guides are of the highest realm."

O'Hara thought of how Teagan had said that Nan protects him.

She clucked her tongue, the way Dina used to. "Not her." She then took one hand and patted her other forearm, over a tattoo of a geometric pattern of intertwined circles, triangles and other obscure shapes. "The highest density."

O'Hara studied the tattoo on Teagan's arm, but did not understand its significance.

"Your journey is far from complete."

"I miss you," he said, submitting to the possibility that he might somehow be speaking to Dina directly.

A warm smile appeared on her face. "You don't have to miss me. I am with you. And I am with you in this form as well." She ran her hands over her chest and torso, then her legs, as if smoothing out wrinkles on her clothing. "We are all one."

"I want to see you."

"You will." She took hold of his hand and leaned forward, close enough so that he could feel her breath against his face. "You must go to the land you have traveled to."

"Lebanon?"

She clucked her tongue. "In your dreams." She gave a slight nod. "It will be made clearer to you, in the days ahead. But it is where you will find answers. But not to the questions you will think you are there to ask."

"I don't understand."

She rested her forehead against his and closed her eyes. "It is okay to not understand," she whispered.

With his eyes shut, he imagined it was Dina's skin he felt. He shifted his head so that their lips met. They remained like that for some time, lips pressed against each other's. She wrapped her arms around his shoulders as he turned to lay her down. Without opening their eyes, they began to undress one another, slowly and with care.

When they began to make love, O'Hara felt an electric charge pass through him. He opened his eyes to find Teagan's beautiful face giving in to the passion as they moved together. He shut them and saw Dina before him. She pulled his head down and kissed him.

When they were finished, they lay there in each other's arms, Teagan asleep with her head on O'Hara's chest, psychically and emotionally exhausted. He did not suffer the same inner turmoil or guilt that he had felt in the past. He understood how much she had given of herself to make it happen, now feeling the truest gratitude and wanting to be closer to her because of it.

He listened to her softly snore. Her face appeared younger now than when she was awake. There was an innocence about it, and he had the urge to protect her. The sun was setting and a deep orange slice of light cut across the darkened room along her torso. O'Hara closed his eyes, and listened to her breathing until he too, fell asleep.

* * *

He cooked a late meal of scrambled cheese-eggs and toast for the three of them. Breakfast for dinner. Teagan came out to eat, but was still exhausted from having channeled Dina. The news was back on the television, playing without sound, when Mick noticed a headline at the bottom of the screen that mentioned Redcliffe. He picked up the remote and unmuted it.

"We now know that the victim of the attack in the bayside suburb was thirty-nine-year-old Israeli national Rafi Ben-Ezra," the female newscaster's voice stated over a photo of the café where the shooting had taken place. The block was still cordoned off by yellow police tape. "No further information is known about the gunmen at this time, but they are believed to be armed and dangerous. The phone number at the bottom of the screen has been set up jointly by the AFP and QPS, where any and all information that might help lead to the apprehension of the gunmen can be reported anonymously.

"Grubs," Mick said to the television. "There's only one bloke you need to be looking for."

Teagan stood. "I'm buggered. I am going to turn in early."

O'Hara thought to reach out and touch her, but hesitated. She offered a tired smile and ran her hand over his shaved head. "Night," she said, then turned to Mick. "Night Mick."

"G'night, Tea," Mick said.

O'Hara stood and followed her into the bedroom. "You alright?" he asked.

She turned and nodded. "I'm just really tired."

"How much do you remember of it?"

"Everything up through Rafi coming forward."

"Do you remember Dina?"

She took a deep breath. "I remember what we did, physically... but I don't have any memory of what you might have spoken to her about."

"Wow."

"I've honestly never channeled before."

He waited for her to elaborate.

"It took such a physical toll on me. I wouldn't have guessed."

He stepped toward her and placed a hand on the small of her back. "Anything I can do for you?"

She reached up and touched his face, smiled and shook her head.

He nodded. "I'll let you get some rest." He turned to leave the room.

"Will you sleep in here?" she asked.

He looked back at her.

"No point in pretending it didn't happen," she added.

"I'll make sure to be quiet when I come in."

She smiled and slipped under the covers, into bed.

EIGHT

"I need to get something from the cabin," he told Bob, who was drinking coffee at the kitchen counter with Mick.

"Not a good idea," Bob replied.

"It's for Teagan."

"I don't care who it's for."

"She's not responsible for this mess," O'Hara said. "And there's no manhunt for her."

Bob shot him a questioning glance. "Which manhunt are we talking about?"

"What do you mean?"

"The law or the people that are trying to kill you? Because those people surely know about Dina, and her name is listed as the most recent legal owner of that property."

O'Hara didn't answer him.

"Maybe you and I should have a chat before you start giving in to her cabin fever."

"That's not what it is," O'Hara snapped back. "It's holistic meds. She's not feeling well."

Bob shot him a skeptical look.

"Where'd you go, anyway?" O'Hara asked.

"Not that it's any business of yours, but I had to see a doctor."

"Then don't give me shit about getting her meds."

"If it's holistic there's gotta be a health food store you can pick it up from. Cabin's a bad idea."

"Nah, it's something specific, and it's already there."

"Whatever." Bob frowned and picked up the half-filled coffee pot and topped off his mug. "Wanna finish this off?"

"Sure."

Bob took a mug down from an overhead cupboard and filled it. He set the pot in the sink and handed O'Hara the coffee across the counter. "I did some digging while I was gone. Met a contact."

"And?"

"Let's step outside," Bob said.

O'Hara followed him out through the sliding glass doors.

"I mentioned some of the details you gave me about the gunner in Redcliffe," he said in a quiet voice, once he had shut the door behind him.

"And?"

Bob nodded. "The bit about him having two different colored eyes piqued their interest. Apparently, there's been talk over in Ukraine, and popping up in intelligence channels elsewhere about some nasty Russian mercenaries. One guy among them with a very pale-colored eye."

"What are the odds it's the same guy?" O'Hara asked.

"Longshot, I know." Bob shrugged. "Over there the Ukrainian soldiers talk about this guy's unit almost like folklore, though. They call them *Vovkulaka*, which basically means werewolf in Ukranian." He touched his chest. "My take on that – and my contact agrees – is that he's likely a Russian and in some way connected to the Volk Group. *Volk* also means wolf, in Russian."

"I remember," O'Hara said.

"This Vovkulaka unit is responsible for serious war crimes. The kind of shit that hasn't been heard of since the Serbs in Bosnia."

"The guy was definitely trained-up. Rafi was done before I even recognized his gun." O'Hara tucked his hand under his armpit, the way the gunman had done. "And with the knife, there wasn't even a moment for me to fight back."

"The eye. The fact that he was a professional. The ability to catch a guy like Rafi unprepared. Even the werewolf-wolf connection with Volk Group." He nodded. "You never know."

"Why would they pull a guy like that from an active warzone and send him after me in Australia?"

Bob stuck a finger in the breast pocket of his coat and pulled out a cigar wrapped in plastic. He peeled the plastic from around the cigar and stuck it in his mouth. "Why someone like that would be tasked with the job of killing you?" Bob searched his pants pocket for a light, finally finding a lighter. "Because so far nobody else has been able to do it."

"Don't bullshit me," O'Hara said.

"If The Baker holds you even partially responsible for blowing up his brother in Beirut, I'd say that's reason enough. Assuming he was behind the botched attempt in Africa, he might want someone that'll get the job done."

O'Hara glanced at the outside windows of Teagan's bedroom. The shades were drawn. "They can send who they want."

"I told you I'll help you out." He took another drag from the cigar. "But, no more of this cowboy shit. It's gotta be a more sophisticated approach than the way you've been operating up until now."

"Help me how?"

"Well..." Bob's face grew serious. "I came back with one name."

O'Hara looked at him.

"Sasha Filenkov."

O'Hara shook his head, to suggest he didn't recognize the name.

"But to find him, it'll mean we have to go pay your friend the prince a visit."

"What's his connection to Prince Ahmed?"

"An interest in NEOM."

"And where is this Sasha?"

"Lately, Egypt. Just like the prince," Bob said.

O'Hara thought of what Dina had said, when Teagan channeled her. Something about traveling. He nodded. "I'm open to hearing you out about this guy," he said. "But in the meantime, I'm still taking Teagan to the cabin."

Bob shook his head. "Make sure you get everything you need this time."

The first thing O'Hara noticed while traveling down the gravel drive was how much taller the grass had grown in the short time since he had last been there. It was vibrant green under the overcast sky. The air was thick and moist, and the ground was damp to walk on. Only the sound of the waterfall in the distance could be heard.

"I don't know," Teagan said as they neared the bottom where the driveway leveled out.

"You don't know what?" Bob said.

O'Hara looked at her.

"Maybe we should forget it," she said.

"We aren't coming back," Bob said.

"I'll go in," O'Hara said. "Where is it?"

He didn't want to have to tell her that he had Mick's .45 caliber Springfield MDX tucked at the small of his back. It only carried six rounds with a seventh in the chamber, but it gave him a sense of confidence.

"I don't know," she said again.

"Where is the stuff?" O'Hara asked.

She looked out the window, scanning the property. "There's a small black pouch in the top drawer of the dresser. In the bedroom." She wasn't looking at him. Her eyes were fixed on the far end of the property, where it dropped off down an embankment toward the nearest stream. "A vial of pink salts and another with black paste."

"I'll be back in a minute," he said and opened the truck door. He was holding the house keys in his hand. As soon as he shut the door, Bob pulled the car around so that it was facing the driveway, leading up toward the nearest road.

O'Hara wasn't sure which he heard first. Teagan's muffled shout from inside the car or the zipping sound of a round passing his ear, but he didn't have time to decide as he saw the large caliber hole it formed in the sidewall of the truck bed. He stooped low and dropped the keys, drawing Mick's gun and firing three times in the direction the shot would have come from. He ran toward the cabin and kicked in the front door, diving onto the floor and swinging it shut behind him. With the lock broken and the wood splintered around it, the latch wouldn't catch. He heard the roar of an engine and peeked up over the nearest windowsill to see the back of Bob's truck clear the peak of the hill and turn out of sight. He was relieved that Teagan was no longer there, and wondered if Bob would call the cops, despite everything else about their situation. If so, he would have to drive some distance before he picked up any cellular service.

He thought he heard movement out in the yard. A twig snapping, leaves rustling. He tried to replay in his mind the cadence of shots he had fired. He thought it had been three, which would mean he had four rounds left. He needed to make them count.

He scrambled across the floor, keeping low until he reached the kitchen, where he rose just enough to peek out one of the windows. A man in a black cap, sunglasses and holding an assault rifle was crossing the yard with his weapon trained on the house. It could have been Jorge Posada from Redcliffe, but he wasn't sure. The man appeared to be alone.

O'Hara removed a carving knife from a block set on the counter and turned it in his free hand so that the flat side of the blade rested along his forearm. He flinched as shots burst through the front door, knocking it open on its hinges. O'Hara fired two shots back and crawled into the bedroom. He now had two bullets left, at most.

He considered escaping through the rear door, but knew it would be locked, along with the screen door beyond it. Having to unlatch it might create just enough noise to get himself killed. He slid across the floor with his back against Dina's bed and kept as still as he could with the gun aimed at the doorway. His ears were popped from the percussion of the rounds being fired, but he thought he could feel the vibration of footsteps against the floorboards.

Time seemed to slow as he looked around the bedroom. This home Dina had dreamed up from nothing and manifested with the idea that the two of them would spend their life together in it. He thought of the splintered door and broken glass. The walls shot up. The damage felt like a violation of her memory. He considered the possibility that if he didn't move, he was sure to die there on the floor. This brought him to terms with the fact that, while he was ready to die, it couldn't happen in such a way, cowering on the floor like hunted prey. He climbed to his feet and leaned his back against the wall, straining to listen. Hearing a noise, he reached his hand out and fired a shot. A deafening silence followed. The smokey scent of the spent cartridge was strong. He was down to his last bullet.

He crept across the room and slid the window open, hoping to give the impression he had escaped, then stepped into the closet and waited. A burst of suppressed gunfire from outside the room tore into the mattress and the wall behind it. Clumps of stuffing rose in the air. O'Hara remained still.

He saw the muzzle creep into view, aimed at the open window, and fought the urge to reach for it and give away his position. As it continued to move past the open doorway, he aimed the MDX where he expected the man's head to soon appear. The gun retracted out of sight and he sensed his position had been compromised. He conjured a last image of Dina's face as he dropped low in a crouch, leaned out and fired his last bullet. Return shots were fired and the bedroom window shattered. A round went through the wall and across the closet over O'Hara's head. He flashed back to the streets of Bel-Air as he prepared for what he knew was next.

Out of options, he dropped Mick's gun and gripped the carving knife in his dominant hand, then lunged from the closet ready to swing at the air. As he did so, the gunmen stepped into view and they clashed, too close for any shots to be fired. O'Hara grabbed a hold of the man with his free hand and tried stabbing him in the ribs with the knife. The gunman released his grip on the rifle, which hung from a shoulder strap, and blocked the hit. His pale dead eye confirmed who it was.

O'Hara headbutted his nose, feeling the cartilage pop. The man bit down on O'Hara's neck and started thrashing his head around. O'Hara screamed out and found the man's face with his free hand, then forced his thumb deep into his eye socket until he felt blood run down his wrist.

The man released his grip and stepped back, drawing a sidearm from the small of his back. O'Hara swung the knife down hard across his forearm, nearly severing his hand and causing the gun to drop.

O'Hara picked the pistol up off the floor and fired four shots into the man's chest, knocking him back against the wall where his knees buckled and he fell in a seated position. His orbital socket was a cave of pooled blood and only the pale eye remained, staring across the room at nothing. O'Hara heard the sounds of a vehicle outside.

He walked to the closet and picked up Mick's Springfield, tucking the empty gun at his waist as he moved toward the front of the house. He peeked through the window, considering whether he might shoot himself with the attacker's gun if it were the police outside. Bob's truck was idled at the top of the drive.

O'Hara walked back into the bedroom and retrieved the pouch of salts and black paste from the dresser, then exited through the front door. When he emerged from the cabin Bob drove the rest of the way down to the house.

"Are you alright?!" Teagan yelled through the open truck window as they parked.

O'Hara reached up and felt his neck. "Yeah," he said. His shirt was drenched in blood.

Bob left the engine running as he and Teagan climbed out of the truck and walked over to O'Hara. She touched him, assessing him for further injuries.

"Your neck," she said.

He nodded, beginning to feel the onset of an adrenaline dump.

"I'm sorry for taking off," Bob said. "I didn't know where the shots were coming from. I didn't want to just sit there taking fire."

"You did the right thing," O'Hara said. He looked at Teagan, then back at Bob. He gestured over his shoulder toward the cabin. "Your werewolf is in there."

"Dead?"

O'Hara nodded.

"Alone?"

"Yeah."

Bob walked across the yard and entered the cabin.

"I tried to yell out," she said, once Bob was gone. "Warn you."

"I heard it," he replied. "Thanks."

"I'll clean all of this up." She touched the bite wound on his neck. "You might need a stitch."

"I'll be alright." He pulled the pouch from his pocket and handed it to her.

She brought it to her chest before sticking it in her pocket. "I'm so sorry."

O'Hara shook his head. "This guy wouldn't have stopped hunting me." He scanned the base of the tree line. "Do you know anything about the nearest neighbors? It got loud with the shooting."

"They're far enough away to where I've never met them." She looked around, as though she might spot someone in the woods.

Bob walked out of the house slipping a phone into his pocket. "I'll come back and get this cleaned up. Let's get you two out of here."

"It's him," O'Hara said.

"I snapped a pic to confirm," Bob said. He opened the driver's side door of the truck. "Get in."

When he reached the end of the gravel path Bob turned in the opposite direction, away from Yandina and climbed the dirt road further into the bush, knowing that any cops, and most other vehicle traffic would have to come by way of the town. Teagan knew a route of backroads, some of which didn't even have names, where they would exit the forest somewhere between Image Flat and Kiamba and make their way back to Bli Bli. Duct tape was covering the bullet hole in the truck bed as they crossed small bridges over running creeks and passed No Trespassing signs, where Teagan explained many of the landowners illegally grew cannabis and would be unlikely to talk to the police even if they did notice the truck drive past.

"When we get to the house, only pack what you can carry. Anything that can be replaced, leave it. You'll need to travel light," Bob said to O'Hara. "We have to get you out of this country before that body is discovered."

"How are we gonna manage that?" O'Hara asked.

"Fly, if we move quick enough."

Outwardly, Bob appeared calm and relaxed. O'Hara knew, by the way he squeezed the steering wheel and constantly checked the rearview mirror that he was in operational mode. "I think it's time to head to Cairo."

Teagan reached out and took hold of O'Hara's hand, and squeezed it.

"What will Mick do?" O'Hara asked. "They'll eventually figure out he's the guy in the videos from Redbank, if not already."

Bob nodded. "He can either go with you, or stay. He's not my main concern."

O'Hara turned to Teagan. "I'm sorry," he said. "Is there anything in the cabin that can lead them to you?"

"My DNA is all over it."

"You might eventually end up having to talk to cops," O'Hara said.

Teagan looked out the window. "I'm coming with you." She was still holding O'Hara's hand. "If I don't, we'll never see each other again."

O'Hara remained quiet. After believing he was going to have to find a way to say goodbye to her, he was relieved.

NINE

"Piece of piss," Mick said, leaning his elbow out the passenger side window, staring out into the dark night. Under a near-full moon O'Hara could clearly see his face in the side mirror from where he sat behind him.

"What is?" he asked.

"Being on the run."

"What are you, forty-five?" Bob asked, turning the wheel to change lanes along the Bruce Highway south.

"Nearly forty-seven," Mick said.

"You're just a kid. I've forgotten more than you've ever learned," Bob shot back.

Mick stared at the old American before a large grin appeared on his face. "You're a hard old cunt, aren't you, Bobby? You've got us covered, huh mate?"

"I may not be as good as I once was, but I can manage to be as good once, as I ever was. I'll get us out of this."

"Bob's your uncle," Mick replied.

O'Hara leaned across to where Teagan sat, hugging her knees to her chest with her feet on the back of the driver's seat.

"Are you sure you don't want to bail? It's not too late," he said. "It kills me that you're roped into this."

"I've felt it coming my whole life. I just didn't know the details." She looked over at him. "You need me around. I know you're struggling more than you let on."

"Struggling?"

Under the moonlight that entered the window the angles of her face looked sculpted from stone.

"With all the death. People taken from you. Lives you've taken." She turned and looked at him with such compassion, it was as if she might cry. "You're so connected. You understand much more than you think. But it's intuition. You're not aware of it."

He placed his hand on her knee and gave it a squeeze.

"Just keep this in mind..." She looked out the open window at the moon. "We signed up for this."

"I wish I remembered the script."

"You don't have to," she replied. "You're writing it."

* * *

After helping Teagan stow her bag in the overhead compartment, O'Hara continued down the aisle toward the rear of the plane. Bob hadn't been able to book them seats near one another on such short notice. When he reached his seat, the one next to it was already taken by man with a hoodie pulled up over his head, sleeping against the window. O'Hara stowed his backpack and did his best not to disturb him as he sat.

From his seat he could see Mick's bleached hair halfway up the plane. Relieved that his friend's passport had cleared security checks while exiting Australia, there was a sense of safety in knowing they would soon take flight and leave behind all that had occurred.

The man beside him sat upright and removed his hood. O'Hara watched him switch his phone to airplane mode and slip it back into his pocket. He had a mess of brown hair and one ear was slightly cauliflowered. An unkempt beard covered a sunburned face.

Once the plane was in the air, O'Hara reclined his seat with hopes of catching some sleep. The stewardesses made their initial rounds with the big steel cart, offering beverages. O'Hara ordered a water. The man beside him ordered two red wines. He waited for the stewardesses to move on down the aisle, then picked up one of the cups of wine and set it on O'Hara's fold-down tray.

O'Hara looked over at him.

"Word on the street is that poets like red," the man said, speaking with an American accent.

O'Hara had the cold feeling that came with the realization that he'd been trapped.

"Nate Killeen," the man said and extended his hand. When O'Hara clasped it, he added, "I believe Bob's mentioned me."

PART 2

TEN

Cairo, Egypt

They rode through gritty blocks of tall, beehive buildings that towered above the bustling streets. Locals walked among the traffic, stopping short and side-stepping like matadors to let vehicles pass. Through the open windows of the microbus the air was thick with the taste of exhaust.

Battered black and white Peugeot taxis navigated the nonexistent lanes while honking their horns, beating their steering wheels in distinct rhythmic patterns. The gray-haired microbus driver explained in a conspiratorial tone to Nate, who rode shotgun and translated what he could for the others, that taxis had their own language of car horn affronts, where different patterns represented different insults. He used an open palm to beat a short burst of code before leaning closer and explaining that it meant 'your mother's...' He then paused and gestured toward his own crotch to indicate the final word.

Nate grinned and told the man to keep his eyes on the road ahead.

On the flight over O'Hara had grown to like Nate. He had a hardscrabble, no-fucks-given personality, claiming to have grown up in Philadelphia before enlisting in the military and becoming an operator, then a contractor. That was how he met Bob. O'Hara knew there was a chance the whole backstory was bullshit, but Nate definitely had that East Coast vibe about him. In the end it didn't matter if he was telling the truth. What mattered was the rapport they had built by the time they had landed, and the bit of information he was willing to share about Bob.

"Old dog's a legend," Nate had said in a whisper, sipping from his second airplane cup of red. The loud hum of the aircraft engine drowned out their words from being eavesdropped on. "Trust me."

"Says the spook."

"Alright, here's one for you, and then I'm done." Nate finished the wine and set the cup inside O'Hara's empty one. "Back in the mid-eighties he was posted in Moscow. Was a different set of rules over there. Apparently, the barons didn't even expect you to recruit anyone. They knew it was impossible. The KGB had the city on lock. The most guys were getting away with were dead drops. Brush passes. Clandestine meetings with agents already in place..." Nate nudged O'Hara with his shoulder. "But Bob being Bob recruited a whale. He had first met her in Cuba, but she ended up back in Moscow while he was there."

"She?" O'Hara asked.

Nate nodded. "Apparently, she was a knockout. No doubt he would've been able to turn on the charm. One thing led to another."

"That'll complicate things." O'Hara was sure that must have been the wrong turn Bob spoke of.

"The heart wants what it wants. Even so, he ran her for years. Eventually she got posted to DC, so Bob got himself relocated stateside, to be near her." He looked at O'Hara and lowered his voice. "I don't know how much you know about eighty-five. They call it 'the year of the spy'. Aldrich Ames. Robert Hanson."

"I remember the names."

"Ames was in charge of CIA's Russian counter-intelligence. So, when he turned, he handed over a list of all the Russian agents that were spying for the Americans. On that list was Bob's old lady."

"Damn," O'Hara said.

"The guilty Russians each started getting called back home for fake reasons... promotions, whatever. Then, once back, a bullet in the head." Nate made a pistol with his fingers. "Knowing she'd be sure to get that call back to Moscow, Bob pulled off one of the smoothest moves of his career. He manipulated the situation to appear as though she had recruited him."

O'Hara leaned back.

Nate nodded. "Saved her life. Probably got her promoted, too."

"Holy shit."

"See what I mean?" Nate said. "You're in good hands with the old dog."

"Is she still alive?" O'Hara asked.

Nate shrugged. "I don't even know who she is. If she's still alive she'd be a legend over there, though. Because if she was a considered a whale, then flipping Bob would have been like harpooning Moby Dick."

The microbus passed through a series of down-trodden neighborhoods where it was common to see homes missing front doors and windows without glass. The driver masterfully maneuvered down alleyways that were barely wider than the vehicle itself, where herds of people gathered in the lanes and brought traffic to a halt for long stretches. Many of the men in these parts had thick beards that hung half-way down their chest and were dressed in the long traditional *gallibeya* robes. The women donned loose-fitting modest outfits with their hair covered by *hijab* headscarves.

In the middle of one intersection, young boys were kicking around a plastic soda bottle as if it were a soccer ball. Behind them, outside a makeshift café a half-dozen goats stood tied to a fence post. Through the open window of the microbus the air smelled of shit. They left this neighborhood across a steel bridge, where they passed over what they would soon learn was the mythical Nile River. Downstream, colorful triangular sails glided across the murky green water like swans.

"*Felluca*," the driver said about the boats, before shouting, "*Ya wallid*!" through the open window and beating out a code of horn-honks. Beside them, an ashy-skin child rode atop the hump of a large galloping camel, guiding it among the automobile traffic by its reins.

"A bloody camel-jockey!" Mick called out. "Dead in the middle of the city! You've got to be kidding me!?"

The smiling boy ignored the honking and hand gestures of the driver.

As they exited the elevated bypass road the driver dragged his finger across the width of the windshield, calling out "*Wust el-Balad*."

Nate turned in the front seat and explained, "That's what they call this downtown area. It means 'center of the city'."

"Is there anywhere we can wet our throats?" Mick asked.

Nate said something in Arabic to the driver whose thin lips curled up into a mischievous grin. He laughed and responded.

"I'm having him drop us at a spot a few blocks from the flat. Bob'll meet us there."

They turned off the main road that ran parallel to the river and passed through multiple roundabouts with high-mounted statues. The architecture of the surrounding buildings could have been lifted straight from Paris, were it not for the sepia tint of the brickwork caused by decades' worth of pollution, rendering the neighborhood a faded remnant of its colonial past.

They entered Falaky Square, a clearing among the dense blocks of downtown buildings with a large parking lot at its center. Crowds of customers swarmed around sidewalk fruit stands hawking everything from bananas and mangos to guava and pomegranate.

Ashraf's Café was located on a corner near the middle of the square, where a small lane branched off from the parking lot. The exterior appeared run-down, the outer walls made up of large French doors, swung open on weathered hinges to allow the steady buzz of conversations to be heard coming from within. They followed Nate down the few steps to the recessed interior, a large cafeteria-style room where a handful of men, each dressed in khaki and sporting thick push-broom mustaches moved among the crowd with beer bottles fanned out in their hands, the bottlenecks wedged between each finger. As they passed tables of customers, without warning they would slam a bottle on the table top, barely breaking stride.

"We might be a bit early," Nate said to O'Hara as a small waiter with an underbite and several missing teeth took note of them.

"*Beeyra*," the waiter asked.

"Fuckin' oath," Mick responded. "Whiskey-*ya* too, while you're at it. I'm parched."

The man gestured toward the busier end of the café, which contained most of the tables and all of the crowd. Nate noticed a smaller seating area to the left, in which four old men were nursing glasses of tea and playing backgammon.

"*Mumkin?*" he asked the waiter, pointing to the empty tables nearest the old men.

The waiter clucked his tongue. "Where games play, alcohol forbidden," he said in broken, heavily accented English. He then waved his hand toward the crowded side of the room. "Any seat, *ya basha.*"

As they looked, they noticed Bob standing before two tables at the far corner of the room.

"He's here," O'Hara said.

They crossed the room to where Bob began pushing the two tables together. He was dressed in a fedora and sports coat, with a smoldering cigar clamped between his teeth. He stepped around the table and embraced each of them in a hug.

"Sit, let's have a quick drink. The flat is just blocks away." He caught the attention of the nearest waiter and made a circular motion with his finger.

"Stella!" the waiter shouted as he shuffled across the room toward a long, water-stained wooden bar that ran the length of the room beneath a cement wall of chipped yellow paint and foggy mirrors.

Bob drew from his cigar and released a cloud of smoke. "There's a good *koshary* spot just up the street. If you're hungry we'll grab some." He removed a cigar from his shirt pocket and handed it, along with a lighter, across the table to Mick.

"Cheers," the Australian said, sticking the cigar in his mouth and snapping the lighter open.

The crowd in the bar had a bohemian vibe, with a mix of patrons of all ages with the looks of artists and intellectuals. Teagan wasn't the only woman in the room, although most of the crowd were men.

"Popular joint," O'Hara said.

"More than one revolution has been plotted from within these walls," Bob said. "A lot of history here."

A waiter returned and set five green bottles of beer on the table. The yellow labels on the bottle read *STELLA* in blue lettering underneath a star and Arabic script.

"There she is," Mick said as they each reached for a bottle.

O'Hara took three long gulps and sat back in his chair.

"The Arabic sounds different here," he said as he eavesdropped on the conversation being had by a group of men one table over.

"Egyptian dialect," Bob said. "Different from what you'd have heard in Beirut or Riyadh."

"It's the most widely understood dialect," Nate added. "Because of the film industry, and music."

As Nate and Bob discussed the details of the flat Bob had arranged for them to stay in, O'Hara reached across and put a hand on Teagan's leg. When she looked at him, he whispered, "You good?"

She nodded. "Just can't believe we're actually here. Cairo."

O'Hara was about to say something when he was interrupted by the hauntingly beautiful sound of the azan echoing among the surrounding buildings and through the open windows of Ashraf's. He knew the muezzin's words by heart and found them comforting and nostalgic. Many of those in the bar rose from their chairs at the call to prayer, settled their bills with waiters and left.

"Making it to the pyramids will be like fulfilling a lifelong pilgrimage," Teagan continued where she had left off.

"Bit of an Egyptologist?" Nate said.

"Not exactly," she replied.

"You'll find no shortage of activities to keep you busy if you're into that kind of thing," Bob said.

O'Hara watched Mick, who had been silent for some time, scanning the crowd in the room, sizing things up.

"Everything alright, Micky?" he asked him.

"Yeah, nah, all good," Mick said. "Just wondering which of these blokes wants to get slapped. Everyone in the bloody city's got a staring problem."

Nate laughed.

"You better get used to it, pal," Bob said.

"I think it's the dreadlocks, Tea," Mick said to Teagan. "You show a bit of hair to these wankers and they're all popping out of their pajamas." He belched in the direction of the nearest table of men. "The piss is alright though." He turned to Teagan. "Enough of these and I'll be walking like an Egyptian."

"Let's finish up and I'll show you the apartment."

Bob caught the attention of a passing waiter, who counted the bottles on the table and tallied the bill. He paid the man in cash, handing him a few large Egyptian pound notes and saying *"Shukran."* He then asked Nate to tell the man to keep the change.

Nate said something in Arabic and the man smiled widely and shook everyone's hand except Teagan's, toward whom he placed a palm against his own chest as a gesture of gratitude.

O'Hara and Mick drained their beers and stood, as the others finished theirs. They walked out onto the busy sidewalk, where a man in a gallibeya was crouched beside the doorway, shining another man's shoes.

They walked along a street called Champollion past a strip of autobody shops where high stacks of spare tires were staggered along the sidewalk and grease-stained mechanics lay beneath jacked-up cars through open garage doors.

Bob nodded toward the opening of an alley among them. "That way," he said.

They crossed the street and entered a crowded lane filled with men and women of all ages, sitting around small outdoor tables and drinking tea or coffee. Many were smoking shisha, which masked the smell of car oil and exhaust with the aroma of sweet, apple-scented tobacco. A haze lingered in the air and the collective hum of conversations brought the alleyway to life with a buzzing energy. Hustling waiters ferried hot coals through the crowd among the small mushroom-like tables, while others balanced trays of glass mugs high above their heads.

A guitarist with wooly hair tied back in a ponytail was playing an acoustic song while an elderly man walked down the lane swallowing burning sticks of fire. A child made rounds, accepting tips in an upturned hat. The musician began to sing in Arabic, a song that reminded O'Hara of the traveling gypsy music of Europe. It must have been a popular ballad, as it wasn't long before the entire crowd in the alley began to sing along.

They exited through the other end of the alley and followed Bob around a corner to a five-story pre-revolutionary, stone building with a glass front entranceway.

"This is you," Bob said. "Number five Hussein Basha Meamar Street."

There was an empty chair resting alongside the marble stairs that rose to the doorway. Bob noticed O'Hara looking at it.

"That's the *bawaab*'s post," he said.

"Every building has a guy who looks after its maintenance," Nate explained. "Mans the door. Runs errands for folks who live there. They call him a *bawaab*."

"Yours has been paid a little extra in advance to mind his business unless you need anything, so you may not see him much." He pulled a keychain from his pocket with a single key hanging from a ring. "There's only one key, so you'll have to figure it out."

"Who owns this place?"

"A friend of a friend," Bob said. "Paid in full. Everything's discreet. That's all you need to know."

They followed him through the glass doors of the front entrance and up another short set of marble stairs to the first floor, where he used the key to open a dark mahogany wood door in the corner of the lobby.

The apartment's interior had the look of a once-grandiose home that would have been a great fit for lavish dinner parties a half-century earlier, but might not have been touched since. Spacious rooms with brass furnishings and tiled floors where two oversized sofas and a coffee table were the only furniture.

"It's only a two-bedroom," Bob said.

"I'll be coming and going," Nate said. "I'll take the couch while I'm here."

"You two can have whichever room's larger," Mick said to O'Hara and Teagan.

There was a small kitchen off to one side of the lounge area, and two doors at the far end of the room. Bob pointed to one.

"That's the master. It opens out onto the terrace."

O'Hara and Teagan opened the door to find a large room with a queen-sized bed and a wooden armoire. A desk and chair, like those found in a children's school, were set beneath the large French windows. They threw their knapsacks on the bed, opened double doors at the far end of the room and stepped out onto a cement terrace. A chest-high, parapet wall overlooked the street they had entered from. Music and singing could still be heard coming from the direction of the alleyway café around the corner.

"I'm going out to get us some koshary," Nate called out to them. "I'll be back in five."

O'Hara touched the small of Teagan's back. "Anything you need while he's out?"

"Nothing that can't wait," she said.

Bob walked out onto the terrace a steaming mug of hot tea in his hand. "We'll need to chat about the days ahead."

O'Hara looked at Teagan. "Mind giving us a minute?"

"Of course," she said and kissed him, before walking back inside.

Bob pulled the doors shut and surveyed the windows in the building above that overlooked them. Their apartment, being on the lowest floor and situated over an underground parking garage was the only one with an outdoor space.

"There's enough residual noise from the street. If we keep our voices down, we don't have to worry about being heard."

They walked to the parapet wall and leaned their elbows against it, looking down the short drop onto the street below. There was a strong waft of roasted garlic coming from an open window nearby.

"ABT holds court at the Semiramis Hotel, just a stone's throw from here, across Tahrir Square."

"Isn't that where the revolution went down?"

"Three blocks that way." He nodded in the direction up the street, as he began to bob the teabag, holding it by the string.

The singing coming from the alleyway café had grown louder and there was a cadence of hand-clapping to the rhythm. An alarm sounded from within Bob's pocket, and he pulled out the cellphone it was coming from and silenced it. He shifted his mug of tea from one hand to the other and removed a small pillbox from his other pocket, flicked the lid open with his thumb and dropped its contents into his mouth. "With all the time zones it gets tricky, keeping track of when I need to take this shit." He then washed his meds down with tea and rested the mug on the windowsill.

"What is it?" O'Hara asked.

"What's killing me?" Bob let out a slight laugh. "Probably karma." He shook his head and looked down the street toward a patch of light beneath a lone lamp, where a stray cat was rummaging through an empty box on the sidewalk. "Shit, it goes so fast, kid." He let out a long sigh. "Don't take it seriously. When you get to where I am, you come to realize there was nothing to stress about."

"Why are you still doing all this, then?"

Bob furrowed his brow, as if thinking of an answer. "Who else will?" He coughed, cleared his throat and spat off the edge of the terrace.

O'Hara wanted to ask him about the Russian woman, but thought better of it. He didn't want to let on that there had been gossiping.

"When am I reaching out to Prince Ahmed?"

"That's what I want to talk about. We'll have you call him tomorrow. Ideally, you're in front of him by the end of the week."

"And this Russian prick, Sasha?"

Bob gestured toward the street. "He's out there. He'll rear his ugly head."

"What else?"

"That's all." Bob lifted his mug from the top of the wall and studied O'Hara. "I was going to get into more details, talk a bit of gameplan, but I'm too shot. I'm gonna head to my hotel."

"Where's that?"

"Zamalek. Small island in the middle of the Nile, just a short walk from here."

"Listen..." O'Hara turned and lifted himself up on the wall. "I'd appreciate knowing what exactly you've got going on. This little ring of spies you're running."

Bob nodded. "It's as you said. Now you've heard it."

"Why are you doing it?"

"To hold the line for as long as it can be held."

"Are there more foreigners like Rafi with you?"

"Nationality..." Bob shook his head. "Those days are done. It's more primal than that. Good versus evil. Light against dark."

"So, it has nothing to do with the wrong turn you took once upon a time? Redemption?"

Bob laughed. "It's always about redemption." He clucked his tongue. "I like you, kid. I've said it before, if you were brought up under different circumstances you could have easily ended up doing what I did for a living."

"Good thing I wasn't."

Bob's grin widened. He reached up and clapped O'Hara on the back. "Don't overthink things. Explore Cairo." He gestured over his shoulder, back toward the apartment. "Take your lady on a date. I'll see you in the morning."

He turned and walked back into the apartment, leaving O'Hara sitting atop the wall.

ELEVEN

It was a short taxi ride out of Wust el-Balad, across the Nile to the leafy island of Gezira, where the neighborhood of Zamalek was located. The first thing O'Hara noticed was the heavily fortified Marriot hotel with its walls and armed guards, appearing more like a prison than a spot for tourists.

26th of July Street, lined with shops and European themed cafes and eateries felt noticeably more upscale and pretentious than downtown. The driver turned north onto a side street and into a neighborhood of mansions, with large properties and wrought iron gates. Teagan pointed to the many different flags being flown before each one.

"Embassy," the driver said in English with obvious pride in knowing the word.

They pulled up alongside a Queen Anne Victorian corner house with an English style garden of roses and high hedges that gave the front lawn a sense of privacy. Nate overpaid the driver to avoid an argument, and sent him on his way.

Bob was waiting at the front gate and let them into the property, guiding them along a paved stone footpath to a side door that led to a garden level apartment.

"In case anyone comes around, the owners think I'm a visiting professor at AUC," he said as he opened the door.

The apartment was a single room of hardwood floors and walls. A loaf of French bread and cheeses were laid out on the counter of an attached kitchenette.

Bob picked up a carafe of coffee and filled mugs, handing them out as he did so. "It's some Yemeni grind I bought at a little hole in the wall, across the river. The guy called it *Gamid*. Apparently, it means 'hard', or 'bad-ass' or something."

Mick slurped his coffee. "Fuckin' oath. This'll wake the dead."

Bob put an arm around O'Hara and guided him outside into the garden. Once they were alone, he handed O'Hara a cellphone. "It's probably best if you walk and talk, with all the consulates and embassies around."

O'Hara nodded. He handed Bob his coffee mug.

"Remember, you're just catching up with an old friend."

"Got it," O'Hara said, then turned and left the property. He walked south and turned east on 26th of July Street, which he took to where the street ended beneath the bridge that connected to downtown. He pulled out his phone and punched in the number he had memorized. The phone began to ring.

"*Ahlan,*" the prince's familiar voice said.

"Prince Ahmed," O'Hara said.

"*Meen?*" he asked.

"It's your old friend, Donovan Burke."

A long silence settled in over the line.

"Hello?" O'Hara asked.

"This cannot be," the prince said in a familiar British accent. "Donovan Burke is dead."

"It's me, *ya Emiri.* I thought you might recognize my voice."

There was a long silence. "Where are you calling from?"

O'Hara stared out at the downtown skyline across the water.

"Cairo," he answered.

The prince made a humming sound in response. "Interesting." Another pause followed. "Coincidental, even."

"No coincidence. I'm here to see you."

"After all this time..." the prince said, sounding unconvinced.

"Yes."

"How did you know to find me in Cairo?"

O'Hara looked over his shoulder at the high stucco wall shielding the Marriot Hotel from the main street. "Word travels," he said.

"Give me something to confirm I am speaking to the real Donovan," the prince said.

"I never had the chance to offer my condolences for Amjad."

An even longer silence settled in.

"I went looking for you," the prince replied.

"I heard."

"You heard. From who, the same people that told you to find me in Egypt?"

"Nobody told me to find you. Just where to find you."

"Who told you I came looking for you?" the prince asked. "When we were there nobody was able to provide any information about you."

"I was being protected."

"From me? We are dear friends, are we not?"

"Of course."

"Of course," the prince repeated.

"I'm sorry for any disruption of your business back there."

"Don't insult me," the prince said. "The business was not important. I am sorry about Dina, my dear. *Inna Lillahi.*"

"Thank you," O'Hara replied.

After another long silence, the prince said, "If you are in Cairo, I would like to see you, Donovan."

"I'd like that."

"I have recently been put in charge of a very important project for The Kingdom. This is why I spend much of my time here in Egypt, when not in Riyadh."

"Congratulations. I'm sure the position is well deserved."

"Thank you, my dear. I will be in charge of all sporting leagues and events within Neom. Have you heard of Neom?"

"I have not," O'Hara lied.

"A new land the Crown Prince has envisioned. Cities and islands stretching from western Saudi Arabia across the Gulf of Aqaba to the Eastern Sinai. Citizens will become Neomians, with passports, and all. It will be his legacy."

O'Hara could hear the excitement in the prince's voice as he spoke.

"What an honor for you to be tasked with such a position."

"I hope Neom will host the Olympics one day. Maybe you will become a Neomian yourself."

"Where do I sign up?" he replied, drawing a slight laugh out of the prince.

"I remember you being a sporty man," the prince said. "We discussed football and the Newcastle United ownership when we first met."

"I remember the conversation. You were off to a match here in Egypt."

"Allah has blessed you with a good memory."

"*ilhamdulillah*," O'Hara said.

"The western border of Neom will extend all the way to the Sinai, and so with the Confederation of African Football having its headquarters in Giza we have decided to establish an office here."

"I look forward to hearing all about it," O'Hara said.

"My dear, are you familiar with the Semiramus?" the prince asked, but continued without waiting for a response. "The hotel on the edge of *Midan Tahrir*. Tomorrow I will be hosting some representatives from a few international corporations who are interested in learning more about our intentions for athletic leagues in Neom." There was a brief pause. "I can see you beforehand if you are able to come to the hotel in the early afternoon. We can lunch together."

"I can make that work," O'Hara replied.

"Very well. Come after the mid-day prayer. I will have someone waiting in the lobby for you."

"I'll be there," O'Hara said.

"*Salaam, ya Habibi*," the prince said.

"*Salaam*," O'Hara replied.

TWELVE

A side staircase led to the horseshoe driveway overlooking the Nile where guests were being dropped off outside the elegant hotel entrance. As O'Hara walked past the well-dressed bell hop and stepped through the revolving door, he noticed there was a metal detector set up with security guards standing on either side. He pulled his cellphone from his pocket and faked as though taking a call. Holding it to his ear he stepped back outside and crossed the street, where he sat with his back to a bush. As he pretended to talk with one hand holding the phone to his ear, he drew the butterfly knife from his pocket and hid it within the bush.

He crossed the street to the hotel and entered through the metal detector, into the grand lobby where, as promised, a well-dressed Arab man in a suit approached him. The man introduced himself as Hussein and asked O'Hara to follow him to the elevators.

They rode the lift to one of the higher floors that required a FOB key to access, and the elevator door opened to a long hallway. O'Hara followed Hussein to the far end where he opened the last door.

Inside was a large suite with a jacuzzi in one corner opposite an entire kitchen with an island counter, on which rested dozens of buckets of KFC fried chicken, and bottles of Perrier alongside a row of crystal glasses. From a couch across the room, Prince Ahmed stood and held his arms wide. He had aged over the years since O'Hara had last seen him. A few strands of his beard were beginning to gray, as was the hair along his temples, beneath his red and white checkered *ghutra*.

"My dear," the prince said, smiling. "Your hair is gone."

"Prince Ahmed," O'Hara replied, and walked forward to great him with a kiss on each cheek, followed by a hug.

"I hope you are hungry," the prince said, and gestured to the buckets of fast food.

"I can see you still follow an American diet," O'Hara said, causing the prince to laugh.

"*ilhamdulilah*. Some habits are hard to break."

"This is a nice hotel," O'Hara said, wondering why the prince would have opted for such a modest suite.

"I have rented out the entire floor, as well as the ones above and below." The prince then said something in Arabic to Hussein, who nodded and left the room. He walked toward the kitchen counter and twisted the cap from one of the Perrier bottles. "Some of my staff stay in the other rooms, but no random guests among the three floors." He poured the water into two of the glasses, and slid one toward O'Hara.

"*Shukran*," O'Hara said, lifting the glass to his lips and drinking.

"If you are in need of a place to stay in Cairo, I welcome you to use one of the suites."

"I appreciate it," O'Hara said. "I may take you up on that if I end up sticking around town long enough."

"Where are you currently staying?"

"With a couple Australians I met, not far from here. They've got a flat."

"Where?"

"Wust el-Balad. I'm not familiar with street names, yet."

The prince nodded, but said nothing.

"Thank you for inviting me over."

The prince frowned. "You know better than to act like a stranger." He held a hand out toward the food. "Please eat."

They filled plates with fried chicken and mashed potatoes and carried their food to the couch.

"Prince Ahmed, rather than beat around the bush, I want you to know I go by a new name these days," O'Hara said.

The prince chewed his food and washed it down with water. "And what is the name?" he asked.

"Danny Marrero."

The prince wiped the corner of his mouth with a napkin and set it down on the table. "Alright, *ya* Danny." He looked up at him. "May I ask why?"

"As you know, someone tried killing me in Africa."

He studied the prince's body language. He didn't so much as blink.

"Where did you obtain this identity?"

"Black market," he answered. "It's a Canadian passport."

The prince nodded. "Did you get it through the Chinese man?"

"Something like that," O'Hara lied, unprepared to discuss Li Yong.

The prince pointed toward a stainless-steel carafe that rested on a countertop beside the refrigerator. "There is coffee, if you'd like. Once you've eaten enough."

O'Hara stood, and carried his empty plate to the sink. "Would you like a cup?"

"Please," the prince replied.

O'Hara took two porcelain mugs from a cabinet and filled them with black coffee from the spout of the carafe.

"My dear, I know it must be a sensitive subject for you to think about, but I would like for you to explain to me what exactly occurred in Guinea."

"I don't mind," O'Hara said.

"And I would also like to better understand where you were taken by this Chinese man, to recover." The prince placed a palm on his chest as O'Hara handed him a mug of coffee.

"How did you know about that?"

"Word travels," the prince said, quoting O'Hara from their previous phone conversation.

O'Hara knew the prince was keeping his cards close to his chest. He considered the possibility that he might even know about what occurred in Australia. Anything was possible at this point.

"I'm afraid it's not a short story."

The prince sipped his coffee, keeping his eyes on O'Hara as he did so.

"What took you so long to contact me?" he asked. "Years."

"It took me a long time to trust anyone, again. It was nothing personal." He looked him in the eye. "It's a vulnerable feeling to be hunted and not know who's after you."

The prince showed no reaction to this comment.

"After the shooting, I was ferried away to a protected compound. That's where I first regained consciousness." O'Hara shook his head. "Where I had to begin processing all that happened. All that I had lost." He sipped his coffee and looked out the window. From the height of the room, he could see far beyond the Nile to the pyramids along the horizon. "I didn't know how or why this might have happened. Who could be behind it."

"And you are worried it was me," the prince said.

O'Hara looked back at him. "I had to consider everyone."

"And have you discovered an answer?"

O'Hara shook his head.

"So as far as you know, it could still be me."

O'Hara didn't reply.

"What reasons would I have to be behind it? I cared for you and Dina. And of course, Amjad…"

O'Hara nodded. "I know."

"What would you do if you found the people responsible for what had happened?"

"Take from them, what they took from me," O'Hara responded.

"And so, you entered this room willing to take my life, if you discovered I had anything to do with what occurred?"

O'Hara sipped his coffee. He looked into the prince's eyes and nodded. "I came here with the hope that you had nothing to do with it."

"*Without a doubt Allah knows what they conceal and what they reveal,*" the prince said, quoting the Quran. He patted O'Hara's knee with his free hand.

"*If you retaliate, then let it be equivalent to what you have suffered,*" O'Hara responded.

A satisfied grin appeared on the prince's face. "*inshallah,*" he said, and patted his leg once more. He slurped his coffee and gestured with his chin. "Please tell me about the Chinese compound."

"That'll be a two-cupper," O'Hara said and stood. He held his hand out. "Heater?" he asked.

"Heater," the prince repeated and handed over his mug.

He walked to the kitchen and refilled their mugs. When he returned to the couch, he handed the prince his coffee and sat. Starting with Dina's arrival in Guinea, he took the prince through a detailed account of all that had occurred on the day of the attack in Bel-Air, and the long recovery that followed in the African bush. The prince didn't say a word throughout the story, and by the time O'Hara had finished, there were tears welled in his eyes.

"Where was Dina buried?" the prince asked, breaking the silence that had settled between them.

"I was told she was cremated."

"Oh?" the prince asked with a look of surprise. "Wasn't she Muslim?"

O'Hara nodded. "Half."

"There is no half-Muslim."

"And Amjad?" O'Hara asked.

"He is buried in Riyadh." The prince stared out the window at a single wispy cloud in the pale blue sky. O'Hara noticed a genuine sadness in his expression.

"He died a hero."

The prince looked at him. Tears balanced along the lower lids of his eyes. He inhaled deeply, and sighed. "A martyr."

O'Hara nodded.

"We weren't blood relatives, you know," the prince said.

"I didn't know that," O'Hara replied.

The prince nodded, and sipped his coffee, then swallowed. "We referred to one another as cousins to keep things simple, and to explain why someone of his background would have been among us in the court." He paused to shake his head. "But this was not the case."

"I will forever be grateful for what he did in those last moments, trying to protect Dina."

The prince nodded, and wiped at his eye. "Much like you did for him in the Beirut nightclub."

O'Hara's thought of that night in Beirut. Uncle Nikolai and the Albanians.

"He cared very much for you, my dear. It was Amjad who recommended that you take over his position in Guinea."

"I didn't know that."

"It is so. I would like to honor his memory by offering you a chance to continue working with me. By offering you a position with my new project in Neom."

"What kind of position?"

"I was thinking it should be something directly under me, involving athletics." He gave O'Hara's bicep a gentle squeeze. "How would you feel about being a talent scout? Recruiting fighters to compete in events held in Neom under my organization's banner?"

"Recruit fighters? From where?"

The prince shrugged and looked away. "You can choose. The world is ours, *ya Habibi.*"

O'Hara studied the prince's expression to gauge his sincerity. He still hadn't mentioned either of the attacks in Australia.

The prince wiped his hands with a napkin. "Anywhere. We can decide upon location once you've decided whether you want the position. The Crown Prince is a major fan of boxing and Mixed Martial Arts, and has already agreed that there will be no sum too great, if it means attracting the world's best athletes to compete in Neom. Now his excellency already knows how to connect with many of the top fighters from other organizations. What I might task you with is discovering new talent. Unknown fighters that could be brought up entirely within the organization, from the onset of their professional careers."

"Street level," O'Hara said.

The prince smiled and placed a hand on O'Hara's forearm. "Danny Marrero, a man of the streets."

"I'm honored that you'd consider me."

There was a knock on the front door of the suite, which seemed to snap the prince from his focused state and drew him back to the present. He stood and walked to the door and opened it.

Outside, in the hall was an effeminate teenager, with stylish hair and a cleanshaven face. They exchanged words in Arabic, and Prince Ahmed looked at his wrist watch. He spoke another few sentences in Arabic and closed the door, leaving the boy outside. O'Hara walked to the kitchen and set his mug in the sink.

"I lost track of time, my dear," the prince said to him. "I have to take this meeting before I begin to get ready for the evening's conference."

"Thank you for lunch," O'Hara said.

"It will be the first of many," the prince replied and held his arms wide. They kissed on each cheek and hugged. "It is good to have you back."

O'Hara placed a palm on his chest. "I'm forever indebted to you."

A wide grin appeared on the prince's face. "Tomorrow afternoon I will be hosting an event for some of the businessmen who will be attending this evening's conference. It will be a pool party, with music and such." He draped an arm around O'Hara's shoulder.

"They're in for a treat," O'Hara said. "Nobody throws a pool party like you."

"You should come. Bring the Australian friends that you're staying with." He guided him toward the exit.

"They'd love that." O'Hara stopped at the front door.

"Can I reach you on the phone number you called me from yesterday?" O'Hara nodded.

"I will send you an SMS with the details and, *inshallah*, I will see you there tomorrow." The prince opened the door. "Hussein is over at the lift and will escort you down to the lobby."

As he turned to leave, O'Hara glanced at the effeminate man outside, who smirked. He was of a slight build and smelled of cologne. The prince said something and motioned for him to enter. As he heard the door close behind him, it suddenly dawned on him that if the prince and Amjad weren't actual cousins, he wondered if they could be lovers.

Down in the lobby, Hussein walked with him toward the front entrance. As O'Hara turned to thank him, he heard a man's voice call out from behind.

"Hussein, isn't it?" the voice asked in a distinct, familiar accent. "How are you, my friend?"

O'Hara recognized it to be an Irish brogue. He turned to find a middle-aged Caucasian man with mostly white hair and a strong, wide jaw. He was smiling and had pale blue eyes that pinched down along the outer ends like an old dog. He nodded at O'Hara, but said nothing.

O'Hara returned a nod and patted Hussein's shoulder, before turning and exiting among the noisy chaos of the Cairo streets.

THIRTEEN

The long sandy road was flanked on either side by fields of farm crop. Ahead, beyond the one story building they drove toward, the three main pyramids of Giza cut a jagged line in the otherwise cloudless, blue sky.

"My God," Teagan said, upon noticing it.

There had been few other places in O'Hara's life that had surpassed its reputation when finally seen in person.

"I love a good triangle," Mick said from the back seat.

They pulled up to a low brick building where a row of Range Rovers and limousines were parked out front. From the street the building looked like a closed-down restaurant, but they could already hear the bass thumping from the beat of electronic music being played out back.

The taxi parked behind the row of vehicles, where a handful of men in traditional Saudi garb were standing in a huddle, holding glass mugs of tea. Each of the men turned and snuck glances at Teagan's body as they made their way toward the entrance.

"Sun's strong out this way," Mick said, then turned to Teagan. "I'll have to get me one of those tablecloth bandanas to protect me skin." He let out a giggle and stared at the group of men until they looked away. "There ya go, gents. G'day."

"Let's not create a scene," O'Hara said.

"Yeah, nah. Best behavior, today," Mick said in an unconvincing tone.

There were two security guards standing on either side of an entrance gate under a tan brick archway. The buzz of conversations could be heard from somewhere beyond. As the three of them reached the gate, O'Hara noticed one of the security guards was Hussein from the Semiramis hotel.

"*Assalamulaikum*," Hussein said.

"*Walaikumassalam*," O'Hara responded.

Hussein nodded at Mick and averted his eyes from Teagan as he stepped aside to let them pass. They entered through the archway and walked down a set of stairs into a sunken pit with a large tiled pool, empty of people. A walkway bridge crossed over the water, connecting a seating area to an empty dance floor.

O'Hara scanned the faces of the guests gathered at the tables, noticing the silver-haired man that had approached Hussein in the hotel lobby the day before. He was deep in conversation with an Arab man.

Toward the back of the property, on an elevated landing a few steps above the rest, Prince Ahmed sat perched looking out over his guests. He was flanked by a handsome man with chiseled features and long hair tied up in a bun. The backdrop displayed massive sand-colored pyramids against a flawless blue sky.

"Isn't man-bun up there the famous cunt from Arsenal?" Mick asked.

"No clue," O'Hara said. "What's his name?"

"Buggered if I know, I follow footy," Mick replied.

They descended the stairs and O'Hara noticed the silver-haired man watching him.

An employee in a white suit invited them to sit at a table near the pool's edge. Mick ordered a round of beers for the three of them. The man paused for a moment, then nodded and walked away.

"I'm pretty sure that guy wasn't a waiter," O'Hara said.

"He is now," Mick replied.

O'Hara gestured up toward the pyramids. "How's this for a place to drink?"

"Amen," Mick replied.

"I think you've been noticed," Teagan said, looking in the direction of the raised platform.

O'Hara turned to find the prince looking his way. He waved.

A man arrived carrying three bottles of Stella, and set them down on the table.

"Guess that other bloke wasn't a waiter after all," Mick kidded, and lifted his beer to his lips. "Shit mate, we missed the part about the dress code. Suits or bed sheets seems to be the go."

O'Hara laughed. "Nobody came dressed to swim, that's for sure."

"No worries, if we're here long enough, I'll be having a skinny dip," Mick said.

Teagan leaned back in her chair and put her feet up on O'Hara's leg. He noticed that the act drew more than a few eyes from among the guests, who seemed to observe her as if she were an exotic animal.

"I'll say, mate. The place is beautiful, but the crowd is a bunch of grubs. Everyone's just sitting around." He sipped his beer. "If this was Queensland, I'd say someone's waiting to be relieved of their Rolex." He giggled. "I could use a new pair of sunnies, too!"

O'Hara looked up at the platform where Prince Ahmed was still entertaining the soccer player. The prince noticed and raised a hand, motioning for him to come up.

"I'll be right back," he said and stood.

O'Hara felt exposed as he climbed the steps to where the prince sat. Men among the crowd seemed to be looking at him with more interest now. As he reached the platform, the soccer player stood from his seat, and Prince Ahmed held an upturned palm out for O'Hara to sit.

"She's all yours," the man said.

O'Hara thanked him and sat, as the man took the stairs down to the rest of the party.

"Do you know Saxon Watts?" the prince asked.

"I know the name."

"We may bring him aboard to serve as a football ambassador to Neom," the prince said.

"No kidding?" O'Hara said, faking interest.

They watched Saxon walk to a table where an attractive woman sat sipping a cocktail.

"This is incredible," O'Hara said to the prince. Behind them the land was covered by wild grass and lush green palms for hundreds of meters, before transitioning to a stretch of desert. Along the far edge of the clearing was a row of weather-beaten buildings like eroded sand castles. Beyond them the size and magnificence of the pyramids took up much of the panoramic view. "There's no way humans built those so long ago."

The prince grinned. He picked up a glass of tea and sipped it, glancing at the pyramids. "Who do you imagine did?"

"Anything's possible."

"Anything's possible with the help of Allah," the prince replied.

O'Hara knew better than to take that bait. "You never fail to throw an excellent party."

"The venue is not much, but I needed the location for its discretion." He nodded toward the crowd below. "Some of the guests would rather not attract attention, and especially not for sharing the same space as one another."

"And here I was thinking I was your only questionable friend, *ya Emir*," O'Hara joked.

The prince smiled. "Would you like a refreshment? I only ask that you don't drink alcohol while sitting beside me in front of everyone."

"A tea would be great, thanks," O'Hara said.

The prince caught the attention of a man standing at the bottom of the stairs and told him to fetch two more teas and a shisha. He turned to O'Hara. "Do you see the table of Englishmen there?" He was looking at a table of men dressed in polo shirts and khaki pants. "They are with the largest transport company on the planet."

"The one that dropped Tom Hanks off on that island?" O'Hara joked.

The prince didn't get the reference.

"They will be making a pitch to his excellency for all business in and out of Neom, but they are looking for an early foothold by securing the contract for sporting events." He turned to O'Hara. "Did you know that was my first line of work for the kingdom? Transport."

"I didn't."

The prince nodded. "It is a special interest of mine."

"I assume they aren't the ones who need discretion?"

The prince clucked his tongue. "But among the guests are everything from high-ranking Egyptian military officers, to billionaires."

O'Hara scanned the crowd to see if he could guess who the billionaires were.

The prince cleared his throat. "Later, everyone will leave and I will privately host the head of *Keta' el Amn el Watani*."

The man returned with the tall waterpipe and set it on the floor between the prince and O'Hara. A second man carried a tray up the stairs with two glasses of tea and a bowl of sugar. The prince took hold of a shisha hose and handed the other to O'Hara.

Prince Ahmed motioned for the men to take the sugar bowl away. "I assume you still do not take sugar with your tea."

"Your memory never ceases to amaze me," O'Hara replied.

"It is one of most dangerous poisons in this world. Sugar." He brought the mouthpiece of the shisha hose to his mouth. "This is another." As he pulled on the mouthpiece the base of the waterpipe bubbled.

"What were those Arabic words you said just a moment ago?" O'Hara asked. When the prince had finished, he drew smoke from his hose. The smoke relaxed his abdomen. "About the guy you're shutting down the party to meet with privately."

"The Egyptian National Security Agency," Prince Ahmed replied as clouds of smoke escaped his lips with his words. "So, my dear, tell me about your Australian friends." He glanced down at where Mick and Teagan were talking and laughing.

"I met them down in Queensland when I went to visit where Dina had been living." Teagan looked up at him, as if sensing being talked about. She smiled and waved.

"She's very attractive. Although her style is odd, if you don't mind me saying so," the prince said. "Are you two in a relationship?"

O'Hara looked at Prince Ahmed, and paused before answering. He didn't want to compromise her in any way. "It seems to be headed in that direction," he said.

"Who is the big fellow?"

"Mick. Good man."

The prince nodded, as if accepting the answer. He drew on the shisha hose.

"I've been thinking in more detail about our idea. Maybe setting you up with a gym."

O'Hara pulled on the shisha and blew a stream out the side of his mouth.

"Does it still interest you?"

"I grew up in and around gyms."

"But would you be comfortable with running a business?" the prince asked.

"I did alright in Guinea."

The prince gave a single nod. "You did." He glanced out over the crowd. "And you endured much, and lost much during that time, which has not been forgotten."

O'Hara didn't reply to this statement.

"Where do you think would be a good location for this... the gym?"

O'Hara shrugged. "There are scrappers in every country, Prince."

The shisha pipe began to gargle as the prince drew smoke.

"Very true. Well, we have time to narrow down our options, consider the finer details." The prince grinned. "I think you've sat up here long enough. Everyone in attendance will now assume you are a person of influence."

"Is that why you asked me up here?" O'Hara replied with a laugh.

The prince winked and stood. "I always take care of those close to me."

O'Hara stood and kissed each of the prince's cheeks.

"I'll be down to meet your friends a bit later," the prince said.

O'Hara nodded and walked down the stairs. As he returned to his table, it felt as though all eyes in the party were on him. A handful of women from the crowd had taken off their shoes and were dancing to the electronic music on the other side of the pool.

"How do these poor girls stay awake hanging out with these boring wankers?" Mick asked. He gestured to an untouched bottle of Stella on the table. "Got you another coldy."

"Thanks," O'Hara said and sat. "Enjoying yourself?" he asked Teagan. She was bobbing her head with the music. "Yeah, we should dance."

"It'll take a few more beers for that," O'Hara replied.

When they finished their drinks, they ordered another round and sat and enjoyed the music. Waiters came by offering candied dates and pastries.

At some point, after an hour or so, a handsome middle-aged man approached the table, dressed in a short-sleeve buttoned-down shirt and slacks. The skin of his face and arms was tanned and a pair of designer sunglasses rested atop his head, holding back a mop of long graying hair like a headband. He placed one hand on his chest.

"I have been told that you are a good friend of the prince," the man said in Slavic-accented English, then turned and gestured toward a table where an attractive middle-aged woman sat alone. "My wife and I ordered a bottle of champagne for your table."

"That's very kind of you both," O'Hara said and stood, extending his hand. "Danny Marrero."

"Sasha Filenkov," the man replied, clasping his hand.

O'Hara was taken aback upon hearing this, recognizing it as the name Bob had mentioned back in Australia. He gave the man's hand a firm squeeze.

"Prince Ahmed suggested that we meet," Sasha said, before extending his hand to Mick, who shook it. He then took hold of Teagan's hand, brought it to his lips and kissed her knuckle.

Mick looked at O'Hara and rolled his eyes.

"The bottle should arrive shortly," Sasha said. "Danny, would you mind accompanying me to the bar?"

"Sure," O'Hara replied. He followed Sasha toward a standalone bar at the far end of the pool deck while the others waited for the champagne to arrive.

Sasha was tall, and had a healthy, youthful look that was only betrayed by the color of his hair.

"You will think this is Russian cliché," Sasha said. "But I like to take a shot of vodka."

O'Hara grinned.

"I hear you are Canadian," he said.

"I am."

As they reached the bar, Sasha ordered two shots of vodka from the bartender, then turned to O'Hara.

"I currently live in Istanbul, and own some land here, out on the Sinai."

The bartender slid two filled shot glasses across the bar to them.

"With Ukraine, it's a difficult time to be a Russian," Sasha said. He picked up one of the glasses. "Which is why I keep a few different countries to call home." He held his glass aloft between them. "It is a pleasure to become acquainted," Sasha said and touched it to O'Hara's.

"Cheers," O'Hara said.

They drank their vodka shots, and set them down on the bar top. O'Hara motioned with two fingers for another round.

"The prince tells me you will be scouting for athletes on behalf of his organization," Sasha said. "I'm sure you know that Russia produces some of the best fighters in the world."

"Most definitely. Especially the beards up in Dagestan," O'Hara said.

Sasha nodded. "The country's success in martial arts is due to Combat Sambo being a staple of our culture."

O'Hara nodded.

"Even our president is a Master of Sport in Combat Sambo." He held his arms outstretched. "I was never a martial artist, myself. I prefer running."

The bartender slid two more shots across the bar in front of them. They each took one.

Sasha touched his shot glass to O'Hara's. "If you want to be introduced to some Russian fighters, though, have Prince Ahmed contact me. I will see what I can do."

"I appreciate that," O'Hara said, and they downed the shots.

O'Hara set his glass down and shook the man's hand.

"I trust Prince Ahmed's judgement," Sasha said, and glanced at his watch. "But more importantly, I trust my own. I knew everything I needed to know about you by the time we reached this bar. It is one of my superpowers." He laughed. "Time is a commodity, though, Danny. I must go back to my wife. Enjoy the champagne."

"Appreciate it," O'Hara replied.

Sasha walked away, taking a different route back to his table so that he could stop to exchange a few words with a group of men in suits.

"Bubbly?" Mick said as O'Hara arrived at their table. He filled a flute glass with champagne.

"What did he want to talk about?" Teagan asked.

"He saw me up there with the prince and mistook me for someone worth knowing," he kidded.

"No kind gesture is a free one among this lot," Mick said.

"Fact," O'Hara agreed.

Teagan was watching the prince as O'Hara spoke.

Mick pointed the lip of his bottle across the pool where a handful of women were dancing together on the other side. "I think I'll have a little boogie. Help balance out the ratio over there." He chugged the rest of his beer and let out a belch as he stood. "Pardon me, dear," he said to Teagan.

They watched as him dance his way toward a circle of women, who laughed and made room for him to enter their middle.

"Micky's wild, huh?" O'Hara said.

"He came into your life for important reasons," she replied.

O'Hara slid his chair closer to hers. "I think you did."

She smiled.

"You regretting that, yet?" he asked.

She bit her lip and shook her head.

Their moment was interrupted by arguing from across the pool. They turned to see Mick facing off with three Arab men. One of the men was older and well dressed, while the others had the obvious look of security guards.

"That didn't take long," O'Hara said. "Stay here," he told Teagan and crossed the bridge over the pool.

As he reached the dancefloor the two bodyguards were yelling at Mick in Arabic until one got too close and Mick punched him in the mouth, snapping his head back. The females scattered and Mick and the man began wrestling.

The second bodyguard circled behind them but O'Hara grabbed a hold of him and tossed him into the pool. The splash drew the attention of the remainder of the guests, who now watched on.

Men started shouting from the other side of the venue as O'Hara leaned down and pulled Mick off the man.

"Fuckin' dog bit me," Mick said, climbing to his feet.

The man hissed something in Arabic, so Mick cold-cocked him, dropping him. He turned to the older well-dressed man. "I don't mind bashing an old cunt, too!" he shouted. When he noticed the other security guard climbing out of the pool, he burst out laughing.

"*Ya* Danny!" Prince Ahmed shouted.

"Let's go," O'Hara said to Mick, pulling on his arm.

"Needed to cool off, did ya?!" Mick asked the wet security guard.

"Danny!" the prince shouted again.

"Go get Teagan," O'Hara said to Mick.

Hussein ran up to them. "The *Emir* wants to see you. Your friend must leave, now!"

"We're leaving," O'Hara said.

"*Yalla*," Hussein said to O'Hara, who followed him across the bridge over the water.

Prince Ahmed was standing at the foot of the stairs that led to his raised platform.

"What have you done?"

O'Hara gestured back toward the dancefloor with his thumb. "Some guys picked a fight with my friend."

"Is that the story you're choosing to tell me?" the prince asked, clearly agitated.

O'Hara nodded.

"And the man that ended up in the water?"

"What do you want me to say?" O'Hara shrugged.

"Come," the prince said and guided O'Hara by the elbow. When they were out of ear shot of any others, he leaned closely and spoke under his breath. "This is why I know you are the right man for the job I am offering. The same reason you were the right man in Guinea."

O'Hara looked at him and thought he noticed the slightest grin on Prince Ahmed's face.

The prince held a finger up before him. "Don't ever embarrass me with behavior like this again."

O'Hara touched his chest.

Prince Ahmed sucked his teeth three times. "Obviously, you must leave now." He then winked, turned and climbed the stairs back to his seat.

O'Hara made his way out front, where Mick and Teagan were waiting for him.

Mick slapped him on the back. "Thanks, mate. Old mate caught the shits that I was dancing with his missus, I think. I didn't understand a word of his gibberish."

"Fuck 'em," O'Hara said. He looked at Teagan. "We might as well check out the pyramids. They're right here."

"I'd love that," she said.

"You don't want to go there now," a man's voice interrupted with the clear cadence of an Irish brogue.

O'Hara turned to find the silver-haired man from the hotel lobby.

"Too crowded. Tourists. Con-men trying to take your money. Coppers shaking down the con-men." The man nodded. "You want to be there for a sunrise. Magical thing to see." He extended his hand. "Shane Malone."

O'Hara clasped his hand. "Danny Marrero."

"Pleasure," the man said. He had a firm grip and an easy smile. He shook hands with Mick and Teagan. "I know a guy that can get you in before the sun's up. While it's still closed-off to the public." He looked at each of them. "If that's something that interests you."

"Shit yeah," Teagan said.

"Consider it done," Shane replied. "Where are you's off to? Can I offer a lift?" He nodded toward a black Mercedes SUV that sat parked with the engine running.

"Over near Midan Tahrir," O'Hara said.

"Hop in," Shane said with a nod.

They made small talk on the ride to Wust el-Balad. Shane poured glasses of whiskey from a crystal decanter set in a center console minibar. He described himself as the part-owner of an aviation company that conducted business across the African continent, delivering goods and supplies to NGOs and other private corporations. He was in Cairo looking to gain a foothold in the Neom project, but there was something in his smooth-talking and charismatic demeanor that made O'Hara suspect he was fishing for something more.

This was confirmed when they reached Tahrir Square. As Teagan and Mick were climbing out of the vehicle and O'Hara was last to exit. Shane grabbed a hold of his wrist and leaned in closely so that the others wouldn't hear and asked if he'd join him for a nightcap at the Amarna Hotel Bar.

* * *

The rooftop bar sat eight stories above a crowded side-street that branched off from the bustling chaos of Talaat Harb Street. A dozen small tables were spread out among the outdoor terrace, where the air smelled of apple shisha tobacco smoke and potted plants lined the parapet walls that overlooked the other rooftops of the city. Make-shift dwellings could be seen on some building tops. People cooking with pots over propane stoves, or sitting on couches.

They sat at a table near the edge of the building.

"Cool little spot up here," O'Hara said.

"It's my favorite bar. Open twenty-four hours. Even through Ramadan, when the government forces all the bars to shut."

"What's the loophole, there?"

"It's attached to a hotel."

The floor was covered in green carpet, worn smooth and dark in the aisles and littered with small burn holes from fallen cigarette ash and shisha coals. A tired man with a face like crag rock sat behind a bar, smoking and watching an Arabic film on a small box television.

Shane was staring off the edge of the building at a rooftop where people were watching television under the night sky.

"Do they live on the roof?" O'Hara asked.

"Some do. Many are the families of bawaabs," Shane said. "Sometimes you wonder if they're the ones that understand what freedom really is. To live simply."

"Managing an aviation company in a war-torn continent isn't simple enough?" O'Hara asked.

"The paths that choose us," Shane replied. "Speaking of... what path leads a Canadian to end up in Cairo, rubbing elbows with princes and oligarchs?"

"The kind of path you wouldn't believe even if I told you."

Shane grinned.

"And you?" O'Hara asked.

"I'm just a Dubliner who took a few risks that paid off."

"Fortune favors the bold," O'Hara said. He was growing tired of the veiled verbal dance they were engaged in. "So, I've been invited here because you saw me shooting the shit with two powerful men."

"The real power is in the nexus points," Shane said. "Where the so-called powerful people connect."

"What do you have going with Prince Ahmed?"

Shane shook his head. "Prince Ahmed doesn't know me from Adam. I was there to butter up a high-ranking Egyptian Air Force general."

O'Hara sipped his beer. "Why's that?"

Shane studied him for some time, then leaned forward with his elbows on the table. "I'll be straight with you. I'm brokering a deal with the general to buy planes from him."

O'Hara leaned back in his chair, wondering why an Irish businessman would need military aircraft.

When the silence grew long, Shane began drumming his fingers on the tabletop. "Is it true you have connections in West Africa?"

O'Hara was caught off-guard by the question. "Come again?"

"You know how it goes, Danny boy. They might not always be true stories, but stories get told."

O'Hara had a sudden desire to leave.

"I'm no threat to you, no matter what you're really doing out here. I'm simply asking because it would be in my own best interest to befriend you if you did have connections in certain West African nations."

"Why the interest in West Africa?"

"Nexus points."

"With Egyptian military planes."

"*Inshallah*," Shane said.

"What kind of people are on either side of this nexus point?"

"I don't do names," Shane said. "Just as I would never speak yours to anyone else."

"Then we've got nothing to discuss." O'Hara sipped his beer. "For all I know you're Interpol."

"I'll tell you what. Run my name through a quick google search. That'll answer any questions as to whether I'm Interpol." Shane pulled out a phone. "Use this, it's a burner phone. Type in Shane Murdock, though, with a 'k' at the end." He punched buttons on the screen of the phone to unlock it and handed it across the table to O'Hara.

O'Hara took the phone and typed in the name.

"Careful what links you click," Shane said. "But have a look at the headlines. Click over to images if you want to confirm the face."

The first result that appeared read *Armed Gang Takes €2.5 Million From Dublin Security Van*. Below that, another read *Murdock and Priest Suspected in €7 Million Brinks Robbery*.

O'Hara looked up at the Irishman. He then clicked the tab on the website that showed image results for the search. Sure enough, the first three mugshots on the screen were of the man sitting across the table from him. Shane had dark hair in the photos and a few less creases across his forehead, but the strong jaw and handsome face left no question as to whether it was him.

O'Hara closed the website and handed back the phone. Shane tapped the screen a number of times and slipped it into his pocket.

"Why trust me with this knowledge?"

Shane drank his beer and sighed. "Once I learned you had been living in Guinea, it took a contact of mine about four hours on an encrypted laptop to figure out about the American who was hanging around Conakry and doing shuttle runs back and forth to the mines in the mountains until he was shot up and vanished." Shane pointed at his chest. "I wonder if you pulled your shirt up, if I'd see some patched over holes." He held his palm up. "Don't do that, though. They'll think we're poofs."

O'Hara stared hard at him.

"To answer your question, Danny boy, I gave you the dirt on me so that you'd know you don't have to fear me. All I care about is whether you still have any contacts at the port of Conakry, and if so, whether you and I might be able to help one another."

"In West Africa, money talks," O'Hara said. "You wouldn't need me."

"That's messy." Shane leaned back. "And quite honestly, you've got that something that lands you at the table with Prince Ahmed bin Tarek. Not many people were invited up onto his little perch today." Shane nodded. "If you help me out, it'll be by choice, not out of desperation. Desperate individuals will sell you out to the highest bidder."

Shane held his palms up and leaned back. "Let's leave it off there for now. You have a think about whether anything I've said piques your interest. There's a lot of money to be made, if so." He removed a pen from the breast pocket of his shirt and pulled a napkin close. He then wrote two series of numbers on it. He slid the napkin across to O'Hara. "Text an answer to the number on the top. It'll be the one I activate tomorrow. I change my mobile every day, so don't bother saving it."

O'Hara studied the numbers written on the napkin.

"It should be a yes or no answer, nothing more."

"What's the other number?"

"Guy called Mansour," Shane said. "Tell him you're my mate, and throw him fifty *g'nee*, and he'll sneak you into the pyramids before sunrise." Shane checked the time on his watch. "Enjoy your night, Danny boy." He stood. "I look forward to your answer."

O'Hara watched the Irishman walk across the empty rooftop bar toward the elevator. He tucked the napkin in his pocket and finished his beer, looking out over the rooftops to where the family still sat watching television under the night sky.

FOURTEEN

Mansour was a small, reptilian-looking guard with beady eyes and rotten teeth. He wore a uniform that could have been mistaken for that of a police officer upon first glance. After accepting the money, he mumbled something in Arabic and let them into the grounds through a side gate in a long and high stucco wall.

The sky was pitch black and only by starlight could they see one another's faces. The rolling hills of sand within the walls of the property were cast in a glow that gave it the look of moonscape. In the distance, floodlights illuminated the southern face of the three main pyramids.

They walked in the direction of the monuments. A paved path led in from the main gates in the distance, where another guard looked to be asleep in a chair. As they climbed the crest of a dune, they laid eyes on the Sphinx for the first time. At such a close distance, the serene expression of its weather-beaten face had a nostalgic energy about it.

Teagan stared at the Sphinx for some time before speaking. "This is where the Atlanteans came to restart."

"Were there once two?" O'Hara asked, remembering his dream.

She turned to him and nodded. "Lions. It's so much older than the pyramids." She touched her fingertips to her brow. "Sekhmet's followers. This was a portal." She let her hands drop. "The biblical flood. This existed before any of it."

"I've been here in my dreams," O'Hara said.

"We both have." She looked over at him, then pointed at the Great Pyramid. "You have a strong resonance with Thoth." Under the starlight she took on the luminescent highlights of an apparition. "It is why Dina bought the statue."

O'Hara felt a heaviness in his chest at the mention of her name. He thought of the being Thoth that had appeared in his dreams and wondered how Dina could have known about him.

"We were here long ago," she said. "Before the reset."

"The reset," he said.

"Come." She beckoned him forward, and walked toward the sunken pit in which the Sphinx lay.

With large paws outstretched before it like a guardian of the desert, the majestic monument was smaller than O'Hara had expected. Its head, despite the impressive details of its face and cobra's hood, seemed small compared to the body.

"It is because it was carved from within the original lion's head," Teagan said in barely more than a whisper.

O'Hara looked at her realizing she might have read his mind.

"*Can you read my thoughts?*" he thought.

She took a deep breath and let it out slow. "Do you hear the humming sound?" she asked.

He paused to listen, then shook his head.

"Come," she said and walked along the retaining wall around the Sphinx. She climbed down into the pit. He looked around to make sure the guard in the chair was still asleep in the distance, then followed her. By the time he reached her she was standing at the base of the statue.

"Have you heard the legend that there's a hall of secrets under this?" She rested her palm against the stone paw. "It's true, but not like most people assume. There's nothing physically beneath it."

She took another deep breath. "This is powerful," she said, and patted the stone. "Right here."

"You alright?"

She nodded. "There is something about this exact spot..." She paused, as if needing to catch her breath. "I am receiving a flood of information, almost faster than I can process." She looked at him. "This is what must have been meant all along. The record is not three-dimensional."

O'Hara watched her, seeming possessed by an energy that made her feel like someone he was just meeting for the first time.

"Here you can tap into the infinite records. Source." It was only then that he realized her Australian accent had vanished. She was speaking in an unfamiliar cadence he had never heard before.

She closed her eyes and reached out a hand to touch his face.

"This is the real reason we came...."

He closed his eyes and heard the humming sound she had mentioned. As he focused on it, he realized it was coming from within his own head. He then felt a tickle in his feet that traveled from the ground up through his leg. He dropped to one knee, placing his palms on the earth.

There was a white glow within his mind when he closed his eyes, and a comforting warmth overcame his body. He began to see a montage of images and scenes, as if watching a movie. A young woman and man, hugging one another, smiling. Somehow, he understood that he had seen these people before. He then remembered that it was while first observing this exact moment in time, witnessing their unconditional love for one another, that he chose them, and agreed to the journey he was now on.

When he came to, he was walking beside Teagan. He could make out the details of her face by the residual light from the flood lamps reflecting off the base of the pyramid they moved toward. She was holding his hand, as if leading him.

"I think I just blacked out," he said.

"No, you are just tapped in," she said. "Time isn't linear." She looked at him. "I was receiving so much information." She squeezed his hand. "You received more than your conscious mind was able to process."

"Was I unconscious."

She shook her head. "You were silent. Other than that, you appeared normal."

He looked back over his shoulder at the Sphinx. The stars above were beginning to fade as the lowest edges of the sky began to take on a paler shade.

"I learned a lot about you," she said. "About us. This incarnation." She stopped walking and faced him. "You intuitively shift your frequency at such high levels... you just don't know what you're doing."

"What does that mean?"

"You're a lot like Dina was. It's like having a raw talent without training in how to make use of it. You must focus on developing this gift."

She gestured toward the largest of the three pyramids, which sat before them. "Do you think we can climb it?"

O'Hara looked around. "Who's gonna stop us?"

He followed her toward it. The stone blocks at the base of the pyramid were over half the height of a man. He looked up the slope at what seemed to rise forever toward the sky, and knew in his heart that humans couldn't have built this alone. He understood that all he had been told by Thoth was likely true.

"Let's go," she said, and propped herself up the first level of blocks. He followed after her. As they climbed, O'Hara lost all sense of their reasons for having come to Egypt. There was a sense of safety in the night. Anonymity. They were meant to be where they were, doing exactly this.

She stopped half-way up and turned to rest her back against the stone as the dawn call to prayer echoed from all the mosque minarets throughout Giza in the distance. There was no need for words to be spoken between them. He understood that it wasn't the night that blanketed him with that sense of security. It was her. She waited for him to catch up, and leaned in and kissed him. Before he could speak, she had turned away and continued to climb.

At the summit O'Hara was overwhelmed by the realization that he had been here before. It was exactly as he had remembered it from his dream, down to the inscribed names along the uppermost blocks that the missing pyramidion capstone would have rested atop.

Teagan sat down and leaned back on her elbows, looking out across the vast stretch of sands toward the wall through which they entered the grounds. O'Hara stood at the center, under the iron beams that formed a skeleton pinnacle.

"These pyramids generate a frequency that can raise this entire planet's density," she said. She leaned forward and ran her hands along the top of the block she sat on.

O'Hara was stunned by her words, which were almost identical to those that were spoken in his dream. "Where did you hear that?" he asked and sat beside her.

"This wasn't what historians claim it to be," was all she said.

O'Hara looked down toward the back of the Sphinx. The crests of sand mounds were lit up as the red sun breached the horizon over the neighborhood of low-rise dwellings in the distance. He closed his eyes and felt the warmth of the early light against his face. He felt her breath against his cheek and opened his eyes.

Her eyes captured the light with a glowing blend of gray and pink. "Thank you," she said, and kissed him.

* * *

It was hours later and from an unidentified phone number that Shane Malone responded to O'Hara's text message. He arranged to meet at a bar called Café Riche near Talaat Harb Square.

The Irishman was sitting alone at a table up against a wall, under a mounted tricolor Egyptian flag.

"How'd your business with the general work out?" O'Hara asked as he took a seat across the table from him.

"Ears everywhere in this part of the city," Shane said. He then leaned forward and brought his voice down to a whisper. "It cost me nine million that I don't have, but in this world, you rob Peter to pay Paul until you get what you need." He stopped speaking as a waiter approached and said something to them in Arabic.

"*Ahwa turkiye law samaht*," Shane said. "No sugar," he added in English.

The man nodded and looked at O'Hara, who held up two fingers for an answer.

"After a couple months of flying freight across Africa my debt'll be paid in full."

"Where do you find someone to give you a loan like that?"

Shane winked. "Wouldn't you like to know." He leaned closer and lowered his voice. "So, I take it you're interested?"

"I can try to reach out to some folks for you."

Shane nodded. "That's all I can ask for."

"My connect will want to know who the players are. And what's being moved."

The waiter returned with two small mugs of dark coffee and set them down.

"I still won't do names but I can give you an idea."

O'Hara sipped the Turkish brew and gestured for Shane to continue.

"Probably the scariest people on this planet."

"I've encountered some scary people. You'll have to do better than that."

"Fair enough…" Shane pointed a finger at O'Hara. "The real you, under all this Danny the Canadian shite… Your neighbors to the south."

O'Hara sat back in his chair.

Shane nodded. "Follow me?"

"What are you moving?"

"What you'd imagine."

"No humans."

"Never."

"Where does it all end up?"

"It'll be distributed within Africa. Some will make its way into Europe."

O'Hara thought about it for a moment, then nodded. "I'll see what I can do."

Shane grinned. "You're a legend, Danny boy."

When O'Hara left Café Riche, he walked down to the Nile and sat along the water's edge to be away from the crowds and able to hear himself think. He found a spot under the 6th of October overpass and sat with his back against a concrete pillar. He closed his eyes and rubbed his temples as he tried to remember the number he once had memorized, long ago. When he thought he might have it, he dialed the numbers on his cellphone and waited as the phone began ringing.

"*Wéi?*" the familiar voice answered.

"Li Yong," O'Hara replied, relieved. "It's me."

"*Fángdàn*," the man said.

O'Hara grinned. "Yeah."

"My boy... Where are you?" Li asked.

"Back in Africa," O'Hara said.

"I am not there anymore," Li said.

"Where are you?"

"Myanmar. Come see me."

"I don't think that's possible. Long story."

"Everything is long story with you, *Fángdàn*."

"I was hoping you might be able to come see me, actually."

"Where in Africa?"

"Cairo."

"Why Egypt?"

"I'd rather keep it off the phone."

"Are you in danger?"

"No more than the usual."

He heard Li laugh on the other end of the line.

"What phone number is this?"

"My cell."

"How soon do you need to meet?"

"Sooner the better."

"Tell me something, my boy..."

"What's up?" O'Hara said.

"How important is what you have to tell me?"

"Pretty important, I'd say."

"I will call you tomorrow when I land in Cairo."

"Legend," O'Hara said.

"*Zàijiàn*," Li said before the phone line went dead.

FIFTEEN

Bob chose the location, an *ahwa* in Mohandiseen on the west bank of the Nile. The neighborhood was upscale for Cairo standards, with fitness gyms and trendy clothing stores. Even a Starbucks and McDonalds lined the ring road of Shehab Street where the café was located.

"Thanks for meeting me out here," Bob said. He was wearing large sunglasses and a fedora. "Now that you've begun to gain traction, it's best if we don't spend too much time around one another in public."

They took seats along the sidewalk and ordered Turkish coffees and *shisha tufeh* and sat looking out upon the busy road. It was early morning by western standards but Cairo was already alive and bustling. They made small talk until the pipes arrived, then O'Hara brought him up to speed on all that had occurred since they last met.

Bob puffed from the mouthpiece of his pipe hose. "So let me get this straight," he said, pausing to blow a stream of smoke. "You manage to get yourself invited to a gathering of the who's who of international big swinging dicks... and you get in a brawl?"

"That's not all that happened, but yeah." O'Hara said.

"And somehow you still came out of it on good terms with ABT. Made friends with Filenkov. Potentially forged a business partnership with an Irish transnational criminal."

O'Hara pulled from his shisha and blew streams from his nostrils. He picked up his coffee and sipped it. Bob extended his hand. O'Hara stared at it for a moment, then clasped it.

"Well done."

"The theatrics," O'Hara said and took another drag from the shisha. A calm settled into his stomach, relaxing him in a way that made him understand why so many important matters in the Middle East were discussed over the customary waterpipe.

"Depending on how this goes with Shane Murdock." Bob clucked his tongue. "Malone... you may want to ask yourself if Mick's gonna be a liability."

"He may have been out of his league around the caviar and champagne crowd, but when it comes to what we're out here doing, I want him around." He sipped his beer and added, "Shane and Mick are two of a kind."

"Who is Shane transporting for? And what is he transporting?"

"Mexicans."

Bob whistled.

"I don't know what he's moving. I just made sure it wasn't humans."

An attractive woman in a business suit, wearing a hijab walked past and smiled at them. Bob said good morning in Arabic and followed her with his eyes.

"If it's cartel then its drugs. Maybe arms on the return trip." Bob pulled from his shisha and coughed. "So, he only wants you to help him with the port."

"Yeah."

"You're a prick. Wouldn't introduce me to this Li Yong, but you'll introduce a shady Irishman."

"Li Yong wouldn't have any interest in meeting you," O'Hara shot back. "He may not have an interest in Shane, either, once I explain the situation. But we'll see."

"What's the word on Filenkov," O'Hara said.

Bob blew a stream of smoke from his nostrils. "He's like the Slavic Jeffrey Epstein. True scumbag."

"What about a connection to Bel-Air."

"He's linked to some degree. If he doesn't have blood on his hands, he's broken bread with people who do," Bob said.

"That's enough for me," O'Hara said. "Just don't go getting the wrong guy killed. I don't want that on my conscience."

"Sit tight on that. I'll keep digging."

A silence settled in between them as they watched more locals pass along the sidewalk. There was something about Cairo that reminded O'Hara a lot of New York. The pace, and the grittiness of the people. They were survivors.

"So where are we at with ABT?" Bob asked.

"He wants to bring me in on this Neom athletics gig. Run a gym for him and scout fighters."

"He didn't say where."

"My choice, really. I wouldn't mind eventually heading back to Australia, if the storm ever blows over. I felt close to Dina down there."

"We'll have to see how things play out," Bob said.

O'Hara gave a conceding nod. "It's messy. The cabin. DNA. Photos."

Bob clucked his tongue. "I had someone handle that. A pile of cinders is all they'd find."

O'Hara looked at him.

"The firemen got a good job out of it, though."

"Why didn't you tell me?"

"I didn't think you'd be on board with it," Bob said. "Luckily the property was only registered in Dina's name."

O'Hara felt like he had been punched in the gut. He was trying to wrap his head around what Bob was saying, and how it might change things.

"If Australia is where you'd like to set up shop for ABT, then what I'm saying is nothing's impossible. Sunshine Coast might be off limits, but it's a massive country."

"What about the footage from Redcliffe?"

"They'll never tie you to it. Mick might be another story." He leaned forward in his chair and cradled his stomach with one hand.

"You alright?" O'Hara asked.

When he didn't respond O'Hara placed a hand on his back. Bob eventually nodded.

"Been getting hit with these waves of nausea like never before."

"You want to go get checked out?"

He shook his head and stood. "A late morning nap usually recalibrates me."

O'Hara stood.

"I'll hail you a cab," O'Hara said, to which Bob nodded.

"Getting old has its downsides, kid," Bob said with a grin. He extended his hand and they shook. "Let's do this again in a few days. You've got my contacts if you need me."

A Peugeot taxi pulled up beside O'Hara, who opened the passenger side door.

"I'll reach out if I learn anything pertinent about Filenkov," Bob said under his breath.

O'Hara helped him into the back of the taxi. He shut the door and the car drove off.

* * *

The fitness center in the Semiramus Hotel took up an entire floor of the building, with a weight room, an outdoor pool, a sauna and steam room. When Prince Ahmed chose to use it, the entire floor became closed-off to other guests.

O'Hara had thought he was coming to discuss important matters until the prince stepped up on the treadmill and set the pace at a fast walk. He then stuck an earpiece in and proceeded to make phone calls, conversing in at least four or five languages.

O'Hara took the time to lift weights, and then went outside under the sun and swam laps for an hour. When he was finished, he sat along the pool's edge enjoying the warm sun on his skin.

"*Ya effendim*," a man in a hotel uniform said, interrupting his thoughts.

O'Hara opened his eyes to find the man standing with a glass of dark red pomegranate juice.

"*Shukran*," he said, accepting the glass. He climbed to his feet and drank down the juice, then handed the glass back to the man.

"The Emir would like to invite you for a sauna," the man said in English.

O'Hara followed him inside and through a set of doors that led to an empty locker room. The man pointed to a wood door, then gestured toward a shelf of folded towels. O'Hara undressed and took down one of the clean towels and wrapped it around his waist.

When he opened the door and stepped into the sauna, he was hit with a wave of oven-like heat. Prince Ahmed was sitting on the upper bench in one corner with a towel wrapped draped across his lap. He was drenched with sweat and looked almost unrecognizable without his head dress.

"*Ahlan wa sahlan*," the prince said with a smile. "How was your training?"

"Great. Thanks again."

He picked up a wet hand towel and wrung it out over the hot rocks in the sauna, causing them to hiss as the water fell upon them. "I assume you enjoyed the pool party?"

"It felt like being back in Beirut. Apologies once again, for what happened."

The prince made a gesture, as if telling O'Hara not to worry about it. "Do you miss Beirut?"

"Sometimes."

"It was a good moment in time. I used to enjoy hosting the yacht parties." The prince shook his head. "It is tragic, what happened to that city."

O'Hara nodded.

"Do you ever regret leaving Riyadh, my dear?"

O'Hara looked at him. "The gig in Africa wasn't one you turn down," he replied.

"Yes, but we both know you didn't want to leave Dina."

Hearing her name spoken aloud hurt.

"I regret sending Amjad to Guinea," the prince said. "If I knew our time would be cut short, I wouldn't have."

O'Hara looked at him. He wiped sweat from his brow.

"Guinea changed everything, didn't it?" O'Hara said, uncomfortable with the idea that Dina might still be alive, otherwise.

"What are your thoughts about a man being with a man in that way?" the prince asked.

"Like Amjad?"

The prince gave the slightest movement of his chin, which O'Hara took to mean 'yes'.

"I could care less."

Prince Ahmed nodded.

"Are you...?" O'Hara asked, unsure of how to finish his question.

The prince clucked his tongue. "It is *haram*."

"He wasn't your actual cousin, though?" O'Hara asked.

The prince was avoiding eye contact. He took a deep breath and sighed, with a pained expression. When he looked up at O'Hara, tears were welled up in his eyes.

"I sent him to his death," Prince Ahmed said in barely a whisper.

"That's not true."

"I think about him every day." He used the end of his towel to dab at his eyes.

"Me too," O'Hara said.

"Dina, as well."

"Thank you."

The prince took a long deep breath and sat upright, as if fixing his posture might help him regain control of the room.

"I think this is why when you made contact with me, I welcomed you back." He looked at O'Hara. "You remind me of my time with him. You were with him on his last day."

"Ahmed was one of the bravest friends I've had. It takes great courage to openly be what he was within the Kingdom." O'Hara picked up the wet cloth and wrung it out over the rocks, creating another wave of hot steam.

"I have two wives. Children." The prince pursed his lips. "Amjad and I had a close friendship since we were boys. Throughout the rest of our lives, it remained."

"Close friendship," O'Hara said.

Prince Ahmed grimaced. "How does hearing this make you feel?"

"I can hear in your voice, how much you cared about him," O'Hara replied. He understood what the prince was hinting at. "What did the Crown Prince think?"

Prince Ahmed nodded. "So long as it wasn't addressed or acknowledged, it didn't exist."

A long silence settled in over the room.

Prince Ahmed nodded. He wiped at his eye with his knuckle. "Our bond is made stronger by knowing the secrets of one another."

"I am a vault when it comes to that."

"I know. But, now I want something in return." the prince said. "Who is Danny Marrero and where did you obtain this identity?"

O'Hara wiped his palms against his towel, realizing there was no avoiding the question. "Where to begin..."

The prince kept his eyes locked in on O'Hara's face, unblinking as if studying it for signs of dishonesty.

"After I was ambushed in Guinea, there was no denying that someone was out to kill me. I had an opportunity to purchase a fake passport. Saw it as chance to go off the grid, and hopefully keep myself alive. I never learned who provided it. They were contacts of a friend."

"The Chinese man?" Prince Ahmed asked.

"Yeah," O'Hara lied.

"He is a well-connected fellow," the prince said.

O'Hara nodded. "He has a far reach."

"Did you request Canadian?"

O'Hara shook his head. "It worked with my accent."

"And you used this document to enter Australia?"

O'Hara nodded. "It was where Dina had been living. I was desperate to feel close to her."

The prince nodded. "And did you find what you were looking for?"

O'Hara thought for a moment before answering. "Yeah... I think I did."

"I am glad." The prince wiped sweat from his brow. "Maybe Australia is where we should establish your gym." He sat upright and patted O'Hara's knee. "I will be in Riyadh for the next month. But let this be a topic we discuss in more detail when I return."

O'Hara nodded.

"Is there anything you need before I leave town?"

"Are you able to arrange me a meeting with Sasha Filenkov?"

Prince Ahmed stared at O'Hara for a long moment before responding. "I can do this, my dear," he said and stood. "Please feel free to use the facilities as long as you wish. They know not to open it back up for guests until we have vacated the premises." He patted O'Hara's shoulder and exited the sauna.

SIXTEEN

The taxi came to a stop at the foot of a narrow strip of sandy earth that continued uphill and disappeared around a bend in the distance. There were patchy remnants of paved road at points along the lane, among the ankle high clouds of dust that were being kicked up by donkey wagons and the occasional automobile. The taxi driver declared that they had arrived at Darb al-Ahmar, and made it clear that he had no intentions of driving any further.

The base of the hill was swarmed with vendors. Folding tables and stacks of wooden crates filled with local produce were arranged in the shadow of a stone archway that looked like a medieval gate to a part of the city trapped in time. Beyond the ancient passageway was a mosque that looked more like a military armory from the times of the crusades. Along the narrow, cobblestone road that cut a path beside it were artisans hawking intricately stitched tapestries and richly dyed fabrics and silks.

The muezzin's call to prayer resonated from the armory-mosque, across the low rooftops of the old quarter, followed by the echoes of several more azans sung from other nearby minarets. People began spilling onto the street from shop fronts and alleys, many of them funneling through open doorways into the base of the building. Unlike in Wust el-Balad where it was common to see men in jeans and t-shirts, in this neighborhood everyone wore galibeyas. Women entered the mosque through a separate door from that of the men, all with their hair covered by hijabs.

O'Hara moved against the current of worshippers, weaving his way among a maze of twisting alleys, looking for the restaurant. It wasn't until, in exchange for a five-pound note, a young boy in a red Mohammed Saleh jersey directed him to a nondescript hole-in-the-wall from which the rich scent of spices could be smelled from down the block.

As he approached the opening Li Yong stepped out, holding a bowl and chopsticks and slurping a mouthful of noodles. He was wearing designer sunglasses and dressed in a suit with the top few buttons of his shirt undone. When he noticed O'Hara he smiled widely, handed the bowl of food to someone inside the doorway and stepped toward him with his arms held wide.

They embraced in a tight hug.

"You look good, *Fángdàn*!" He spoke perfect English without much of an accent.

"You're looking healthy, too, uncle," O'Hara said, and clapped his back.

Li Yong laughed and patted his own flanks. "Healthy from eating too much. They said this is the best Malaysian food in Africa, because of all the Asian Muslims that come to study at Al-Azhar." He gestured with a thumb toward the opening in the wall behind him.

"What's the verdict?" O'Hara asked.

Li shrugged, as if conceding. "Outside of my restaurants in Guinea, maybe," He laughed. "Are you hungry?"

"I could eat."

Li placed a hand on O'Hara's shoulder. "Let's get you something. Then you can tell me what I am doing here in Egypt."

They stepped through the doorway into a room where the scent of peppers and fried oil, roasting meats and vegetables, was so strong that it made entering feel like they had passed through a portal to another part of the world. Gone were the lingering traces of car exhaust that was only ever masked by the always-present shisha smoke that settled over most blocks in the city. This one-room kitchen smelled like the campfire cooking during his recovery in the Guinean bush.

Li Yong ordered two bowls of Assam Laksa and two glasses of tea, which they carried outside and drank, sitting on the curb of the street while their meals cooked.

O'Hara studied his friend as he pulled a pack of cigarettes from his pocket and shook one loose. He grabbed it from the pack with his teeth and stuck the rest back in his pocket. "What's up?" he asked.

"I owe you so much, man," O'Hara said.

Li removed a silver zippo and flicked the lid open, lit the end of his smoke and snapped it shut. "Did you accomplish what you had set out to do in Amsterdam?"

O'Hara nodded his head.

"Then you owe me nothing." He closed one eye as he drew from the cigarette and exhaled the smoke through his nostrils. "It's been difficult. Missing her, yes?"

O'Hara looked down at the dusty road between his feet. Li reached over and rubbed the back of his neck.

"She didn't go anywhere," he said. "Just waits in a place we can't see with our two eyes."

O'Hara said nothing.

"I light incense for her every day," Li added.

Hearing this made O'Hara choke up with emotion.

"What have you been doing for money out here?"

"I only recently arrived. I've made the rounds since leaving Africa." He sipped his tea. "Europe down to Australia. Then here."

Li Yong's eyebrows raised. "I have family in Australia."

"You have family everywhere," O'Hara said.

Li closed one eye and pointed his cigarette-holding hand at O'Hara. "How did you get a visa?"

O'Hara replied and made a gesture with his hand to suggest he might not have. "I'm Canadian these days."

Li nodded.

"What about you? What's the deal over in Burma?"

Li stubbed the cigarette butt out on the curb and dropped it in his empty tea glass as one of the workers brought out the two bowls of food. O'Hara finished his tea and she took both of their empty mugs.

"It's where a lot of business can be done."

"Business?"

Li slurped his food and nodded as he chewed. "Supply chain."

O'Hara chewed his food, the veiled answer needing no further explanation.

"Are you there full-time?"

Li shook his head. "Myanmar. Singapore. Sometimes Guinea."

"You must've been promoted," O'Hara said.

Li cleared his throat and spit onto the street. "*Fángdàn*, I'm not here house-hunting in Cairo. Why I am here?"

"Supply chain."

Li Yong tilted his head and arched his brow.

"Guinea."

Li Yong went back to eating his Laksa. "What needs to be brought in?" he mumbled through a mouthful of food.

O'Hara shrugged. "I can only assume at this point."

"Who is moving it?"

"I know the man who would move it once on the continent." He waited for Li to look over at him before adding, "The ones bringing it in are Mexicans."

Li Yong looked across the street at nothing in particular and picked his teeth with a thumbnail.

"Have you ever done business with cartels?" O'Hara asked.

"No. But my people have."

"Where?"

"Vancouver."

"Are you interested so far?"

Li held his hand up and rubbed his thumb against his first two fingers and hummed an affirmative. "Tell me everything about this man who will move the goods once in Africa," Li said.

"His name is Shane Malone," O'Hara said, before diving into the rest of what he knew about the man, including his time spent in Ireland and the UK as Shane Murdock. Li listened and chain-smoked cigarettes. Every so often he'd nod his head at a detail or point that O'Hara made.

"Military planes from the Egyptian air force?" he asked, skeptically, once O'Hara was finished talking.

"Yes," O'Hara replied.

Li nodded, and frowned in thought. "I have a counter proposal for this Irishman. If he agrees to it, I will help him gain access to the port of Conakry."

"When do you wanna meet him?" O'Hara knew Li only dealt with people face-to-face when it came to this type of thing.

Li Yong looked O'Hara in the eye. "Time is money, my boy."

O'Hara pulled his cell phone out and found Shane's number.

* * *

Shane was dressed in a suit and was holding a leather briefcase as he shook Li Yong's hand, then O'Hara's, and asked them to follow him up the gangway onto the ferry.

He had chartered the Nile riverboat for the three of them to speak privately without risk of being listened to. They climbed to the top deck, where a minibar was stocked with bottles of imported red wine, champagne on ice and bourbon. There was no bartender.

"I'll pour, what'll you have Mr. Li?" Shane asked.

"Red, thank you."

"Danny?"

"Yeah, same."

Shane used a corkscrew to pop open the bottle and set two long stemmed glasses on the bar top. He poured the wines and then poured himself a few inches of bourbon into a highball glass.

Li Yong studied the Cairo skyline along the east bank, a mix of curved mosque domes and minarets among boxy high-rises with unfinished top floors.

"You know all that's an insurance loophole," Shane said.

"What is?" O'Hara asked.

"Something to do with keeping the building unfinished by having an open top floor. The building owners can forever escape certain payments or fees, something like that." He turned to Li. "I didn't hire a captain as a matter of privacy, but I still can if you would like to go downriver."

"This is fine," Li Yong said.

"Shall we sit?" O'Hara asked, at which point they all took seats at a U-shaped booth of cracked leather upholstery, near the minibar.

From inside his jacket pocket Shane produced three cigars.

Li accepted one and studied it, then looked at Shane. "Gurkha His Majesty's Reserves," he read from the label.

Shane smiled with his jaw set in that way that made it look like he was chewing something. He offered one to O'Hara who accepted.

"Seven-fifty a smoke," he said. He set a cigar cutter on the table between them.

Li picked it up and sliced the tip off. He handed it to O'Hara and then pulled out his zippo and lit the other end, turning it in the flame to catch all sides. He took a few puffs and released smoke into the evening air.

"Thank you," Li said, to which Shane nodded.

O'Hara cut and lit his cigar, then handed the lighter back to Li.

"So, gentlemen, I'm hoping that this marks the start of a lucrative relationship. Not just a one-off deal and a handshake." Shane sipped his bourbon and set the glass down on the table, before lighting his cigar.

"How many planes will you have leaving from Guinea, and who will be flying them?" Li asked bluntly.

"Six. I have pilots that already work for a front company I own. Four planes will be legitimate. They will transport medical supplies and food throughout Africa. I have secured contracts with an NGO that works in rural areas a few hours out of Conakry. The two remaining planes will transport what we are here to talk about."

Li smoked his cigar in a way that he only ever removed it from his mouth to sip wine. He stared at Shane through the wisps of smoke that rose from its end.

"May I ask for the details of your port connections in Conakry?" Shane asked.

"You can ask, Mister Malone. But you won't receive the answer you are looking for," Li replied. "I don't need your business. It is you who needs me."

"Fair enough," Shane said. He tapped ash from the end of his cigar into a glass tray. "Then would you mind telling me what is required to arrange for certain shipments to enter the port without inspection?"

"We must know the details of the shipment. Container numbers, things like this. For private vessels it's a bit different."

Shane looked at O'Hara, then back at Li.

"I won't make assumptions," Li began and rocked forward so that his elbows rested atop his knees. He pointed toward Shane's briefcase with one of the fingers that held his cigar. "But know that if there are any recording devices in there, that my people are aware that I am meeting you. If we are being set up in any way, you and those close to you will... you know the rest."

Shane opened his briefcase to show Li that it was only filled with a manila folder, which he removed and offered to Li.

"All I have in here Mister Li are some glossy photos of the aircraft I am purchasing. You can keep them if you'd like, as a token of my trust and gratitude."

Li accepted the folder and removed the photographs. He closed the briefcase and flung it over the rail, where it hit the water with a loud splash.

"We don't have to make threats so early on in our relationship," Shane said. "There are plenty of countries that would lock me up tonight if they got a hold of me. I am here in good faith, trying to broker a deal that can make us all loads of coin."

"What are you offering in exchange for helping your shipment enter Guinea?"

"Ten million per container."

"How often?"

"We would like to eventually grow to twenty-four times per year. The hope is for a new shipment every couple of weeks." He drew from his cigar. "Things would start off slower, obviously."

"Some people in the Guinean government will need to be paid-off," Li said. "I will need eleven million instead of ten."

"I will speak to the shippers," Shane said.

"Who are they?"

"I promised to protect identities."

"You can guarantee me eleven now by taking the extra million out of your own cut. Then go work the math out with the Mexicans, however you must."

Shane looked at O'Hara. After some time, he gave a slight nod and said, "For you... I will do that."

"I assume it's drugs you're bringing in?"

Shane nodded. "Mostly."

"Arms?" Li asked.

Shane held up his thumb and forefinger in a way as if to suggest 'a little bit'.

"I will need advanced notice on any shipments that contain freight other than drugs."

"You have my word," Shane said.

Li looked at O'Hara, then back at Shane. "Are you a pilot, Mr. Malone?"

"I am."

"We will also need you to be willing to provide one of your planes should we ever need them to travel within Africa."

"If we reach a deal, that can be a part of it."

"You can tell your Mexicans that if this business is conducted successfully for at least six months, there might be more business we can do together in southeast Asia."

Shane nodded. "I will pass that information on to them."

Li sat back and pulled hard on the cigar. He blew smoke toward the sky.

"My money is to be cash. American dollars, nothing else. I want six-million up front as a token of your faith, once the Mexicans agree to the terms. Within one week. If you make good on this payment, the first shipment you bring in will only cost you five million." He tapped his cigar against the edge of a glass ashtray. "From then on, it becomes eleven per shipment."

"How much notice will you need to make arrangements for the first shipment?"

"Once you pay the six, I will have everything ready within seven days."

Shane extended his hand. Li shook it.

"We have a deal," he said. "Now, if you don't mind, Mr. Malone, once you have finished your drink it would be appreciated if you would give me and Danny some time to discuss matters in private."

Shane appeared confused. "You want me to leave?"

Li nodded.

"Of course, take your time." He shot down the last of his bourbon and stood.

"Thank you for the beautiful cigars, and the red," Li said.

O'Hara stood and shook Shane's hand. "We won't be long."

Shane winked. "The boat's yours until midnight if you need it." He looked at Li Yong. "I look forward to doing business."

"Likewise," Li said.

"Gentlemen, enjoy the evening." Shane exited the deck down the gangway.

They moved to the railing along the edge and watched him climb into a waiting car.

"You don't fuck around," O'Hara said.

"It's business *Fángdàn*," Li replied. He pulled once more from his cigar and walked back to the table where he stubbed it out in the ashtray. He picked up the wine bottle from the bar and filled their glasses with what remained. He read the label. "I will be buying this one again."

"What are your thoughts on Shane?"

"He will be a man of his word."

"What about the Mexicans?"

"Real gangsters want no attention. If they're making money, they're happy. I can fulfill my part of the deal."

O'Hara sipped his wine.

"We are partners in this, you and I," Li said.

"Nah, I'm just making the connects."

Li waved a finger. "That connection earns you commission like any good sale should. Every time one of their shipments passes through Conakry successfully, you will be a million dollars richer."

O'Hara patted the man's ribs.

"You deserve to start relaxing," Li said. "Enough with the fights and the shootouts." He touched a finger to O'Hara's head. "You're a master at knowing who to know, and then at tricking them into wanting to know you. That is a skill that can't be taught or learned, my boy. Utilize that, and get rich. No more dirty hands." He wiped his palms against one another as if cleaning them and then held them up for O'Hara to see. They were smaller than average, but thick. "You know when the last time I shot a gun was?" He gestured toward O'Hara with his chin. "Bel-Air. Laying on top of you with all your holes. These days if there's a problem, I don't grab a gun. I tell someone else about it and by the time I wake up the next morning the problem is gone."

"My man."

"*Fángdàn*..." Li Yong touched a finger to his temple. "This will always be your most dangerous weapon."

SEVENTEEN

The Greek Club was located just around the corner from the flat, through an easy to miss doorway off Talaat Harb Square, up a narrow stairwell on the second floor. Beyond the initial fine dining room, decorated in a pre-revolutionary style with a piano player and crystal chandeliers, was an outdoor courtyard enclosed by surrounding buildings.

Li Yong had reserved the courtyard for what he told the owner would be a private event. When O'Hara arrived with Teagan and Mick, he was already sitting out there among several stone water fountains, smoking a cigarette and drinking a glass of wine. He stood and hugged O'Hara, then shook hands with Teagan and Mick.

"I come all the way to Egypt to eat in a Greek restaurant," Li kidded.

"I'm keen for some good Greek," Mick said. "I've been living on those mashed beans all the locals seem to love. Mashed beans in a bowl. Mashed beans in a sandwich. You wonder why everyone's smoking that shisha all the time. Probably to cover up the smell of farts."

Li laughed.

"It's called *fuul*," Teagan said with a grin.

"They must see me walk up and think, give the big fool some *fuul*."

O'Hara picked up a bottle of Obelisk Egyptian red wine from the table and poured three glasses, then topped off Li's with the last of it.

"Li knew Dina well," he said to Teagan.

"I cared about Dina very much." Li made a hand gesture toward O'Hara. "*Fángdàn* is like a nephew to me."

"Dina was like my sister," Teagan said.

"Then that makes you my niece," Li replied.

She smiled affectionately.

"What was that you just called him, Li?" Mick said. "*Fong Tong*."

Li looked at O'Hara. "*Fángdàn* means bulletproof." He made the shape of a gun with his fingers.

"Oh, right," Mick said. "Yeah, he had a few holes punched in him, didn't he."

"I don't know how he survived," Li said.

"You're the reason I did," O'Hara said.

"Ancient Chinese secrets?" Mick asked.

O'Hara draped his arm on the back of Teagan's chair as a waiter brought out plates of grilled halloumi cheese, hummus, toasted flat bread and spanakopita, and spread them along the table.

"Please eat," Li said.

"Too easy," Mick assured him and loaded a plate with food from each of the dishes. "So, what is it you do, Mister Li?"

"I'm a businessman. I own restaurants. Hotels." He brought an unlit cigarette to his mouth. "And you?"

"I was a bit of an entrepreneur myself," Mick said with a mouthful of halloumi. "Now I'm just on walkabout with me mate." He punched O'Hara in the shoulder. "A bit of a gypsy."

"I know what you did for him down there," Li said in a serious tone. "I respect you for it."

Mick raised his wine glass and said, "Cheers," before taking a drink.

"In my culture, family is everything." He paused to gesture toward O'Hara. He then pointed toward Mick. "One of the most important things we can have around us is a..." He paused again, snapping his fingers, then batting his hand at the air. "I forget the English word. We must have friends that become close like family. We must be willing to die to protect them." He then glanced at O'Hara and added, "When I say *Fángdàn* is my nephew, I mean it. I am honored to meet his new family."

Teagan smiled and ran her hand along O'Hara's forearm.

"To Uncle Li," Mick said, raising his glass.

"Stand up," O'Hara said and stood from his chair, holding his arms wide.

Li stood and O'Hara wrapped him in a tight hug, lifting him off the floor.

"Everyone should be lucky enough to have an uncle like this guy," he said. He was feeling good from the wine.

Li struggled to laugh until it ended in coughs.

"Sit, sit," Li said. "The waiter thinks we are weird."

They all looked at the staring Egyptian waiter, who averted his eyes from them.

"Ah, old mate's just wondering why we didn't order the mashed beans," Mick replied.

They sat back down and ordered more bottles of wine along with the main course, and for the first time in a long time, O'Hara allowed himself to get drunk and do nothing more than appreciate their company, without a worry over what might lie ahead in the days or weeks to come.

As the night went on, Li regaled them with stories of Mandalay and the lawless lands further north in the Golden Triangle of Myanmar, near the Chinese border. Mick told hilarious stories of the Australian underworld and some of the more colorful characters he had gotten to know in prison. All the while, O'Hara relaxed and took it all in. He watched Teagan, captivated by the two men's knack for storytelling and knew that he was among kindred souls.

* * *

The next morning, they woke with the dawn call to prayer singing through open windows. The sky was ashen gray and already the smell of burning tobacco was strong in the air. O'Hara brewed coffee and they drank it in bed, holding one another.

"There's a heaviness looming. I thought it was to do with Bob being sick, but it's more." She was wearing one of O'Hara's t-shirts.

"What's up?" he asked as the strong brew began to lift his hangover.

Teagan shook her head. She was cradling her coffee in two hands and inhaling the steam that rose from it. It was the first time he noticed the crow's feet along the edges of her eyes.

"Just a looming heaviness," she repeated. "A weird feeling is all. Please be extra careful out there."

She rested her head against his shoulder and he kissed the top of it.

"If you want me to channel Dina again, I can try."

He massaged her neck, but didn't respond.

"Like in Bli Bli, I mean."

"I know what you mean."

She ran her fingernail along his leg. It wasn't until he looked at her that he saw the tears in her eyes.

"What if I just want you to be you?" he asked, and set his empty mug down on the dresser.

She reached up and touched the side of his face and brought it closer to hers. He kissed her, then took her mug and set it down beside his. She slipped out of her nightshirt and they made love with the low rising sun to the east casting a hazy orange glow across the room through the open window.

* * *

An old brown Toyota Yaris sedan pulled curbside in front of the Excalibur Diner on Talaat Harb Street and O'Hara climbed into the passenger seat. Bob was behind the steering wheel, wearing a ball cap and tinted prescription glasses.

"Driving in this fucking city," he complained as he hesitated three times before finding the right opportunity to pull the car out among the flow of traffic. He beat the horn out of frustration, making O'Hara laugh.

"It's like a city of New York cabbies," O'Hara said.

"Go figure," Bob said. "Just think how many of them were probably Egyptian."

"You're looking a bit pale. You should get out in the sun more. Get some vitamin-D."

"Just tired is all." Bob changed lanes and another car honked its horn. "Go fuck yourself," he said with his hand out the window.

"Where'd you go?" O'Hara asked.

Bob glanced over at him as though hesitant to answer. "Kraków," he said. "How's your Chinese Uncle settling in?"

"He pretty much made Shane his bitch."

"Don't sleep on Shane. Being the link between a cartel and a triad makes him a powerful bitch."

"Sounds like a quick way to end up dead."

"Unless you're good at what you do. He's got the wings."

O'Hara shrugged. "You gain any good intel in Poland?"

"Mostly about Ukraine, which is a shit show. But yeah, I learned a few things about our little hunt."

"Like what?"

Bob entered a large roundabout and exited across a bridge over the Nile, where at all four corners large lion statues stood guard.

"Oddly, it seems ABT is clean, with respect to what went down in Bel-Air." He frowned. "I had thought maybe he had set you up, but there's no evidence to support that. He might be a real friend, after all."

"I hope so," O'Hara said.

Bob glanced at him, then back at the road. "Our man down at the cabin in Queensland. He's Volk Group. Not that you hadn't figured as much." Across the bridge, Bob turned north in front of the Cairo Opera House and traveled the ringed road that ran beneath the tree-lined streets of Gezira Island.

"What about Sasha Filenkov?"

"It's hard to tell how deep his ties are to Moscow. They were once strong, before he got on the wrong side of the Tsar." Bob coughed. "He got the boot from London, after Ukraine started up. He's been living in Istanbul, mostly. Watch him, though, because a ho-ligarch like him will do anything to get back in the good graces of the mighty."

"Most of what you've told me, I already knew."

"Fuck me, how did you do prison time without patience?" Bob grabbed a cigar that was resting at an angle in the car cupholder and stuck it in his mouth. He rolled down the window and bit off the tip and spit it out. "I never said I had intel to be shared with you, anyway." He held the cigar clamped between his teeth and lit it with a lighter. He drew smoke from the cigar and dropped the lighter into the cup holder.

O'Hara rolled his window down to let out the smell.

"You probably just let in worse air."

The comment made O'Hara grin.

"I have another stogie if you want one."

"I'm good," O'Hara replied. "You know you're grumpy as fuck, today."

Bob batted a hand at the air in O'Hara's direction. "Listen, I need you to memorize a few words of Russian."

"Why?"

"With it being confirmed that Russians are behind the attempts on your life, in case you're ever in a situation where they catch up with you. Kidnapped. Detained. Anything like that. If you say this to the right Russian it may save your life."

"Even Volk Group?"

"If it's The Baker you might be fucked. But it would still be worth a shot as a last resort."

"Did you learn something that makes you think I'll end up in a situation like that?"

"They've tried killing you three times." Bob shook his head.

"And what exactly will saying these words do for me?"

"It's old Cold War slang. It might at least buy you some time. Keep you from eating a bullet and getting thrown in an unmarked grave."

"Let's hear it."

"*Vampir, adin, devyat, sem, dva, pesht.*"

"What the hell is all that?"

"A series of words that'll make sense to the right people." He dropped ash from the cigar out his window. "If you're lucky."

"And to the wrong people?"

"It'll sound like gibberish. Give it a go."

"Let me hear it again," O'Hara said.

Bob repeated the words, this time in a cadence as if teaching a nursery rhyme to a toddler. O'Hara repeated them, slightly bobbing his head with each word.

"*Molodets*," Bob said. "Again."

O'Hara repeated the words.

"You have a good memory. Not a bad accent, either. Now keep repeating it until it's become that annoying song you can't get out of your head.

"What's it all mean?"

"Vampire, one, nine, seven, two, Pest."

"And what's that mean?"

Bob clucked his tongue. "Don't worry about that. Just make sure you drill the words into your brain. Pretend you need to know it like your life depends on it." He crossed another bridge off the island and entered the west bank neighborhood of Dokki.

"*Vampir, adin, devyat, sem, dva, pesht*," O'Hara said.

"Yes." Bob moved his cigar to the cadence as if he were conducting an orchestra.

As O'Hara was reciting the Russian words to himself, Bob hit his thigh to get his attention.

"You need to memorize one more sentence. This one can be in English."

"Go ahead," O'Hara said.

"Margarita must know, Professor Woland is a wolf."

O'Hara repeated the sentence, then asked, "What?"

"Russian grammar is too complicated. You'll fuck it up. Whoever you're saying this to will know how to get it translated if they don't already understand English."

"Margarita must know, Professor Woland is a wolf." O'Hara nodded to himself. "*Vampir, adin, devyat, sem, dva, pesht*."

"That's it, kid."

"Sometimes I think you play up this spy shit," he said.

When he received no reply, O'Hara looked over at Bob, who was now wincing, holding his chest with his free hand. He had dropped the lit cigar onto his lap and was veering into oncoming traffic. O'Hara snatched the cigar and tossed it out the window, grabbed the steering wheel and straightened the car's course.

"Bob, whats up?!"

Bob didn't answer. He curled forward with his face toward the wheel, but managed to hit the brake enough to slow them. Cars honked their horns. O'Hara stepped over the middle console and steered the car toward the side of the road while stepping on Bob's foot atop the pedal. The front tire jumped the curb and he pulled on the emergency break. He hopped out of the car and ran around to open Bob's door.

"I'm alright," Bob hissed, still in obvious discomfort.

O'Hara realized he was likely having a cardiac episode, and grabbed him under the leg and back and pushed him over the center console into the passenger's seat, then climbed in behind the wheel. "Do you know where the nearest hospital is?"

Bob gave a slight nod of his head. "Tahrir Square," he said among a series of grunts. "Just south of it."

O'Hara peeled out into traffic, speeding through Dokki back toward Gezira in the direction of Wust el-Balad. He sped through intersections, weaving in and out of lanes, talking to Bob about anything that would keep him responsive. His mind was on autopilot as he drove, unable to make sense of how he even knew his way until he found himself entering the big roundabout at Tahrir Square. He exited off a main road to the south, and saw what looked to be a hospital.

"Is that it?" he asked Bob, but received no response.

He looked over and Bob's eyes were rolled back in his head. His tongue was sticking out.

"Fuck!" O'Hara shouted and reached a hand out for Bob's neck. He felt under his jaw for a pulse, then pulled to a screeching halt at the curb outside the hospital building.

Jumping out, he circled around to Bob's door, screaming out for help. He dragged Bob out and lay him on his back on the sidewalk where he began to perform chest compressions. Bob remained unresponsive. The skin under his eyes and along his bulbous nose had taken on a shade of gray.

O'Hara could hear the sounds of help arriving from somewhere behind him, but his thoughts were frozen. Without realizing it, as he pressed down repeatedly on Bob's chest, attempting to keep the blood flowing through his friend's heart, he found himself moving to a subconscious rhythm and muttering the words "*Vampir, adin, devyat, sem, dva, pesht*" over and over until a hospital employee dressed in scrubs pulled him away. Two men lifted Bob up onto a stretcher and rushed him into the building.

EIGHTEEN

The sound of a key in the door caught their attention. The knob turned and it opened with Nate entering the room. O'Hara set his coffee down and walked over.

"I'm sorry," he said.

Nate nodded. "Appreciate it. You guys alright?"

"Yeah." O'Hara took a clean mug down from a cabinet and poured a cup for him.

"Now what?" he asked.

Nate let out a sigh. "I'll make sure the right people are made aware so that they can arrange for him to travel home."

"Colorado?"

"Yeah."

"What about here? Are we done?"

"Stay the course," Nate said. He had the glazed over eyes of someone who had woken up after being knocked unconscious. He walked over and took a seat on an empty chair at the table with Mick. "ABT is your guy. Roll with that until you hear from me."

O'Hara looked at Teagan, who was watching Nate as if waiting for him to say more.

Nate reached up and patted O'Hara's shoulder. "When I get back from the funeral, we'll reassess."

"When'll that be?"

Nate sipped his coffee. "Depends on a few things."

"How long is this place paid for?" O'Hara asked.

"You've got plenty of time, here."

O'Hara nodded. "How can I get in touch with you?"

"I know how to find you," Nate said.

"What if we leave Egypt?"

"I'll see you before that." Nate gulped down the rest of his coffee and stood. "You have anything you hadn't passed to him yet? Anything pertinent?"

O'Hara shook his head. He thought of asking Nate about the meaning of the Russian words Bob had him memorize, or the line about Margarita, Professor Woland and the wolf.

"Alright then, I just wanted to do a face to face before I bounce. I'm gonna head." Nate extended his hand and shook with O'Hara and Mick. He gave Teagan a hug, and turned and left the apartment.

O'Hara knew the man's sadness too well. He wouldn't have wished it upon his enemy.

* * *

The ahwa was filled with the rich scent of strong coffee, twice boiled in the Turkish tradition. Li Yong sat on a chair on the sidewalk, smoking a cigarette with his legs crossed. He was watching an artisan across the walkway stitch a colorful pattern of Quranic calligraphy onto a tapestry.

O'Hara hung up the phone and put it in his pocket.

"He's apparently made arrangements to land his planes at a strip in the mountains."

"How will he get there from Conakry?" Li asked.

"His problem."

A waiter brought out two steaming cups of Turkish coffee. They each accepted one. Li used his thumb to flick ash from his cigarette.

"Everything there is ready to go from my end," Li said.

"Will you be over there at all?"

Li sucked his teeth and shook his head. He hit O'Hara with the back of his hand, a habit of his. "Which is what I wanted to talk about before I go. Why don't you to come to Burma?"

"It's a shit-show, no?"

Li shrugged and dropped his cigarette butt on the sidewalk, stubbing it out with his foot.

"You'd be safe there with me."

O'Hara took a sip of coffee and ran the grit against the roof of his mouth with his tongue.

He patted O'Hara on the thigh. "If you come over, I will introduce you to the General."

"Which general?"

Li smiled widely. "*The* general."

O'Hara waited for him to elaborate.

"Will you come?"

"I'll try to visit, at some point."

"It will be good for this new business you mention about searching for fighters."

"How so?"

Li laughed. "Ah, *Fángdàn*. Lethwei."

"What's that mean?"

"Burmese kickboxing. The most lethal fighting style you will ever see."

"Lethwei," O'Hara repeated. "Never heard of it."

"The art of the nine limbs." Li slapped his arm. "Trust your uncle..."

O'Hara put a hand on the back of Li's neck and gave it a gentle squeeze.

Li finished his coffee and set the mug on the table. He stood and O'Hara did as well.

"Go see Shane and tell him to fly to Guinea and rent a room at my hostel in Bel-Air. Chan is running it, now. He will be his point of contact going forward. No phones. Anything that needs to be discussed must happen face-to-face."

"I'll make sure he knows."

The two men hugged, clapping one another on the back.

"Once you've got your business sorted here, we will book your flight to come see me."

O'Hara nodded and watched as his friend turned and crossed the street to where a Malaysian driver was waiting in a parked car.

* * *

The next morning O'Hara bought a ticket at the metro station underneath Tahrir Square and rode it south to the Mar Girgis station, where he met Shane Malone. They walked among the pale cobblestone alleys of the old Coptic quarter of the city, among the high rampart walls, through cloisters and past churches, where O'Hara brought the Irishman up to speed on who he was to contact in Guinea.

The smells of burning incense lingered among the narrow passages of the old town, reminding O'Hara of Bronx churches from decades past. As they walked, they made small talk. As if to honor their dependency on one another's discretion, Shane disclosed stories of prison time he served in Dublin as a young man and again in England, years later. Before O'Hara could offer up any of his own stories, he was interrupted by his phone vibrating in his pocket. He pulled it out and brought it to his ear.

"Meester Marrero," a voice said in English. "I was told to reach out and check on you by our friend the prince."

"Mister Filenkov?"

"Please. Sasha," the Russian man replied.

"It's good to hear from you. How've you been?"

"I am well, my friend. Are you still in Cairo?"

"I am." O'Hara was looking at Shane as he spoke.

"I was wondering if you would like to come be my guest on the Sinai. Prince Ahmed's conference will be held in Sharm el-Sheikh in a few weeks' time, and I will be staying at my property just north of there, near Dahab. You are welcome to bring your friends, if they are still in town with you."

"That's very thoughtful of you," O'Hara replied.

"A friend of the prince is a friend of mine. I will be here enjoying the Gulf of Aqaba until the conference. You can reach me on this number I am calling from. Just give me a day's notice, to have rooms prepared."

"I appreciate that, Sasha. I'll call you back later today, once I've spoken to the others."

"*Khorosho*. Speak soon, my friend."

When O'Hara hung up the phone, Shane asked, "Filenkov?"

"That Russian from the pool party."

"Yeah, I know. Watch out for that one," Shane said. "I wouldn't be rushin' to be around any Russians, these days."

O'Hara grinned at his word play.

"He just invited me out to the Sinai. Near some town, Dahab."

Shane gave a nod. "Beautiful out that way." He put his hands in his pockets and shrugged. "Why don't you let me fly you's out there. A token of appreciation for the introduction to Li."

O'Hara looked at him. "I'd rather keep you and I from sharing any travel records. Going by road might be easier."

"*Inshallah*, we can manage to keep off any records." Shane winked. "The good thing about out here, lad... is when the money talks, Allah listens. I didn't choose this part of the world by accident."

O'Hara studied the Irishman, trying to discern whether he was being a friend or an opportunist. "*Inshallah*," he replied as they continued walking in the direction of the metro station.

* * *

The stars were crisp and bright once the sun had set and they stood among the shadows of the rooftop. The moon appeared near full, and bathed them in a luminescent glow. In the distance across the rooftops of Giza the pyramids were like small apparitions against the black sky.

Nate drew from a stick of hash and blew rings of smoke toward the sky.

"It's been a while," he said. "Hash hits different."

"How was it?"

"Nate drew hard once more, causing the ember to glow red. "Was an honor to carry the coffin. The world lost a legend. You don't know the half."

"Are you still on the books?" O'Hara asked. "Or have you left like Bob did."

Nate looked at O'Hara and narrowed his eyes. His lids were heavy from the drug.

"I need to know who I'm dealing with. Otherwise, I want out."

"I think we're done with your little Rambo mission," Nate said. "If that's what you mean."

"Bob promised to help me find anyone involved."

"Bob's dead, brother."

"What about Sasha Filenkov?" O'Hara asked.

Nate looked at him and took one last hit of his spliff, before flicking it off the edge of the rooftop.

"I say you take him up on that invite and get to know the prick. Find out for yourself." Nate held a fist up for O'Hara to knock knuckles with. "You won't be alone. We're always watching."

NINETEEN

Just north of the town of Dahab, a former hippie-trail paradise that now attracted outcasts, fugitives and artists, was a Bedouin settlement called Assala, where a tribe of once-nomadic peoples had since established a semi-permanent village. This tribe of hardened men and women, dressed in traditional garb and violet colored head wraps, ran the coast from Sharm el-Sheikh up to Nuweiba like a mafia. Drugs, arms, even people were moved about the lawless peninsula under their watch.

O'Hara, Teagan and Mick waited at a café along a sand swept boardwalk where plastic tables and chairs were set up along the beach near the water. They drank Bedouin tea, a mix of black leaf and a desert sage called *marmareya*, and looked out over the marbled patterns of blue and turquoise water to where the reef ended and a stark line divided it from the darker shade of the sea beyond.

There was no mistaking the Russian when he crossed the boardwalk and stepped onto the sand. A hefty mountain of a man in dark sunglasses and dressed in a t-shirt and shorts, with a shaved head and a stern expression, he noticed O'Hara and approached the table.

"Meester Marrero," the man said. "Please join me. I will take you to Meester Filenkov."

They rode through narrow dirt lanes with high cinderblock walls on either side. Private courtyards could be seen within many of the plots, where woven rugs were spread out in the open around firepits. Chickens roamed freely behind most houses and horses and camels were tied up near water troughs at the intersections.

They exited the cramped alleys and rode along a sandy road of hardpacked earth with desert to one side and the pristine turquoise gulf water to the other, until they saw the property up ahead, surrounded by high stucco walls with an electric security gate at the front. A two-story stone mansion with a small helicopter parked on the roof stood out from the otherwise rocky landscape.

Within the walls stood an extravagant fountain large enough to be a swimming pool set in the center of a horseshoe gravel drive. Sasha was waiting between two stone pillars atop the front steps. He was shirtless, wearing only board shorts and flip-flops and his graying hair was held back on his head by a pair of sunglasses.

The SUV circled the fountain and rolled to a stop at the base of the stone steps. Sasha walked down to meet them as the driver opened the rear doors to let everyone out.

"Some place you've got here," O'Hara said and shook the Russian's hand. "You could probably house everyone in the village."

Sasha laughed as he then shook Mick's hand and introduced himself. "I bought the land and had the villa built once I realized Neom will likely extend this far east." When he got to Teagan he brought her hand to his lips and kissed her knuckle like he had when they first met.

"You better be careful, mate, the natives'll be bathing in this fountain," Mick said.

"It's funny you say that," Sasha replied. "That fountain used to be saltwater. I had a small shark in it, but one day I came back after a few weeks away and it was gone."

Teagan glanced sideways at O'Hara.

"Did you track down the men who did it?"

Sasha gave a helpless shrug. "These Bedouins aren't the types you want to pick a fight with, if you can avoid it."

"They're cool with you living here?" O'Hara asked.

Sasha held his hand up and rubbed his thumb and fingers together. "Money is the *mallik* around here." He half-turned toward the front door. "Come I will show you the house."

They followed him through the large arched doorway into an open front room with a curved staircase that rose along one side to the second floor. There were recessed stained glass windows set in the walls, and a large tapestry of men on a unicorn hunt, which hung down the entire length of the wall opposite the stairs.

"I bought this piece from a museum," he said, pointing to the tapestry. "It reminded me of my own life's journey. Always chasing the magic."

"Wanker," Mick whispered about Sasha under his breath.

"Wait until you see this, though," Sasha said and led them into a parlor room, where a stone sarcophagus rested in the middle of the room. The features of the carved mummy face were slightly eroded but were those of a man, with arms folded across his chest and holding unrecognizable objects in each hand. There were sofas against the base of the walls, arranged much like a viewing room of an art gallery.

"Is this real?" Teagan asked.

"It is. From the Eighteenth Dynasty, when Akhenaten reigned." He turned to Teagan. "History is a passion of mine."

"I can see that," she said.

"Who was in it?" O'Hara asked.

"He is believed to have been a member of the royal court."

"Now he's a member of your lounge room," Mick said with a giggle.

"The mummy is no longer inside," Sasha responded, not picking up on the sarcasm.

"It must have cost you a fortune," O'Hara said.

"If you have it, why not spend it?" Sasha asked. He pointed back toward the stairwell in the first room. "I will show you the upstairs later. Come, let's drink."

Sasha walked through the mummy room to a large kitchen that would have been better fit in a restaurant, all stainless-steel appliances and marble countertops. A chef in a white apron was preparing food. A man in a linen suit stood behind a fully stocked bar along one side of the room, and through a wall that had been retracted accordion style, was an outdoor patio that overlooked the Gulf of Aqaba.

In the distance, across the teal sea was a mountain range, cutting a jagged line across the cloudless blue sky. Noticing where O'Hara's attention had been drawn, Sasha tapped his shoulder and pointed at the mountains.

"That's your friend's country," he said. "The Kingdom."

"That there is Saudi?" O'Hara asked in disbelief. "It's so close."

"*Da*," Sasha replied. "Do you think you could swim to it?" he asked.

"If I had enough time," O'Hara kidded.

The large Russian driver that had picked them up in Dahab was sitting on a lounge chair facing the sea, holding a glass of brown liquor.

"More guests will be arriving, but it will only be a small gathering today." He called out in Russian to the bartender.

The man produced a bottle of vintage Dom Perignon and uncorked it with a loud pop. He lined up several crystal flute glasses and filled them all. The cook helped hand them out to the guests.

Once everyone had a glass Sasha raised his in a toast and welcomed them to his Desert Dacha, as he called it. The cold champagne was refreshing under the hot sun, and the slight breeze off the ocean was enough to keep them from sweating if they remained within the shade.

Ambient house music played from speakers, hidden throughout the landscaping.

"You his bodyguard, mate?" Mick asked the large Russian driver.

The man nodded and sipped his champagne.

"Right-o," Mick said once he realized that was all the response he was getting. "Chatty bloke," he said to O'Hara.

"Pavel has been with me since I first broke into the hemp industry," Sasha said. "We are from the same block of apartments in St. Petersburg."

Pavel confirmed the statement with a grunt.

"Speaking of hemp," Mick said. "Got any of that kind of thing to twist up into a joint?"

"The Bedouins in Assala have beautiful hashish," Sasha said. "I can have some delivered if you like."

"I'm always up for a bit of a burn," Mick said. "Say mate, where do you take the helicopter?"

"Sharm, mostly. Sometimes over Mount Sinai."

A conversation could be heard coming from behind them. O'Hara turned to find a middle-aged gentleman with gray hair, standing at the entrance to the patio alongside a younger, olive-skinned man. As they were handed glasses of champagne by the bartender, the gray-haired man looked over at Sasha and smiled. He was of average height but thick in the neck and shoulders, with a bit of a belly that caused his untucked linen shirt to hang away from his waist. The younger man had his dark hair combed back in a ponytail, and wore a tight-fitting shirt that showed off a muscular physique.

"Am I the only female here?" Teagan asked.

Sasha placed his hand on hers. "It makes you stand out that much more."

Teagan shifted uncomfortably in her seat.

The two men descended the stairs and walked over. The gray-haired man extended his hand to O'Hara and said "Fyodor Metchikov," before moving on to shake hands with the others, repeating his name for them.

"Fyodor used to be a diplomat, but now does liaison work, helping Russian businessmen navigate the muddy political waters of certain countries."

"As you know," Fyodor said with a warm smile. "We must support those among us who represent our country in a positive light."

The younger, muscular man introduced himself as Tony.

"Tony the Turk, we call him," Sasha said playfully. "My dear friend and a very successful nightclub owner in Istanbul, which as you already know is where I spend much of my time."

When Tony shook Teagan's hand, he stared into her eyes for a long awkward moment.

"What are you doing, mate, trying to read her mind?" Mick asked.

Tony looked at Mick, and offered his hand. "Tony," he said.

Mick clasped his hand and nodded. "The Turkey," he said.

"What?"

Mick released his hand without saying anything and skulled the rest of his champagne. "Sasha, you have any lager or spirits up at that bar? I thought you Russians put vodka in your cereal." He glanced sideways at Tony. "Too much more of the Frog piss and Muscles here might wear on me."

Teagan slipped her arm around O'Hara's elbow and took a step closer to him.

"Help yourself," Sasha replied to Mick. "The barman will serve you anything you like."

"Cheers," Mick said and walked up the steps toward the bar.

"I hear you are a Canadian," Fyodor said to O'Hara. "I lived and worked in Ottawa for a few years."

"Is that why your English is so good?"

Fyodor shook his head. "I lived in New York City, as well as Washington." He then made a gesture with his hand. "I have been speaking English for many years."

O'Hara finished off what was left in his champagne glass and set it on the nearest table. If it was true about New York, Fyodor likely would have spent plenty of time in the Bronx, with the Russian Embassy residence being located in North Riverdale.

"You must have been the man, to get postings like that," he said.

Fyodor laughed. "They were different times, in those days." He shrugged. "Although it seems as though things are headed back in that direction." He gestured with his chin toward O'Hara. "And what brought you out here?"

"I met Sasha at a pool party in Cairo," O'Hara said. "He was kind enough to invite us out."

"What were you doing in Cairo?" Tony asked.

He looked at the Turk, whose confidence bordered too closely on cockiness for O'Hara's liking.

"Business," he answered.

"Business?"

"Yeah, none of yours."

Tony smirked.

"Gobble, gobble, gobble," O'Hara heard Mick say.

He looked over to find Mick descending the stairs with a bottle of vodka and a stack of shot glasses. "Not to stereotype," he called down the stairs. "But I reckon there's enough Ruskies to justify making potato the flavor of the moment."

"I like this man," Sasha said. "Australians rarely disappoint when it comes to being up for a good time."

"Cheers," Mick said. He looked at Tony and added, I thought about bringing some gravy for you, but couldn't find any."

It was obvious that Tony didn't appreciate the attention. "You have a problem?" he asked.

"Settle down ya goof," Mick said.

"Enough, lets drink," Fyodor said.

Pavel returned with a plate of pickled cabbage and cucumbers. Sasha and Fyodor grabbed a pinch of the food with one hand and raised their shot glasses in the other. They all shot the liquor, followed by a mouthful of the vegetables. The glasses were immediately refilled, and they drank another round of shots.

Teagan hissed from the burn of the alcohol. Fyodor laughed and placed a hand on her shoulder. "Pace yourself, Miss Teagan. Sasha here will be legless in an hour."

Tony pulled a plastic bag filled with cocaine from his pants pocket. "I have other things that will keep our legs under us," he said to her.

"No thanks," she said.

The Turkish man shrugged, and poured a small mound of powder onto the back of his fist, then snorted it. He handed the bag to Sasha, who laid out a long line on the table, which he leaned over and sniffed.

"Good. Good. Yes." He looked at the rest of the group. "Who else?"

Only Pavel nodded, so Sasha laid out another few lines for him and the bodyguard.

Sasha started dancing to the house music being played from the speakers. He looked at his watch. "The ratio will be more balanced soon. I have sent a man down to the resorts in Sharm to offer invitations to beautiful people. He has already confirmed fifteen that are coming."

"Where's your wife?" Teagan asked.

"On the yacht, somewhere," Sasha replied without breaking from his dancing.

Mick leaned in close to O'Hara's ear and whispered. "We should let them get blind off the booze and coke and take them for all they're worth."

O'Hara laughed and pulled his head back to look at Mick. "And go where with it all?"

Mick glanced up at the helicopter for a moment. "Shane said he'd pick us up when we're ready."

"You're out of your mind," O'Hara said.

A waiter came down the stairs carrying a large tray of wine glasses filled with an assortment of reds and whites. "Shiraz and Pinot," he said.

O'Hara and Teagan took a glass of red each and thanked him. Mick took two.

Voices could be heard in the kitchen area, laughing. When O'Hara turned there was a group of trendily dressed late-teens or twenty-somethings being escorted through the house by the cook.

"Is this the lot from Sharm?" Teagan asked.

"Must be," Sasha said, before taking another shot of vodka and chasing it with a pickled cucumber. "Now I will have a body to keep me warm at night."

"Or bodies," Tony said with a smirk.

"You're old enough to be their father," Teagan replied.

"Well," Sasha said void of emotion. "Maybe if their actual father did a better job, they wouldn't be here."

Teagan looked at O'Hara with a horrified expression. He put a hand at the small of her back.

"Helicopter!" an attractive blonde among the group said, pointing to the roof of the house.

As the hours passed and dusk settled in over the gentle waters of the gulf, the music grew louder and carried across the private strip of beach beyond the patio. O'Hara and Teagan walked down to the water's edge with their shoes off and stood with their feet in the sea. The coral reef began a few meters out and extended at least fifty yards before dropping off. The water was shallow so that even under the dying light of the setting sun the ocean was translucent. Halfway out on the reef there was a darker oval patch of water where a naturally formed rock pool existed.

"I wonder how deep that is," he said.

"It is deep enough to swim laps!" Sasha's loud voice called out from behind. They turned to find him descending the last few stairs onto the sand. He was holding a half-filled bottle of Vodka in one hand. "I go out there some mornings for exercise. You can actually dive down pretty far. It connects to a network of caves underneath."

Sasha's eyes were glassed over with one staring lazily off to the side.

Teagan leaned close to O'Hara and said, "I'll be back, I've gotta pee."

"I'll chill here," O'Hara said.

As she climbed the steps back to the patio, Sasha turned the bottle up to his lips and drank long enough for air bubbles to gurgle. He held the bottle out to O'Hara, who at first declined, until Sasha said, "Come on, you're not going to reject an offer of my hospitality." He slurred his words.

O'Hara grabbed the bottle and took a swig before handing it back.

"*Khorosho*," Sasha said. "You know I am quite surprised you are still with Prince Ahmed."

"He's always been good to me," O'Hara replied.

Sasha started laughing. "Yeah, yeah. Is it like the Godfather movie with Marlon Brando?"

O'Hara looked at him, confused.

"Keep your friends close, but your enemies closer," Sasha added in a mock-American accent.

"I'm not following you," O'Hara said, knowing that if he sounded uninterested Sasha wouldn't be able to resist the urge to elaborate.

"You know the Saudis are not to be trusted."

"Nobody is, these days." O'Hara moved a shell around under the water with his toe.

"Very true," Sasha agreed.

"You're talking as if you know something about Prince Ahmed."

"I know many things about him."

"Like what?"

Sasha turned the bottle up and drank the vodka for a few long seconds. He handed O'Hara the bottle who put it to his lips and faked a sip. He passed the bottle back.

"As you know, I am an outcast in Russian society. I was in London because I could not remain in my country and maintain my business empire. Now, with this Ukraine mess, I have been kicked out of the UK, also." He drank from the bottle and stared out toward the Saudi Arabian mountain range across the gulf. "But when you are a Russian billionaire, you don't stop knowing people. And you don't stop hearing the whispers."

"Sounds like you have something you want to say."

"Never trust anyone that won't get this drunk in front of you."

"Alright," O'Hara said, blowing him off.

"Because if they won't do this, it is likely that they have something they are scared to reveal to you. When we drink this much, our lips become weak."

O'Hara watched him out of the corner of his eye.

"I have heard you were betrayed."

"Come again?"

"I have heard there was a Russian that wanted you dead. For what reason I don't know. But that in exchange for something..." he stopped and hiccupped. "Your Saudi friends told the Russian where you could be found."

O'Hara stepped in front of Sasha, staring into his eyes.

He offered the bottle, which only had an inch or two of vodka left in it. O'Hara didn't acknowledge it. He had the sudden urge to call Bob, and was hit by a wave of heaviness when he realized why that was no longer an option. He looked up toward the terrace to see if he could spot Teagan, but didn't see her among the guests.

Sasha was now staring through O'Hara. It was clear that he was more than intoxicated, and this made O'Hara question how credible his words could be.

"Who's the Russian that they told about me?"

Sasha hiccupped and batted his hand at the air, mumbling something in Russian. "The motherfucker," he said, stressing the English curse. "Annenkov."

O'Hara ran a hand over his head and turned away from Sasha. He looked back and asked, "How do you know this?"

Sasha shrugged. He finished the last of the vodka and tossed the empty bottle on the sand. "I'll get more," he said and turned to walk but lost his balance and fell face first in the sand.

O'Hara helped him to his feet, but after another few steps Sasha fell again. He crouched down and rolled him on his side.

Sasha said, "*Blat,*" and let out a long groan. His chest heaved once and he vomited.

"You good?" O'Hara said. He shook the man's shoulder to make sure he was out of it, then removed a cellphone from his pants pocket. He looked up toward the crowd at the party to make sure nobody was watching, before turning and hurling it out into the water.

He thought to carry the man back up to the house, but decided to leave him where he lay. Pavel could come get him. Back up on the patio it seemed as though anyone that wasn't dancing to the music was busy sniffing drugs.

He found Mick at the bar with a French woman that had come up among the crowd from Sharm, and asked him if he had seen Teagan anywhere. He hadn't.

He then ran into Pavel and told him where to find Sasha. The Russian mentioned having told Teagan about an upstairs bathroom earlier when she had been looking for one.

O'Hara climbed the curved staircase to the second floor, which consisted of a half-dozen large bedrooms on either side of a long hallway. Many of the doors were left open and the rooms were empty. At the far end of the hall O'Hara noticed one was shut. He listened for a moment before opening it.

He peeked his head in to find Teagan cowered on the floor in the far corner of the room beyond a large bed. On the white duvet cover was a trail of red splatter. He pushed the door open and hopped across the bed to where she sat.

She was crying and shaking, unable to speak. Broken shards of glass were scattered around her feet and she held the broken stem of a wine glass in one hand. The narrow end was covered in blood.

"What's wrong?! What is it?!" he asked her, crouching down and assessing her for any obvious injuries. He noticed her shirt was torn.

She shook her head in response, but couldn't bring herself to speak. He then heard a moan from behind, and turned to find Tony the Turk leaning against the wall behind the door, holding his hands to his bloodied chest. His eyes were bulging with a look of disbelief as he glanced down at his chest and let out a short grunt of a word in Turkish.

"What happened?" O'Hara asked Teagan.

"He followed me up here," she said and stopped to catch her breath. "He tried raping me."

O'Hara looked back at Tony, then took the glass stem from Teagan and set it down. He stood and shut the door, then pulled the balisong from his pocket and flicked it open. He pinned the Turk's head to the wall with his free hand and calmly nicked his carotid artery with the sharp blade. He then walked back to Teagan, as blood sprayed from the man's neck in spurts.

In a matter of seconds Tony collapsed to the floor, dead.

O'Hara helped her to her feet and hugged her. "Don't worry," he said and sat her on the bed. He pulled the phone from his pocket and dialed Mick's number. "You've done nothing wrong," he added as the phone began to dial.

"Aye," Mick answered.

"You need to come upstairs. Last bedroom on the right."

"Be right up," Mick said and hung up the phone.

O'Hara was comforting Teagan when Mick opened the door. He stepped in and closed it, looking at Tony's slumped body and the pool of dark blood surrounding it.

"I'd say the Turkey's done," Mick said.

Teagan went to speak, but O'Hara interrupted her.

"She came up to use the toilet and he tried raping her," he said.

"Then he got what he deserves," Mick said. He crouched down for a better look at Tony. The muffled bass of the electronic music could be felt through the floor. "You alright?" he asked Teagan.

"No," she said.

O'Hara gestured toward the body. "We gotta get outta here before anyone comes up and sees him."

"We can stick him under the bed," Mick said.

"Yeah, but we'll never get the mess cleaned up in time."

"Call Shane," Mick said. "Get that plane ready."

He pulled his phone out and dialed Shane's number.

"Danny boy," the Irishman answered on the first ring.

"How quick can that plane be ready to go?" O'Hara asked.

"Anytime. Everything alright?"

"No," O'Hara said.

"Okay, no more over the open line. How soon do you need?"

"Now."

"Understood. I'll be where you left me."

O'Hara hung up the phone and nodded at Mick.

"How are we getting back to the airstrip? Nuweiba isn't the next town over."

"We'll have to slip out of here and walk to Assala town. Catch a ride from there."

"Bugger that, mate. We'll steal a car," Mick said.

O'Hara gave a conceding nod. He looked at Teagan. "You picking up any vibes on this?"

She shook her head.

He was about to hug her when the bedroom door opened. They turned to find Pavel standing there, holding a stumbling Sasha up with one arm around his waist. When Pavel saw everyone inside, he froze and went to speak, but Mick rushed him.

Pavel let go of Sasha, who stumbled and slipped in the puddle of Tony the Turk's blood.

Mick hit the big Russian and began strangling him. As he struggled to defend himself, Pavel reached toward the small of his back and drew a pistol. O'Hara lunged forward and grabbed his wrist, then punched him hard in the face, buckling his knees. Mick had a tight hold around the man's neck and eventually choked him unconscious. He took the gun and shut the door.

"Piece of piss," Mick said. "Now what?"

"Tony!" Sasha said, as if only just noticing the dead man for the first time. O'Hara hit him hard upside the head with an open hand, knocking him out cold.

"Fuck, these Russians are a mess," Mick said and shook his head.

"Let's go," O'Hara said. "There's still plenty of this guy's crew to worry about. We don't need them up here looking around."

"What about my shirt?" Teagan asked, holding the part that had been torn.

"Check around, maybe the wife has something in one of the drawers."

"Fingerprints?"

"Too late to worry about that," O'Hara replied. "Wash the blood off your hands."

Teagan washed her hands in the bathroom sink. Mick found a drawer with t-shirts folded within and tossed one to her. She put it on.

"I want you and her to go first," he said to Mick. "Draw less attention that way."

"We shouldn't split up," Teagan said.

"We'll meet outside the gate. I'll be right behind you." He grabbed Mick's arm. "If anything pops off, make sure you get her to that airstrip."

"Let's go, Tea," Mick said.

O'Hara kissed her. She winced.

Mick handed O'Hara the pistol and walked out, with her following behind. O'Hara checked the gun, a Glock 43 nine-millimeter, compact and concealable. He ejected the magazine to make sure it was full, and cocked the slide back just enough to see the brass of a chambered round. He slid the mag back into place until it clicked and then tucked it at his waist. He walked to the window and peeked out from behind the drape. When he saw Mick and Teagan enter into view across the driveway, he left the room.

When he got downstairs there were people dancing in the room that had the sarcophagus. He walked toward the front door avoiding eye contact with anyone until he felt a hand grip his arm. He turned to find Fyodor standing there with an unlit cigar in one hand.

"I thought you all had left," he said. "Where have you been hiding?"

"I'm just looking for my crew," O'Hara said. "You seen any of 'em?"

Fyodor shook his head. "All I know is Sasha went a bit heavy on the drinks and Pavel had to help him upstairs to bed."

O'Hara could smell vodka on the man's breath.

"Come. Smoke with me." He placed a hand on O'Hara's shoulder.

"I'll meet you out there," he said.

"Down by the beach," Fyodor agreed and exited the room.

O'Hara turned and walked toward the front entrance. As he was reaching for the doorknob, he heard a shout from upstairs and looked back over his shoulder to find Pavel at the top landing with a gun in his hand. He was screaming something in Russian. A man from among the crowd rushed forward to grab O'Hara.

O'Hara dropped him with an elbow to the jaw, sending the crowd into a frenzy.

He didn't want to lead anyone to where the others were waiting so he ran back down the hallway, through the kitchen and out onto the terrace, pulling his cellphone out and dialing Mick as he went. Pavel was shouting in Russian and chasing him.

"Talk to me," Mick answered.

"I'll meet you at the airstrip. Go now!"

"You in trouble?"

"Get Teagan out of here!" He hung up the phone.

Outside, the music was loud and at first the crowd didn't seem aware of the commotion that had just ensued. O'Hara pushed through the bodies toward the steps leading down to the beach.

Gunshots echoed through the air causing many of the guests to drop to the floor or scramble for cover. O'Hara glanced back over his shoulder just long enough to see Pavel, still in pursuit with his gun aimed toward the sky overhead.

O'Hara took the stairs in a single leap. There was a whistle and the popping sound of a bullet hitting the water, followed by a delayed crackle. He turned and fired two shots back.

"What are you doing!?" a voice yelled.

O'Hara aimed the gun in the direction it came from to find Fyodor standing there. Another shot flew past his head. He turned and saw Pavel at the top of the stairs with the pistol aimed in his direction. He crouched and fired a shot, hitting the bodyguard in the thigh and dropping him down the remaining steps onto the beach.

He pointed the gun at Fyodor, but saw that he was unarmed.

The music was no longer playing, replaced by shouting and screams. O'Hara wondered if someone might have discovered Tony's body. He looked at Fyodor once more before turning and sprinting through the shallow water that covered the reef. More gunshots echoed through the air. He returned fire without breaking stride. A bright beam of spotlight swept across him once, then back. The reef ended and O'Hara plunged into the water. He heard popping sounds as more bullets hit the surface. He fired shots back into the darkness until the Glock's magazine was empty. He let go of the pistol, took a deep breath and began swimming. When he resurfaced, he kept only his eyes and nose above the water so as not to compromise his position. Behind him he could hear shouting in both Russian and Arabic.

He figured himself to be at least a couple hundred yards off shore but without a plan. He had run into the ocean out of desperation, and to draw attention so that the others could escape. Across the gulf, he could make out the silhouette of the Saudi Arabian mountain range against the night sky and wondered if he could reach those shores without drowning. He lowered his head and began swimming in that direction.

In time his feet grew heavy so he kicked his shoes off and let them sink. Not long after that, he ditched his shirt. When he turned back now, he could no longer recognize Sasha's property and figured he must have drifted farther than he realized. The salt had begun to burn his eyes, and the more he swam the more the currents spun him around and disoriented him, stripping his ability to know whether he was swimming toward or away from the Egyptian shore.

When his muscles needed rest, he flipped onto his back and floated, staring up at the night sky. The constellations were like he had never seen before. The Milky Way a brushstroke of white dust that seemed so close, as though he might be able to reach up and swat stars if he tried. As he considered this, he wondered if he could be hallucinating.

He was unsure of how long he had been swimming. An hour, maybe. His vision was wrapped by a halo of blurry haze from the salt in his eyes. A star blazed across the blackness, leaving a seared trail in its wake. He prayed to Dina, letting her know he loved and missed her, and asked her to protect him so that he might see Teagan again in this lifetime. He then apologized for the thought as the heaviness of fatigue banked down on him, tempting him to give in and rest.

I am with you always, he heard a voice say. It was unfamiliar and seemed to have come from within his own head.

"Who," was the only word that he could manage aloud. His throat was parched and his voice raspy.

I am with you always, the voice repeated, but this time in what he was sure was that of Dina's as he remembered it.

"Where are you?" he asked, but received no answer. "Please protect Teagan," he whispered. Once the words left his mouth, he was overcome by a feeling of warmth that displaced the cold of the ocean water. Where his teeth had been chattering moments earlier, it now felt like he had been injected with a narcotic.

He was swept up among a sudden swell that carried him for many feet. A flash of lightning brightened the night sky for just long enough that O'Hara saw the Egyptian coastline in the distance.

"Don't leave me," he pleaded.

He was wrenched from his dream state when he swallowed a gulp of seawater and nearly vomited. The fatigue was overwhelming and his lungs strained to catch a breath. He was shivering as he attempted to swim, and figured he was becoming hypothermic. Thoughts of sharks lingered, but he knew there was nothing he could do about it if there were any nearby.

His pants were making it difficult to swim so he stripped them off. Every bone in his body now felt like it was rattling as he dug deep and forced his limbs to stroke through the water. Whenever his muscles cramped, he allowed the tide to carry him, hoping it was moving in the right direction. The air above the water's surface felt like a thousand pin pricks against his exposed skin. The pain brought forth a surge of adrenaline, and this is what he utilized in a last-ditch effort to swim as hard as he could.

TWENTY

There was a memory of having crashed into the reef's edge with what felt like the force of a car wreck, his leg and one side of his torso shredded against the coral. The salt felt like acid in his wounds. He remembered being in the back of a pick-up truck. Soaking wet and sprawled out while a Bedouin in a purple headwrap sat on the bed wall holding a rifle. Slipping in and out of consciousness with every bump in the road, he faded out. There was a vague recollection of being dropped on a cold cement floor, and feeling too exhausted and dehydrated to open his eyes.

He woke to the worst headache he ever remembered having experienced. Within seconds his body was shivering, his skin covered in goosebumps and his damp underwear feeling like an ice wrap. He stared at a spiderweb crack in the cement ceiling, wondering where in hell he might be. The room was windowless with a single bulb dangling from the ceiling by an extension cord. There was a hole in the floor with a role of damp toilet paper, near the corner. A heavy metal door with no handle was the only outlet.

He felt his body for signs of abuse. The only wounds he discovered were the coral scrapes along his torso and thigh. The door opened and a man dressed in a *gallibeya* and purple headwrap entered, carrying a tray with a cup of water, another one filled with hot tea and a piece of flatbread stuffed with *fuul*. The man set the tray on the floor and turned to leave.

"*Inta Masri*?" O'Hara asked him.

The man stopped, turned to him and stared at him for a long moment.

His brain was foggy and he had trouble remembering the Arabic. He asked in English, "Where am I?"

"*Masr*," the man answered, using the Arabic name for Egypt.

O'Hara began to shiver, and knew he needed to get his body temperature up. He picked up the water and drank the entire glass, then took a sip of the tea. Feeling the warmth travel through him made him wish for a hot bath.

A couple of hours later the door swung open and a man stumbled in, pushed from behind by a Bedouin who then shut the door. The man stared at O'Hara, squinting until his eyes adjusted to the dim lighting.

"*Inta meen*?" the man demanded with a snarl.

O'Hara didn't answer.

"*Eah da*?!" the man shouted and stepped toward O'Hara, leaning down to where he sat against the wall.

When the man's face was close enough, O'Hara rocked forward onto one knee and grabbed a hold of his ankles and dumped him on his side. He began bashing the man's head with heavy fists until his body went limp.

The door swung open and two Bedouins entered with rifles aimed at him. O'Hara raised both hands in the air and stood, stepping back. They began to shout at him in Arabic.

"Fuck off,' he said.

One of the Bedouins swung his rifle behind him where it hung from its strap. He bent down and grabbed a hold of the unconscious man's feet and dragged him out of the room. The second man backed out with his gun aimed at O'Hara. He pulled the door shut, followed by the slide of a bolt lock.

No food or drink were brought in for what O'Hara believed to be the remainder of the day or night. He did pushups and handstands against the wall. He meditated. At some point the door opened and a man slid another tray in with water, tea and a *fuul* sandwich.

He ate the food and drank the water, then used the hole in the floor for a toilet. He saved the tea to be savored and sipped slowly as he did his best to quiet his mind. He wanted to scream out, ask for answers as to where he was or why he was being held, but he refused to show them any weakness. All he had left was his mental fortitude. He sipped the brew and tried to remember words from the languages he had since allowed to grow rusty. French. Mandarin. Albanian. Words from past lives.

When he eventually drifted off to sleep, he dreamed of being with both Dina and Teagan at the same time. They were sitting in a circle around a campfire. Behind them in the dark of night, several moons hovered along the horizon. As he observed them, he came to realize they might not have noticed his presence. Their eyes could have been clones of one another's. Dina was about to speak when a loud bang startled him awake.

A slice of blinding light penetrated the blackness of the room, and O'Hara was forced to shield his eyes with his arm. He felt a kick to his ribs, and rolled away from the attacker. Someone shouted at him in Arabic. He tried to see them, but could only make out silhouettes against the bright backdrop. He closed one eye and lined up the shape of the body and sprung to his feet, landing an uppercut to the man's jaw. The man dropped and O'Hara was hit from behind by someone else. A bolt of pain shot through the base of his skull as all went dark.

He felt warmth against one side of his body and heard the crackling of burning wood. He opened his eyes to find himself lying face down on a rug with a blanket covering him. He lifted his head and looked around. More rugs hung as vertical wind-breaks under a star-filled night sky. Shadows danced along the woven walls.

Across a campfire sat a man with a goatee and the purple head wrap. He was smoking a twisted joint of hashish.

"*Btitkellem Araby*?" the man asked.

O'Hara clucked his tongue. "Where am I?"

"Sinai," the man said. He drew from the joint and exhaled smoke through his nostrils.

"*Sijin*?" O'Hara asked, remembering the word for prison.

The man nodded. "You harmed a prisoner and my guard." His English was heavily accented.

"Can I make a phone call?" O'Hara asked.

The Bedouin man clucked his tongue.

The man dropped what was left of his joint into the fire and looked up. He then stood and walked out of sight behind one of the rug walls.

O'Hara heard the man speaking to another in Arabic. He cradled his face in his hands and attempted to massage the pain from his temples with his fingertips. When he heard the man return, he didn't look up.

"Tea?" a different voice asked him in English.

O'Hara looked across the fire to find Fyodor Metchikov sitting cross-legged, pouring a glass of tea from a cast-iron pot. He offered the glass over the fire to O'Hara, who accepted it. Fyodor poured himself a cup.

"I need to speak to Prince Ahmed bin Tarek," O'Hara said, unable to think of anyone else that might carry the same influence among the Bedouins.

Fyodor sipped his tea, then shook his head. "He can't do anything for you."

O'Hara took a drink of tea.

"You are a murderer." Fyodor smoothed out a wrinkle on his pant leg. "You have also shot a second man."

"Where are my friends?"

"Gone."

"Gone from Egypt?"

Fyodor grinned. "Gone."

"They've done nothing," O'Hara said.

He nodded.

"I'm here to learn who you really are, before I have the Bedouins hand you over."

"Hand me over to who?"

"Depends how you answer." Fyodor sipped his tea. "To the Egyptian government. Or to Islamic State. These Bedouins have strong ties to I.S. in the Sinai." Fyodor nodded. "They would be rewarded handsomely for a western prisoner, who I suspect to be an intelligence officer."

"Intelligence officer," O'Hara scoffed, to mask the terror he felt. "Fuck you," he said. That's when he thought of Dina's voice. How he heard her at sea, like an angel sent to save his life. It gave him a sense of confidence.

"You assholes have been trying to kill me for long enough. Do what you gotta do."

"Do you not fear death?"

O'Hara shook his head. "Most of those who matter to me are already on the other side waiting."

Fyodor stood. "Very well, then."

O'Hara sent a silent prayer out into the universe. His thoughts were focused on Teagan, hoping she might somehow sense them. He thanked her and promised to look after her as best he could, once he had made it to where Dina was. He wished he could see her once more, but was at peace with his understanding of what he thought might exist beyond death. He believed that they would reunite in time.

He looked down at the fire. The logs were leaning against one another like a teepee. A shadow moved in his peripheral, and he turned to find several Bedouin men emerge from behind the rug walls.

So, this is how it ends, he thought. So anti-climactic. With no other tricks up his sleeve, he cleared his throat and said in a calm voice, "*Vampir, adin, devyat, sem, dva, pesht.*" He had not spoken the words since the day Bob died, and surprised himself with how easily the cadence helped him remember.

Fyodor was almost out of sight beyond the wind-break, when he heard O'Hara's words and stopped. He looked back and held up a hand to halt the Bedouins who had now grabbed a hold of O'Hara's arms to lift him to his feet. "What did you say?" he asked O'Hara.

O'Hara repeated the Russian words.

Fyodor gave an order in Arabic. He felt a sharp jab in his neck, and his vision blurred. His final memory was of his legs giving out.

He woke up in darkness, feeling the fabric of a hood against his face. There was a musty smell and the muscles of his neck were sore. His ears popped and he swallowed hard to clear them. The vibration of the engine was loud and calming. He was sure he was lying on the floor of an aircraft of some sort.

He felt someone's fingers against his neck, checking for a pulse. He lay still until they were gone, wondering where he was being taken. Wherever it was, Bob's Russian words got him there. He visualized both Teagan and Dina before him in the darkness, wondering which of them he would see first.

TWENTY-ONE

The hood was removed and at first O'Hara could see nothing. He was cold, his head ached and he had been drooling. Wondering how long he had been unconscious, he went to wipe the spit from his chin but found his wrists bound to the armrests of a chair.

The lights dimmed and his eyes slowly adjusted to the room. He noticed an IV hooked up to one of his arms, and followed the tubing to a hanging bag of liquid solution.

"Vitamins and medicine," a voice said in a Slavic accent. "You will feel better soon."

O'Hara blinked until his vision cleared enough that he could make out the wooden round table before him. Beyond that, it was still blurry. A gray door was just a few shades darker than the polished cement wall around it. There was a large drain hole in the floor.

"Where am I," he said to whoever had spoken to him. He was dressed in hospital scrubs.

"You will know soon enough," the same voice replied from behind.

He turned to find a man in a white doctor's coat. He was short, with a gray beard and eye glasses resting low on a bulbous nose.

"Are you a doctor?"

The man nodded.

"Unbind my wrists," O'Hara said.

The doctor shook his head. He studied something on the IV bag. "Are you beginning to feel better?"

"You want me to feel better, tell me where I am."

"*Zatknis*!" someone ordered from behind.

O'Hara arched his neck to see a soldier dressed in black fatigues standing at the wall behind him, holding an assault rifle.

"Are we underground?" O'Hara asked, but he was ignored. His eyes were now adjusted to the artificial light that shone from a recessed hole in the ceiling. Across the wooden table were three empty chairs facing him.

The doctor looked at his watch.

The door handle turned and it swung inward. A man entered wearing an olive-green army jacket and pants, with black boots. He was middle-aged and pale-skinned with a shaved head. He scowled at O'Hara as stepped aside and held the door open. Through the doorway was a dark corridor.

O'Hara maintained eye contact with the man, unwilling to give him the satisfaction of breaking his stare. "You gonna be the one to tell me where the fuck I am?" he asked.

The man stared hard at him. O'Hara heard several more footsteps outside the door. Four more armed guards filed to either side of the doorway and stood at attention. The next person to turn the corner and enter the room was Fyodor Metchikov. He was dressed in a black suit, and nodded at O'Hara when their eyes met.

"Where am I?" O'Hara asked him, but received no answer.

That was when the next man appeared in the doorway. He was small in stature, but the energy surrounding him was anything but. The way he moved his compact physique, like a coiled spring, emanated a sense of power and confidence. This man needed no introduction, and when they locked eyes, O'Hara felt a sense of panic. They were eyes that had seen the worst of what existed in the world. A cold stare that O'Hara had only witnessed among convicts and killers.

Everyone in the room stood at attention except O'Hara, who was bound to the chair he sat in.

The president was dressed in a pressed suit and his infamous face was void of emotion as he turned and held his hand out in the direction he entered from. It was clasped by another smaller hand as an elderly woman walked into view. Her hair was combed neatly into a tight silver bun and she wore a suit jacket and matching business skirt. Her face was without makeup and her eyes were the pale blue of glacial ice.

The president led her into the room, at which point all the soldiers and Fyodor saluted him. He pulled a chair from under the table and helped her into it, then made a gesture with his hand for the others to sit. He asked the doctor a question in Russian, which the man answered before leaving the room. The president then took the middle chair, opposite O'Hara.

He spoke Russian to the soldiers who each saluted him and all but one left the room. The last man out pulled the door shut behind him. Remaining inside were the president, the woman and the bald man sitting on either side of him, facing Fyodor and O'Hara. The remaining soldier stood at attention against the wall.

"Do I need to introduce myself?" the president asked. He spoke in slow English with a heavy accent.

O'Hara shook his head.

"General Annenkov," he gestured toward the bald man. "Not Anakovich like many of the American politicians and media continue to call him."

O'Hara looked at the General, now realizing that this was The Baker. The man behind the Volk Group and, if so, the man responsible for Dina's death.

"Colonel Limonova." The president then held a hand out to introduce the old woman.

O'Hara acknowledged her with a slight nod.

"You already know Fyodor Antonovich."

"Metchikov," O'Hara said, finishing the man's name.

The president didn't seem to like that O'Hara had spoken. "Introduce yourself," he demanded.

O'Hara cleared his throat and looked at Colonel Limonova.

"Daniel Marrero," O'Hara said.

"From?"

"Toronto, Canada."

The president took a deep breath and sighed.

"If you continue to lie to me, this room will be the last place you will know in this lifetime."

"Where are we?"

The president narrowed his eyes. "Introduce yourself."

"Donovan Burke." He paused. "Boston," he added, when he realized they expected more.

The president continued to stare him down. After a long wait, he asked, "Is that your final answer, Poet?"

O'Hara's heart sank, and a chill settled at his lower back. He maintained eye contact, but had never felt so outmatched. He was stuck in check-mate. After all of the hard men and dangerous criminals, killers and gangsters that he had encountered throughout his life he was finally in the presence of absolute power. O'Hara sensed in that moment that he was unlikely to leave the room alive, no matter how he answered.

"O'Hara Poit," he heard himself say, as if spoken from off in the distance. "From the Bronx. New York City."

The president gave a satisfied nod. "Now we can begin."

There was a knock and the door opened. One of the soldiers had returned holding a tray of glass mugs and a porcelain teapot. One of the tea mugs was already poured. He set the tray down in the middle of the table, and said something in Russian to the president, who nodded. The soldier then took the filled cup and set it in front of O'Hara, before proceeding to fill the others from the pot.

"Tea," the president said.

"Why was mine already poured?" O'Hara asked.

The soldier pulled a knife from a cargo pocket on his pants and cut the binding on O'Hara's arm that wasn't hooked up to the IV.

O'Hara studied the tea, comparing it to the color of the others that had since been poured. "No, thank you," he said.

The president glanced sideways at The Baker, before returning his attention to O'Hara.

"You were in Beirut during the explosion."

Figuring he would soon be executed no matter how he responded, O'Hara nodded.

"Our general's brother was a victim of that tragic event."

"Condolences," O'Hara said to The Baker, who stared back at him with hatred in his eyes.

"General Annenkov believes you to be among those responsible for the explosion."

"Is that why the general has been among those responsible for the repeated attempts on my life? Responsible for killing the love of my life, among others?"

The president slowly exhaled, as if to resist losing his composure.

Thinking that he could be staring at the man who ordered Dina's murder filled O'Hara with a feeling of unexpected rage. "You'll have to do better than the guys you've been sending so far, motherfucker," he said to Annenkov.

The Baker slammed his palm against the tabletop.

The president made a hissing sound. "We already have. Look at you. Do you think you really have a choice as to whether or not you drink your tea? Do you think anyone even knows you are here?"

As quick as O'Hara's confidence had risen, it was gone.

"Tell me about your relationship with the Crown Prince."

O'Hara looked at Fyodor, as if the man he had met in Egypt might offer a lifeline. He was met with a cold stare.

"I have met him a few times. There is no relationship."

"You were living in Riyadh, after Beirut."

O'Hara nodded. "I am friends with Prince Ahmed bin Tarek. I have spent very little time around the Crown Prince."

"Are you telling me the truth?"

"You've spent more time with him than I have. Go ask him yourself."

The president made a steeple with his fingers.

"Is he the one who told you I was in Guinea?" O'Hara asked.

The question was met with silence.

"There is something that doesn't make sense to me, about all of this." O'Hara looked at each of them, one at a time. "You have tried to kill me several times. You have killed people close to me. Why am I now sitting here, when you can just get it over with."

"Because I didn't give the order to kill you," the president said. "If I had, it would have been successful the first time."

O'Hara looked at The Baker.

"You?" O'Hara asked.

The Baker cursed in Russian and looked at the president.

"I was brought here after speaking that Russian sentence to Fyodor," O'Hara said.

Putin glanced at Fyodor, then back at O'Hara. "Speak it again."

O'Hara closed his eyes and recited it once silently in his head before speaking. "*Vampir, adin, devyat, sem, dva, pesht,*" he said.

Upon his speaking the words, Colonel Limonova shifted position in her seat. O'Hara looked at her. Her face was as still as a statue, but he noticed sadness in her eyes.

"How do you know these words?" the president asked.

It was in that moment that O'Hara realized who she must be.

"I was made to memorize them by a man I knew."

The president said something in Russian to Colonel Limonova, who softly cleared her throat.

"Bob," she said, speaking for the first time.

"He recently passed away," O'Hara said.

Colonel Limonova's lip twitched and her eyes grew misty, but she otherwise did not react. "How did you know him?"

"He was a friend."

"He was a spy," the president said.

O'Hara looked at him, eventually confirming with a nod.

"Are you?"

O'Hara shook his head.

"You wouldn't admit it if you were."

"I don't expect to walk out of this room, alive," O'Hara said. "I'd have no reason to deny it if I were."

"Don't you want to try your tea?" the president asked.

"I'd rather a bullet in the head."

This comment brought a slight grin to the president's otherwise stone-faced expression.

"Do you know the reason Bob made you learn this sentence?"

"He knew he was dying. He thought it might help keep me alive if the Russians who have been trying to kill me were to ever catch up with me." He gestured at his bound arm. "Which you have."

"Did Bob explain his relationship with Colonel Limonova?"

"He was in love with her."

When he said this, tears welled in Colonel Limonova's eyes.

"She was his handler," O'Hara added.

"How do you feel about that?" the president asked.

"I could tell he never stopped loving her."

Colonel Limonova wiped one eye with her knuckle.

"How do you feel about the fact that he betrayed your country."

"Love causes people to make difficult decisions," O'Hara said. He then looked at Colonel Limonova. "I'm guessing you are Margarite, then?"

A quizzical frown came over her face. "Anya is my name."

O'Hara glanced at the president, whose eyes narrowed.

"He told you Margarite?"

"He told me to tell Margarite that professor Woland is a wolf."

The president's eyes widened. He sat back in his chair, and cursed in Russian, crossing himself with his right hand. He looked at Colonel Limonova.

"A wolf?" he asked.

"Obviously this means something to you," O'Hara said. "I don't understand it."

The president began knocking his knuckles on the tabletop, breaking from his calm and confident demeanor. He made a disgusted sound as if spitting. He took a deep breath and by the time he exhaled he was back in control of himself. He turned his attention to The Baker and asked him something in Russian.

The Baker responded defensively, holding his palms up as if denying something. The president nodded and spoke to Colonel Limonova next.

She nodded and stood as the soldier in the room opened the door and let her out.

Before making her way toward the door, Colonel Limonova stopped and turned her attention to O'Hara. "Thank you," she said.

"Yes, ma'am," O'Hara replied.

She left the room and the soldier shut the door behind her.

The president was looking at his hands, picking at a hangnail on his thumb. They were small hands, but strong and with calloused knuckles like O'Hara's. They appeared to be trembling. He said something more in Russian without looking up, and Fyodor slid his chair back and stood. The president then looked up and spoke Russian in a soft but stern voice to The Baker.

"Vladmir Vladmirovich," The Baker said, before going off into a tirade of Russian sentences.

The president stared at the man but did not respond. He didn't need to. His eyes said it all.

O'Hara watched as Fyodor circled the table behind the The Baker, who was still protesting. Fyodor pulled a .22 caliber pistol from inside his suit jacket and held it to The Baker's head, then pulled the trigger.

Even for a .22, the shot rang loud in the small, windowless room and it caused O'Hara to flinch. The Baker slumped sideways in his chair, with blood dripping from a hole at the back of his head. Bone fragments and brain stuck to the wall.

The president wiped his palms against his pant legs and stood. He picked up his chair and brought it around to O'Hara's side of the table. He picked up the untouched cup of tea that had been sitting in front of O'Hara, and offered it to him.

O'Hara glanced at the blood splatter along the wall. "No thank you," he said.

The president shrugged and set the mug down on the table.

"Your old friend Bob..." he began, and paused to straighten the lapel of his suit jacket. "He was doing important work for us decades ago."

"I know."

"We had not heard anything from him in a long time."

"I was under the impression that he was retired."

The president nodded. "And yet he somehow he had the ability to ensure that one last bit of intelligence was passed to his handler." He looked at The Baker's body with disgust. "How did he come upon this information?"

"I don't know what you mean."

"What was your relationship to him?"

"He found me. Claimed to be a friend of a friend."

"A friend of which friend?"

"An Israeli friend."

"The one who was killed in Queensland?"

O'Hara looked the president in the eye. "You ordered that hit."

"No," he said.

"Then who did?"

The president didn't blink once. "Did you ever witness Bob and your Israeli friend together?"

"At the same time?"

The president nodded.

O'Hara thought back, but couldn't come up with a single memory of them having been in the presence of one another.

"Did they speak of one another?" the president asked.

"Of course," O'Hara said.

"The Israeli," he said. He said something in Russian over his shoulder to Fyodor. "Did he ever speak of Bob?"

O'Hara's mind was overwhelmed by a flood of memories. Real ones. Assumed ones. He had trouble differentiating between the two. In truth, he couldn't remember a single time that Rafi had spoken of Bob by name, or mentioned anything specific about him. He had left several times to meet a contact. He had important information to pass along the day he was killed in Redcliffe. But O'Hara was now second-guessing his own memory.

"Your friends were intercepted on their escape from the rat Filenkov's mansion. They are also detained."

"Are we still on the Sinai?"

The president let out a slight laugh.

"Where are we?"

"If there were windows, you'd be able to smell the Black Sea from here."

"Russia?"

He didn't respond. "Your friends will be released. You will have Bob's ghost to thank for that."

"How do I know you are being honest?"

"You don't," he replied. "But you eventually will, when you see them."

O'Hara waited for him to elaborate, but he didn't.

"You aren't going to kill me?"

The president poked out his lip and gave a slight shake of his head. He cleared his throat and spat on The Baker's body. "This message Bob had you deliver. It saved all of your lives."

He thought of how Bob had said it might do exactly that one day, if he ever found the need to speak it. "How?" he thought aloud.

The president leaned his head closer and stared into O'Hara's eyes. "Maybe he was just that good at his job."

O'Hara looked at Fyodor, who still hadn't spoken a word.

"Fyodor Antonovich will come see you when the time is right. You will only deal with him going forward."

O'Hara looked at the president. "What?"

"Carry on living your life. You will know if you are ever needed. We have a proverb in our culture. In English it is something like..." he leaned his hands on his knees and spoke Russian to Fyodor.

Fyodor cleared his throat and said, "Work is not a wolf. It will not run into the forest."

The president nodded and looked at O'Hara.

"I don't understand," O'Hara said.

"It means relax for now."

O'Hara looked at his arm, still with the IV attached. "I'm not a spy."

"*Da, Da.*"

"Who is Margarite?" O'Hara asked. "Professor Woland?"

The president made a strange whistling noise with his mouth and stood. "I will leave you with one idea to consider." He placed a hand on O'Hara's shoulder. "With everything you have told me, it is probably in your best interest to be wary of any Israelis that enter your life. I would assume they will be hunting whoever killed that friend of yours in Australia." Without speaking another word, he then turned and left the room.

O'Hara looked at Fyodor.

Fyodor carefully pulled the IV needle from his arm, then cut the binding around his wrist. "You can't return to Egypt."

"Why?"

"Because of the dead bodies left at the mansion."

"Bodies?"

Fyodor didn't elaborate.

"Take me wherever the others are," O'Hara said.

The Russian helped him up from the chair. His legs felt stiff and his insides ached from the drugs in his system.

He looked at The Baker's body one last time. "What will you do with him?" he asked.

"He died in a plane crash," Fyodor replied. He stepped out of the room and returned holding a hood. "Do you want to be sedated?"

O'Hara shook his head.

Fyodor nodded and slipped the hood over O'Hara's head. In the blackness he felt the Russian's hand grip his elbow, and guide him toward the door.

EPILOGUE

Mudjimba Beach - Queensland, Australia

Out past the wave breaks where the dark turquoise swells appeared like rippled glass out toward Old Woman Island, and the sky along the horizon was blended stripes of pink and indigo, the rip was strong and O'Hara had to swim hard against the pull to not be swept out into the depths.

He performed his underwater exercises, the movements he had learned while recovering in the lakes of the Guinean jungle so long ago, appreciating the burn in his muscles. To one direction was what looked like the edge of the earth. To the other Teagan walked along the packed sand where the dampness captured the colors of the sky. As she entered the water, her body was fit and tanned.

In the distance Mick sat atop a cooler filled with beers near the sand dunes. He was leaner since Egypt and had grown out a long beard to match the fake identity he re-entered the country under. Beside him on a spread blanket, Li Yong reclined on one elbow and smoked a cigarette. Down the coastline to the south the silhouette of Nate Killeen could be seen wading at the sandbar with a fishing rod in hand.

O'Hara rode a wave in to where Teagan stood neck deep in the sea. He wrapped his arms around her waist and they kissed. Her eyes were the color of moonstone under the fading light. She rested her chin on his shoulder and stared out toward the water.

"Everything alright?" O'Hara asked.

She made a humming sound that he couldn't decipher.

"What is it?"

"Something's off." She was looking toward the island.

"It's never a good thing when you start talking like that," he kidded, but her comment left him unsettled.

"*Fángdàn!*" Li Yong called out and waved at them to come in. He tapped his wristwatch with his other hand.

O'Hara nodded and turned to Teagan. "We better head in. You gonna be alright?"

She nodded.

They walked along the sand to where the others sat. Nate returned holding a large pink snapper by the gills in one hand. Mick stood and opened the lid of the cooler to hand out fresh beers.

"This one's yours, Li. Can we throw it in there?" Nate asked, holding out the fish.

"Nah, mate! Not with the beers," Mick said, disgusted. "Is that what you do back in Philly?"

"There's only two left, ya prick. Drink 'em. Here, pass me one."

Mick handed him a beer.

"Put the fish in."

"Too easy," Mick said and pulled out the last beer for himself.

"What time's this fight, I'll need a shower," Mick said.

"Seven," O'Hara said.

"This Burmese kid is on a different level," Li said. "A real killer."

"How'd you find him?" Nate asked.

"Guarding a poppy field near the Thai border. They would gamble and fight on their lunch breaks." Li stubbed out a cigarette in an upturned seashell he had been using as an ashtray.

Teagan leaned close to O'Hara's ear and whispered. "I don't feel so good. I think I might need to go home."

"Of course," O'Hara said and stood. He helped her to her feet. "I'll see you's over at the gym around six-thirty."

"I'll give you two a lift home," Nate said and pulled his shirt on over his head. He reached down into one of his boots and pulled out a Sig Sauer pistol, which he tucked at his waist. "I'll go get the car started." He picked up his boots and carried them toward the tree-lined path that led to where the vehicles were parked along Mudjimba Esplanade.

Li Yong and Mick packed up the cooler while O'Hara helped Teagan beat the sand off the blanket and towels.

"Whose is this?" Teagan asked, picking up a book that was under one of the towels. She studied the cover. "Is this yours?" she held it out to O'Hara.

O'Hara shook his head and took hold of it. He asked Li and Mick if it was theirs, to which they each shook their head.

The book was white with an image of a black cat on the cover and the title *The Master and Margarita* by the writer Mikhail Bulgakov. A panicked feeling settled in his gut as he looked up and down the beach in either direction. A few surfers stood along the sand in the direction of Marcoola, but otherwise they had the beach to themselves. He tried remembering if there were any point since arriving that their belongings had been left unattended. He wasn't sure.

"Maybe Nate left it," Mick said.

Teagan put a hand on his shoulder. "I feel like I'm going to be sick," she said, holding her stomach with her other hand, and taking a deep breath.

"Okay, we'll go," O'Hara said. He opened the book and began thumbing through the pages until he got to the title page and stopped.

Inscribed at the top of the page in black ink was a written note in a strangely familiar handwriting.

Nothing is what you've been led to believe.
The old man played everyone.
Keep your head on a swivel.
The answer is in Colorado.

Below that was a marking that froze O'Hara stiff. A symbol that only one person in the world could ever know the significance of. A dead person. He looked up and down the beach again, then down at the shamrock, drawn in red ink.

"You alright?" Teagan asked.

He ignored her. He fanned through the rest of the book's pages, stopping at random ones when his eyes caught familiar names. Margarita. Professor Woland. He shut the book and said, "Let's go."

He started up the sand at a quickening pace. Mick and Li Yong trailed behind carrying either side of the cooler.

"What's wrong?" she asked again, struggling to keep up with him.

As they reached the path and walked between the timber railings and thick stretches of bushland of pandanas trees on either side, his mind was racing. They reached the crest of the hill and began their descent toward the nearest road and watched Nate climb into his car. He pulled the door shut.

They had only made it another step or two, when it happened. O'Hara wasn't sure if it was the thundering sound or the blinding flash of light that came first, but something caused him to shield Teagan with the frame of his body just as Nate's rental car exploded into a cloud of smoke and flames. All the windows blew outward and shattered glass was sent flying in all directions. When he looked back, each of the doors had been blown open on their hinges, and billowing plumes of black smoke escaped all openings and curled toward the sky.

He felt Mick's hands grab him and lift him to his feet, as Li Yong did the same for Teagan. They were screaming at him, their voices muffled as they ushered them down the sidewalk away from the blast.

The last thing O'Hara saw when he looked back at the skeleton car was the outline of Nate's head among the dark smoke and flames. It was slumped over with his body trapped upright by the seat belt.

He had become too familiar with death and loss to feel much of anything in the moment. At least not consciously. What he did understand was that this was how it ended for people in the life they lived. Final goodbyes were rarely exchanged.

As the four of them hurried down the esplanade, O'Hara looked back one last time at the bonfire engulfing the car. Sirens could now be heard somewhere in the near distance. He would see Nate on the other side.

Now, he needed to go to Colorado. He needed to find Red.

ACKNOWLEDGEMENTS

This novel couldn't have been written without the unconditional love and support of my wife, Georgie and our three daughters, Scarlett, Savanna and Stella. It is due to our family's adventurous, at times semi-nomadic lifestyle that I am exposed to the kinds of places and situations that spark the ideas I write about. The early drafts of this novel were crafted while living near the beautiful beaches of the Sunshine Coast in Queensland, Australia.

Throughout my journey toward becoming a writer, there have been authors, mentors and friends whose work I have turned to for inspiration and wisdom. I'd like to give a special thanks to Gregory David Roberts, Junot Díaz and Colin Broderick for the incredible impact they have had on my life.

I'd like to also thank the following people who contributed to this project: Ferd Beck, artist David Colon, my parents, Tom & Lisa McCaffrey, my brother Mark, my sister Jackie, Rob Buffington, James Poit, Mitch Hanna, Andrea Couture, Danny Velasquez, Bryan Rhodes, Devin Hallock, Eileen Cotto, Anthony Day, Veronica McCaffrey, b. Frank, and Nigel, Sarah & Anita Moss.

ABOUT THE AUTHOR

Luke McCaffrey is a writer from the Bronx, New York, who has spent time living in Egypt and Australia. He is a former Denver firefighter who spends his free time in the forests and mountains of Colorado, where he resides with his wife, three daughters, and two dogs.

NOTE FROM LUKE McCAFFREY

Word-of-mouth is crucial for any author to succeed. If you enjoyed *Bulletproof*, please leave a review online—anywhere you are able. Even if it's just a sentence or two. It would make all the difference and would be very much appreciated.

Thanks!
Luke McCaffrey

We hope you enjoyed reading this title from:

www.blackrosewriting.com

Subscribe to our mailing list – *The Rosevine* – and receive **FREE** books, daily
deals, and stay current with news about upcoming
releases and our hottest authors.
Scan the QR code below to sign up.

Already a subscriber? Please accept a sincere thank you for being a fan of
Black Rose Writing authors.

View other Black Rose Writing titles at
www.blackrosewriting.com/books and use promo code
PRINT to receive a **20% discount** when purchasing.